SUN, SAND, SEX

SUN, SAND, SEX

LINDA LAEL MILLER

JENNIFER APODACA

SHELLY LAURENSTON

BRAVA

KENSINGTON PUBLISHING CORP.
http://www.kensingtonbooks.com

BRAVA BOOKS are published by

Kensington Publishing Corp.
850 Third Avenue
New York, NY 10022

ISBN-13: 978-0-7582-1096-8
ISBN-10: 0-7582-1096-5

First Kensington Trade Paperback Printing: June 2007
10 9 8 7 6 5 4 3 2 1

Printed in the United States of America

CONTENTS

ONE LAST WEEKEND

Linda Lael Miller

One

"One last weekend," insisted Ted Brayley, the Darbys' long-time friend and now their divorce lawyer, facing the couple across the gleaming expanse of his cherrywood desk. "Just spend one weekend together, at the cottage, that's all I'm asking. Then, if you still want to split the proverbial sheets, I'll file the papers."

Joanna Darby sat very still, but out of the corner of her eye, she saw her soon-to-be-ex husband, Teague, shift in his leather wingback chair, a twin to her own. Distractedly, he extended a hand, not to Joanna, but to pat their golden retriever, Sammy, sitting attentively between them, on the head.

"I don't see what good that would do," Teague said. At forty-one, he was still handsome and fit, but he was going through a major midlife crisis. He'd sold his highly successful architectural firm for an obscene profit and bought himself a very expensive sports car, and though there was no sweet young thing in the picture yet, as far as Joanna knew, it was only a matter of time. Teague was a cliché waiting to happen. "We've settled everything. We're ready to go our separate ways."

Ted sat back, cupping his hands behind his head. "Really?" he asked, with a casual nod toward Sammy. "Who gets custody of the dog?"

"I do," Teague responded immediately.

"Not in this lifetime," Joanna protested.

Teague looked at her in surprise. It always surprised Teague when anybody expressed an opinion different from his own; he was used to calling the shots, leading the charge, setting the course. Somewhere along the line, he'd forgotten that Joanna didn't work for him. "*I* was the one who sprang him from the pound when he was a pup," he argued. "He's my dog."

"Well," Joanna answered, making an effort not to raise her voice, "*I'm* the one who house-trained him and taught him not to eat sofas. I'm the one who walked him every day. I love Sammy, and I'm not about to give him up."

"Joanna," Teague said darkly, "be reasonable." Translation: *Agree with me. You* know *I'm always right.*

"I'm tired of being reasonable," Joanna said, examining her unmanicured fingernails. "I'm keeping the dog."

Teague rolled his blue eyes and, shoved a hand through his still-thick, slightly shaggy dark hair.

A corner of Ted's mouth quirked up in a smug little grin. They'd both known Ted since college, and they both trusted him, which was why they'd decided to let him handle the divorce. Now Joanna wondered if a stranger would have been a better choice, and Teague was probably thinking the same thing. "I guess you *haven't* settled everything," Ted said. "Sammy wouldn't be the first dog in history to be the subject of a custody battle—but would you really want to put him through that kind of grief?"

"Joint custody, then," Teague grumbled, a muscle bunching in his cheek. "We'll share him. My place one week, Joanna's the next."

"Oh, right," Joanna scoffed. "I'd never see him unless you had a hot date."

Sammy whimpered softly, resembling a forlorn spectator at a tennis match as he turned his head from Joanna to Teague and back again. He wasn't used to harsh tones—the Darby marriage had slowly caved in on itself, by degrees, after Teague and Joanna's only child, Caitlin, went off to college. There had been no screaming fights, no accusations—or objects—flying back and forth. This was no *War of the Roses*.

It might have been easier if it had been.

"One weekend," Ted reiterated. He gestured toward Elliott Bay, sparkling blue-gray beyond his office windows. "You've got that great cottage on Firefly Island. When was the last time you went out there, just the two of you? Walked the beach? Sipped wine in front of the fireplace? Really talked?"

Joanna felt a sharp pang, remembering happier times. She hadn't been to the cottage in months—not once since she'd holed up there the previous summer, after Caitlin's wedding, to finish her latest cookbook, with only Sammy for company. Teague had gone on a sailing trip, off the coast of Mexico. It had been a lonely time for Joanna, endurable only because she'd been buried in work.

Now Teague got up from his chair, went to the windows, and stood with his back to the room, looking out over downtown Seattle and the waters beyond. "Are you a divorce lawyer or a marriage counselor?" he muttered.

Sammy started to follow Teague, paused in the middle of the spacious office, then turned uncertainly to look at Joanna.

She blinked back sudden, burning tears. Gestured for Sammy to go ahead, to Teague. Instead, he came back to her and laid his muzzle on her lap with a sad sigh.

As Joanna watched her husband, an unexpected question popped into her mind. *When did we lose each other?*

She'd loved Teague Darby since her first day of college, when he'd knocked on her door in their coed dorm and introduced himself. They'd married early in their senior year at the University of Washington, and Caitlin had been born a week after graduation. Joanna, having majored in business and intending to attend culinary school after college and eventually open her own restaurant, had happily set aside those plans to stay home with Caitlin and help Teague start his company. The early years had been hard financially, but he'd worked out of their converted garage behind their first tiny house, and they'd been happy.

So happy.

They'd given Caitlin a secure, sunny childhood. While they'd both wanted more children, it simply didn't happen. The disappointment surfaced only occasionally; after all, they had a beautiful daughter, a good life together. What more could two people ask for?

And they'd loved each other passionately.

There had been no single inciting incident, no affairs, no traumas, nothing like that.

As the company grew, expanding at a breathtaking rate, so did the demands on Teague's time. They'd moved into progressively larger houses until they'd finally ended up in a mansion on Mercer Island, hired a housekeeper, and entertained lavishly. But they'd still had time for each other, even then. They'd *made* time.

Secretly, Joanna had always thought of the cottage as home, not the mansion. And the idea of going to Firefly Island for a last weekend with Teague broke her heart. They'd both been living in the main house, Teague on the first floor, Joanna on the second, and the place was so large that avoiding each other was easy. It would be more of a challenge at the cottage.

"If you won't do this for yourselves," Ted said evenly, "or for Caitlin, then do it for Sammy. The poor dog is beside himself."

Since Teague's back was still turned, Joanna took the opportunity to dry her eyes with the back of one hand. Sammy looked up at her with limpid brown eyes, imploring.

"I'll do it," Joanna said, resigned.

"Okay," Teague said, at exactly the same moment.

Ted consulted his watch. "The next ferry leaves in an hour," he said.

"An hour?" Joanna marveled. "But I'd need to pack a bag—and Sammy's food—"

"You have clothes at the cottage," Teague reminded her, "and there's a supermarket on the island. I'm sure they carry Sammy's brand of kibble."

Joanna opened her mouth, then closed it again. The truth was, she'd gained five pounds since her last visit to the cottage, and she wasn't sure her island clothes would fit. Since she was too proud to admit that, she decided to take her chances. Most likely, the experience would be a total bust anyway, and she and Teague would both be on the next ferry back to Seattle. She probably wouldn't even be there long enough to need a toothbrush.

Teague made that pretty much of a sure thing when he added, "Come on, Sammy. Let's get this over with."

Inwardly, Joanna seethed.

Ted gave her a sympathetic look as she rose. Teague and Sammy were already on their way out, though the dog paused every few steps, looking back, clearly waiting for Joanna to follow.

For Sammy's sake rather than Teague's, she did.

Leaving the suite housing Ted's office, they took the elevator down to the underground lot, where Teague's sports car was parked alongside Joanna's stylish but practical compact.

Rather than subject Sammy to another debate, Joanna didn't insist that the dog ride with her instead of Teague. The ferry terminal was only minutes away, and once they were aboard the large, state-operated boat, the ride to Firefly Island would take less than half an hour.

Teague had the top down on his high-powered phallic symbol, and Sammy loved an open-air ride, whatever the weather. Although the morning had been pristinely sunny, one of those days that seem to mock Seattle's reputation for unrelenting rain, the sky was darkening now, its gray tone reflected by the choppy waters of the bay.

In the old days, Joanna thought, with a quiet sigh, she and Teague wouldn't even have considered taking two cars to the cottage. If Caitlin was going along, she'd have had at least one friend with her, and they would have all crammed themselves into Teague's big SUV. On the occasions when Sammy and Caitlin stayed home, in the expert care of the recently retired Mrs. Smills, their housekeeper, they would have stayed in the car for the short duration of the crossing, willing the boat to go faster.

Back then, as soon as the front door of the cottage closed behind them, they'd have left a trail of clothes behind them, laughing as they raced for the bedroom.

Joanna waited in the short line of cars just behind Teague and Sammy—not as many people heading for the island as there usually were on Friday afternoons, she thought—paid her fare when her turn came, and drove into the belly of the ferry.

They practically had the whole boat to themselves.

Joanna waved reassuringly to Sammy, who responded with a doggy grin, but Teague sat staring straight ahead as though they were strangers, he and Joanna, not two people who had raised a child together.

She leaned back in the car seat and closed her eyes. Ted's heart had been in the right place—he hoped she and Teague would reconsider, of course, and decide not to go through with the divorce. Maybe he figured they'd fall into each other's arms, alone in a romantic island cottage, and rekindle the old flame that had once burned so brightly that it glowed within both of them.

When had it gone out?

The last time she and Teague had made love—weeks ago, now—they'd both been satisfied, but nothing more. Two bodies, colliding, responding reflexively, biologically—and then drawing apart. Afterward, Teague had quietly left their bedroom and gone upstairs to sleep in one of the guest rooms.

Remembering, Joanna felt humiliated all over again.

She went to the gym three times a week, but she was forty-one, after all, and soft all over, a little saggy in places. And even though she tried to watch what she ate, she was forever testing recipes for her cookbooks, and that involved a lot of tasting.

Hence the extra five pounds.

Was it the extra five pounds?

A brisk rap on her driver's side window startled her, and she turned to see Teague peering in at her.

She had put the key in the ignition in order to operate the power windows, and she'd done it before she realized she could have simply opened the door.

"I'm going upstairs for some coffee," Teague said, unsmiling. "Want some?"

"No," Joanna said. "Too late in the day for me. I'd be up half the night."

That familiar muscle in Teague's jaw tightened again. "Right," he said. "Keep an eye on Sammy while I'm gone, will you?"

"Of course," Joanna replied. As soon as Teague had made his way to the steel staircase leading to the upper deck, she got out of her car, crossed to Sammy, and stroked his silky golden head. The water was a little rough that day, and Joanna felt slightly queasy.

Boats, even cruise ships, made her seasick.

Teague loved anything that floated, and dreamed of building a craft of his own.

Just one of the many things they *didn't* have in common.

When Teague returned, carrying a steaming foam cup in one hand, Joanna got back in her own car.

Within a few minutes, the captain blew the horn, which meant they'd be docking on Firefly Island soon.

Joanna's spirits rose a little at the prospect of being at the cottage again, even though the place was probably full of dust and in need of airing out. But Teague would build a fire on the hearth in the living room, and she would brew tea in the old-fashioned kitchen, and if nothing else, they could talk about Caitlin or Sammy.

Or they could not talk at all, which was the most likely scenario.

Since it had begun to drizzle, Teague hastily raised the top on his sports car while the first cars to board started off the boat. Sammy seemed to droop a little, as if disappointed.

The cottage was several miles from the ferry terminal, which was little more than a toll booth on that side of the water, and Teague led the way along the narrow, winding road, passing the supermarket without even slowing down.

Irritated, Joanna pulled into the lot, parking as close to the entrance as she could, and dashed inside to buy kibble, coffee, a toothbrush and paste, and the makings of a seafood salad.

By the time she arrived at the cottage, Teague had turned on all the lights and built a fire. With a grocery bag in each arm, Joanna plunged out of the car into the rain, now coming down hard, and dashed for the front door.

Just as she reached it, Teague flung it open and Sammy burst through to greet her, almost sending her toppling backward off the small porch.

Teague caught her by the elbows.

Sammy, meanwhile, ran in mad circles in the yard, barking exuberantly at the rain.

"Damn fool dog," Teague said, with the first real smile Joanna had seen on his face in weeks.

He took the bags from her and shunted her inside.

"There's kibble in the backseat," she said, despairing of her tailored gray pantsuit, now drenched.

"I'll get it in a minute," Teague said, without his usual curtness, heading for the kitchen. "Jeez, Jo, the shopping could have waited—"

Sammy dashed back inside, soaked, and stood beside Joanna to shake himself vigorously. Teague used to joke— back when he still had a sense of humor—that the dog must be part water spaniel, the way he loved getting wet. Throw a piece of driftwood into the sound, and he'd swim halfway to Seattle to retrieve it.

Joanna laughed, forced the door shut against a rising wind, and peeled off her jacket, hanging it gingerly on a hook on the antique coat tree next to the door. *What the well-dressed woman wears to a civilized divorce,* she thought.

And then she didn't feel like laughing anymore.

Teague was back from the kitchen. "Dry off," he ordered. "I'll get the dog food."

Joanna kicked off her sodden shoes and wandered into the living room, with its pegged plank floors, and stood in front of the natural rock fireplace, where a lively blaze crackled. Sammy followed, shook himself again, and curled up on the hooked rug at her feet.

She heard Teague come in and slam the door behind him.

Hair dripping, he lugged the twenty-five-pound bag of kibble past her, retracing the route to the kitchen.

"Twenty-five *pounds*, Joanna?" he asked. "We're spending the weekend, not burrowing in for the winter!"

"I might stay," she heard herself say. "Start that novel I've been wanting to write."

The dog-food bag thunked to the kitchen floor, and Teague appeared in the doorway. For the first time, Joanna noticed that he'd exchanged his suit for jeans and a plaid flannel shirt. In those clothes, with his hair damp and curling around his ears, he looked younger, more like the Teague Darby she'd known and loved.

"We agreed to sell the cottage," he reminded her.

"No," Joanna said mildly, "we *didn't* agree. You said we should sell it and split the proceeds, and I said I wasn't so sure. I think Sammy and I could be very happy here." She looked down at the dog. His fur was curling, too, just like Teague's hair, and he seemed so pathetically happy to be home.

"Not that again," Teague said.

"You travel a lot," Joanna pointed out. "He'd be with me most of the time anyway."

Some of the tension in Teague's shoulders eased. "Maybe *I'd* like to live here," he said. "I could build my boat."

"You'll never build that boat," Joanna said.

"You'll never write a novel," Teague retorted, "so I guess we're even."

Sammy made a soft, mournful sound.

"Let's not argue," Joanna said. "We ought to be able to be civil to each other for a weekend."

"Civil," Teague replied. "We ought to be able to manage that. We've been 'civil' for months—when we've spoken at all."

Joanna felt cold, even though she was standing close to a blazing fire. She turned her head so Teague wouldn't see the tears that sprang to her eyes.

"Change your clothes, Joanna," Teague said after a long time, and much more gently. "You'll catch your death if you don't."

She nodded without looking at him and scurried into their bedroom.

Her wardrobe choices were limited, but she found a set of gray sweats and pulled them on. When she got to the kitchen, Teague had already opened a bottle of wine and busied himself making salad. Sammy was crunching away on a large serving of kibble.

Outside, the wind howled off the nearby water, and the lights flickered as Teague poured wine for them both—a Sauvignon Blanc, to complement the lobster topping their salads.

"I didn't know you still wanted to write a novel," Teague said.

"I didn't know you still wanted to build a boat," Joanna replied. She sat down at the table, and Teague took his usual place directly across from her.

"Why a novel?" Teague asked thoughtfully. "Your cookbooks are best-sellers—you were even offered your own show on the Food Network."

"Why build a boat?" Joanna inquired, taking a sip of her wine. "You can certainly afford to buy one."

"I asked you first," Teague said, watching her over the rim

of his wineglass. She wondered what he was thinking—that she ought to get a face lift? Maybe have some lipo?

Her spine stiffened. "I've always wanted to write a novel," she said. *Weren't you listening at all, back when we used to talk about our dreams?* "And this cottage would be the perfect place to do it."

"It would also be the perfect place to build a boat."

The lights went out, then flared on again.

Thunder rolled over the roof.

Sammy went right on crunching his kibble. He'd never been afraid of storms.

"Remember how Caitlin used to squirm under the blankets with us in the middle of the night when the weather was like this?" Teague asked. He'd set down his wineglass and taken up his fork, but it was suspended midway between his mouth and the plate.

"Do you think she's happy in California?" Joanna mused. "Happy with Peter?"

"They're newlyweds," Teague said. "She has a glamorous job, just like she always wanted. Of *course* she's happy."

"So were we, once." Joanna reddened when she realized she'd spoken the words aloud. She'd only meant to think them, not say them.

"What happened, Joanna?" Teague asked.

The lights went out again, and the fan in the furnace died with a creaky whir.

Teague left the table, went to the drawer, and rummaged until he found a candle. Plunking the taper into a ceramic holder Caitlin had made at day camp the summer she was eleven, he struck a match to the wick.

Joanna figured he'd forgotten the question, but it turned out he hadn't.

"What happened?" he repeated.

She sighed, turning the stem of her wineglass slowly between two fingers. "I don't know," she said softly. "I guess we just grew apart, once Caitlin left for college."

"I guess so," Teague said. "Is there somebody else, Joanna?"

She bristled. "Of course not," she said. "How could you possibly think—?"

In the light of the candle, Teague's features looked especially rugged. Again, Joanna had that strange feeling of time slipping backward, without her noticing until just this moment.

He didn't answer.

She took a gulp of wine this time, instead of a sip as before. "What about you? Have you—well—is there—?"

"No," Teague said in an angry undertone. "What the hell kind of question is that?"

"The same kind of question you asked *me*," Joanna fired back, though she was careful to keep her tone even, for Sammy's sake. "We haven't had sex for weeks. You bought a sports car. Next thing I know, you'll be squiring around some girl barely older than Caitlin—"

"You've got to be kidding," Teague interrupted. "Maybe we're on the skids, but we're still married—and I bought a sports car because I *wanted* a sports car."

"You're forty-one. You've just sold a company you worked half your life to build. You bought a sports car. Enter wife number two, who has probably already targeted you as fair game."

"Good God, Joanna. You *should* write a novel, because you have *one hell* of an imagination!"

"I don't need an imagination. Half the guys you play golf with have trophy wives, while the women who bore their children and helped them build their companies and their bloody *portfolios* are still wondering what hit them!"

Sammy crossed the kitchen, toenails clicking on the tile floor, and laid his muzzle on Joanna's lap.

She stroked his head. "It's all right," she told him. "We're not going to fight."

Teague shoved back his chair and stood. "It's *not* all right," he growled. "What kind of man do you think I am?"

The furnace tried mightily to come back on, but there wasn't enough juice.

"I don't know anymore," Joanna admitted quietly. "Do you think the electricity is going to come back on soon? It's getting cold in here."

"I have no idea," Teague said. "If you're cold, go sit by the fire."

"I will," Joanna said loftily, refilling her wineglass before she left the table.

Sammy trotted after her, his tags jingling hopefully on his collar. The cottage had always been a happy place, with the exception of last summer, when Joanna had cried a time or two. No doubt, the dog expected things to morph back to normal at any moment.

It would be nice, Joanna reflected, to be a dog.

Teague followed and threw another chunk of wood onto the fire, causing sparks to rise, swirling, up the chimney.

Joanna plunked into the overstuffed armchair a few feet away, at the edge of the firelight. She swirled her wine in her glass but didn't drink. "Maybe we should go back to the city," she said. "We could catch the six o'clock ferry."

"Go if you want," Teague replied coolly. "Sammy and I are staying here."

Joanna closed her eyes for a moment, trying to keep from being swept downstream into the Sammy conflict again. "If he's staying," she said, "I'm staying."

To her surprise, Teague laughed. It was a raw sound, gruff and low. "Damn," he said. "One thing hasn't changed, anyway. You're still as stubborn as a toothless old bulldog with a bone."

"Are you comparing me to a toothless *old* bulldog?"

Teague shoved a hand through his hair, swearing under his breath.

Joanna set her wineglass aside on the table next to her chair. "Okay," she conceded. "I might be a little stubborn, but I am *not* old or toothless."

"A *little* stubborn?" He moved out of the firelight and began rummaging again in the darkness. Just when Joanna had decided he was definitely going to strike her with a blunt object or stab her with an ice pick—by her own admission, she'd watched *way* too many episodes of *Forensic Files* and *Body of Evidence*—she heard the staticky crackle of a transistor radio.

He was turning the tuning knob, probably looking for a weather report.

"—ferries temporarily out of commission," a disembodied male voice said, between buzzing bursts of static, "widespread power outages—winds reaching—"

Joanna sat up very straight and reached for her wine again. "We're stranded," she said.

Sammy, lying on the rug in front of the fireplace, rolled onto his back, paws in the air and belly exposed, and snored.

"I see the dog's terrified," Teague quipped.

"Teague, this is serious. What are we going to do?"

"Well, we could tell ghost stories. Or play checkers." He paused. "Or tear off each other's clothes and have sex on the floor like we used to, whenever we came out here without Caitlin and half her Girl Scout troop."

A hot chill went through Joanna, making her ache in some very private places. In danger of spilling the wine, she set it aside again with a thunk.

"Don't be ridiculous," she said.

And suddenly Teague was in front of her, kneeling, parting her legs.

An involuntary groan escaped her.

Teague slipped his hands up under her sweatshirt and cupped her bare breasts in his hands. Ran the pads of his thumbs over her nipples until they hardened.

Joanna groaned again. "Teague—"

He pushed her shirt up, tongued her breasts, then suckled.

"This is—" She paused, gasping. "This won't solve anything—"

He was pulling at the elastic band of her sweatpants, drawing them skillfully down, off, away. "Maybe not," he murmured, raising one of her bare legs and placing it over his shoulder, "but it's going to feel good." The other leg went over the other shoulder. "Don't be quiet, Joanna," he said, sliding his hands under her backside and raising her until she felt the warmth of his breath through the nest of curls at the juncture of her thighs. "Please, don't be quiet."

Clawing at the arms of her chair, bucking against Teague's mouth, sobbing as she reached the first of several shattering orgasms, Joanna was *anything* but quiet.

And the dog didn't even wake up.

TWO

She was so beautiful, lying there asleep on the floor in front of the hearth, her supple body spent by their lovemaking, her features gilded in flickering firelight. The glow caught in her chin-length blond hair, all atangle now, and gleamed on the long sweep of her eyelashes. Joanna was Teague's age—forty-one—and yet she looked so much younger, with her guard down like that.

Teague wanted to stretch out a hand and caress the flawless line of her cheek with a light pass of the backs of his knuckles, the way he'd done a million times before, when things were good between them.

A dog snore ripped the darkness, and Teague smiled slightly, sadly. Sammy was zonked out, too, on the cushions of the window seat built into the bay windows overlooking the water. Not so long ago, Caitlin, coltish and spirited, would have been curled up there with the dog.

Where had the time gone?

One minute, Sammy was a pup and Caitlin was a ten-year-old.

Now, suddenly, the retriever was getting old, and Caitlin was a college graduate and a *wife* living far away, in California. Teague's eyes smarted, and he was glad of the power failure, glad of the darkness, glad Joanna was sleeping and couldn't see how close he was to losing it.

Losing it? He was losing *her*. How had he managed to accomplish *that* marvelous feat? Simple neglect, probably. He'd been so busy, building his career, building houses and office buildings, being a man-among-men and all that other crap, that all the ordinary little things connecting him and Joanna to each other had slowly withered and disappeared.

He didn't know her anymore.

And she certainly didn't know him, if she really thought he wanted to trade her in for a younger model, one of those calculatingly sweet *chicks* with the grapefruit boobs and sleek hair and the acquisitive instincts of a shark on the hunt.

Teague felt betrayed, and for a brief moment, he seethed.

Then he sighed and shoved a hand through his love-rumpled hair. Joanna wasn't a stupid woman—anything but. She'd helped him set up and then maintain the company. She'd raised their daughter, and done a hell of a good job in the process. And in addition to all that, she'd established a successful career of her own.

And yet she was willing to condemn him on the purchase of a *sports car*?

Teague sighed. Joanna had been right earlier: half the couples they'd socialized with over the years had split up, longtime wives replaced by talking mannequins composed more of silicone than flesh and blood and soul. And too often the process started, innocuously enough, with the buying of a sleek, expensive two-seater car.

Joanna stirred in her sleep and stretched, one breast bared by the motion.

Teague took a few moments to admire that breast, then gently replaced the quilt because the room was cold, even with the fire going. Beyond the sturdy stone walls of the cottage, the storm still raged, cutting Firefly Island off from the mainland.

Silently, he blessed the forces of wind and rain and high tides lashing at the rocky shore. Just then, he could have spent the rest of eternity, not just this last poignant weekend, alternately making love to Joanna and watching her sleep.

Sammy made a whimpering sound, chasing rabbits in his dreams.

Teague spoke quietly to him, and he sighed and settled deeper into his slumbers.

The faint jingle of Teague's cell phone, resting on a nearby end table, reminded him that there was no escaping the outside world, not even on Firefly Island in the middle of the storm of the century.

Afraid of waking Joanna, he scrambled for the phone and flipped it open.

"Teague Darby," he said, whispering.

"Dad?"

"Caitlin," he said, his voice warming. "Babe, it's the middle of the night. Is anything wrong?"

"No," Caitlin answered and immediately burst into tears.

"Hey," Teague said as Joanna stirred again, sat up, and yawned. "What's wrong?"

"I keep thinking about you and Mom getting divorced," Caitlin wailed. "I can't believe it!"

"Caitlin?" Joanna mouthed, reaching for the sweatshirt Teague had dragged off over her head earlier and pulling it on.

Teague nodded. "You should be asleep, sweetheart," he told his daughter. "We can talk about this tomorrow."

"I *can't* sleep," Caitlin said. "There are so many things going around and around in my head—"

"Like?"

"Like what's going to happen to Sammy when you two split up? *Tell* me you're not planning to take him to the pound!"

"Caitlin, *of course* we're not planning on taking Sammy to the pound."

Joanna smiled and shook her head, then reached for her sweatpants and shimmied into them. "I'll put the coffee on," she said, then remembered that the power was off and looked stymied for a moment. The pump would work—for a while—so there was water, but the pot was electric.

"Oh, good," Caitlin snuffled. "I was so afraid—"

"Don't be. Everything is okay, honey."

"No, it isn't! You and Mom are getting *divorced*! The *world* is ending!"

If Caitlin's career in advertising didn't work out, Teague figured, she could probably land a part on a soap opera. She had the crying part down pat.

"Honey—"

Joanna approached, took in Teague's naked frame with a lift of her eyebrows, and held out one hand.

Teague gladly surrendered the phone.

"Cait," Joanna said, watching as Teague pulled on his jeans and headed for the kitchen, probably intending to engineer some solution to the coffee problem. "It's Mom."

"Mooooooom!" Caitlin sobbed.

Usually, Caitlin was coolheaded, self-possessed, certainly not given to hysterics.

"Sweetheart," Joanna began, following a prompt from her well-developed intuition, "are you pregnant, by any chance?"

Caitlin gulped. "Yes! And what kind of family is this baby going to have, I ask you? Peter's parents have been divorced since he was ten. Now you and Dad are going your separate ways! What is my child supposed to do for *grandparents*?"

Teague came out of the dark kitchen, brandishing a metal coffeepot they used for camping.

He was a blurry shape to Joanna because her eyes were full of tears.

"Sweetheart," Joanna said carefully, "grandparents don't have to be married to each other to do grandparent-type things."

Teague dropped the coffeepot, spilling water and dry grounds all over the plank floor. He looked so stunned that Joanna laughed.

Caitlin, misunderstanding, was not pleased. "This may be funny to *you*, Mother, but I assure you, it is no laughing matter! My whole life, I've imagined us all having Christmas and Thanksgiving together at the cottage, me all grown-up, with a family of my own—and now—"

"There's a baby—she's—?" Teague croaked.

Sammy, roused from his bed on the window seat, padded over to lap up water and grounds.

"Yes, Teague," Joanna said, speaking over Caitlin's tearful rampage, "our daughter is expecting a child."

Teague sank heavily into an easy chair.

"You're not having a heart attack, are you?" Joanna asked.

"Dad is *having a heart attack?*" Caitlin cried.

"No," Joanna said, very quickly. "No, sweetheart. No. He's just, well—surprised."

"Is he all right?" demanded Caitlin, frantic. Peter could be heard in the background murmuring reassurances, probably trying to wrest the telephone receiver from his bride's hand so he could find out what was going on.

"Teague," Joanna said, "Caitlin wants to know if you're all right."

"I'm—fine," Teague said, poleaxed.

"He's fine," Joanna told Caitlin.

"Joanna," said Joanna's son-in-law on the other end of the line, "Caitlin is beside herself. Listen, if Teague is having a heart attack, we'll catch the first flight out of LAX—"

"Hold it," Joanna said. "Teague is *not* having a heart attack. Sammy is not being sent to the pound. And unless I miss my guess, no planes are landing at Sea-Tac because we're in the middle of a virtual hurricane."

"A hurricane?" Peter gasped.

Caitlin's instant lament could be heard in the background.

"Wait," Joanna pleaded. "I was exaggerating. It's only a very bad rainstorm. Take a breath, Peter. And tell *Caitlin* to take a breath. She could hyperventilate."

"My daughter is *pregnant?*" Teague muttered stuporously, like a man just coming out of a coma.

"Caitlin, sit down," she heard Peter say. "Take a breath.

There is no heart attack. There is no hurricane. Everything is *all right*."

Caitlin sobbed something incoherent.

"Except that you and Teague are getting divorced," Peter translated sadly.

"Well, yes," Joanna allowed. "We are. But it isn't the end of the world."

"As you know," Peter replied, "Caitlin doesn't see it that way."

"Take care of her, Peter. Get her to breathe into a paper bag or something, and if she still doesn't calm down, call her doctor. This is so unlike her. She's usually so practical."

"She's been crying for two weeks straight," Peter admitted.

"And you didn't call me?"

"She said it was nothing, just a mood she'd get over. Or PMS. It really resembled PMS."

Joanna sank into the second chair, remembered what she and Teague had done in it a few hours before, and sprang to her feet again. "Sammy," she said, since Teague was still out of commission, shooing the dog away from the spilled grounds, "don't eat the coffee."

"Joanna, are you *sure* everything is all right? Where are you, anyway? We tried the main house, and the cottage, and finally resorted to Teague's cell phone."

"We're fine. We're at the cottage, but the power is out, and the phone lines are evidently down, too. Put Caitlin back on, if she's able to talk."

There was some shuffling.

Joanna crouched to scoop up the soggy coffee grounds with the first thing that came to hand—Teague's flannel shirt.

"Mom?" Caitlin said.

"Feeling better?" Joanna asked, directing the question not only to her distant daughter but to Teague, who seemed to be coming around.

"Yes," Caitlin said.

"No," said Teague.

"When was the pregnancy determined?" Joanna asked. "And when is the baby due?"

"We did a test yesterday," Caitlin sniffled. "You know, with one of those drugstore kits? I saw my doctor today, and he confirmed it. It's too early to pinpoint the actual due date, but he's guesstimating it will be sometime in February."

"Are you happy?"

More sniffling. "Of course I'm happy. So is Peter." Then, bravely, "I guess we can have Christmas at your place one year and Dad's the next."

"We'll figure something out," Joanna said gently, trying not to think about split Christmases and Thanksgivings because she knew if she did, she'd soon be sobbing as hard as Caitlin had been a few minutes before. "I promise."

"You're cutting out, Mom," Caitlin said, sounding more like her usual self.

"Your dad probably forgot to charge his cell phone again," Joanna said.

"At least I carry one," Teague said.

Joanna hated cell phones, considered them intrusive. But with the regular lines down and Caitlin so upset, she was glad Teague didn't share her sentiment. "Go back to bed, Caitlin. Get some rest. If the storm lets up, I can probably call you tomorrow."

"Wait a second," Caitlin said. "You and dad are at the cottage together. Does that mean—?"

"Tomorrow, Caitlin," Joanna said.

They rang off.

"She's a baby herself," Teague said.

"Caitlin is a grown woman, Teague," Joanna reasoned, feeling the strangest mixture of joy and sorrow. "She has a college degree, a husband, and a good job." *My baby,* her heart said. *My baby.* And she started to cry.

"Come here," Teague said, holding out a hand.

Joanna let him pull her onto his lap. Nestled against him, she buried her face in the curve between his neck and shoulder, breathing in his familiar scent.

She thought of separate Christmases.

Separate birthdays and Thanksgivings.

And she cried even harder.

"Hey," Teague said gruffly, stroking her back, "I think we're supposed to be *happy* about this."

"I *am* happy!" Joanna sobbed.

Sammy, laying his muzzle on the arm of the chair Teague and Joanna were huddled in, gave a low, worried whine.

"It's okay," she told the dog.

"I don't think he believes you," Teague said.

Joanna stroked Sammy's head, brushed some coffee grounds off his nose. "Really," she said. "It's all good."

Teague held her. "Right now," he said, "I like it fine."

Sammy gave a doggy sigh, turned, and went back to his window seat, climbing the special carpeted stairs Teague had built for him when the vet first diagnosed his arthritis.

"This is hard," Joanna whispered.

Teague propped his chin on top of her head. "Somehow," he said, "I don't think that's a comment on my manly virtues."

Joanna giggled moistly.

"Of course, I *did* bring you to three or four screaming orgasms—Grandma."

Joanna laughed and swatted at him.

But he caught her face between his hands and suddenly, his expression was serious. "Joanna, about the sports car—"

She stiffened. Teague had said he didn't have a trophy wife waiting to plant a firm derriere in the passenger seat of his ridiculously expensive ride, and she believed him. But once the divorce was final and he was on the market, it wouldn't be long. He was smart, good-looking, successful, and great in bed—or out of it.

No, it wouldn't be long.

"Just for tonight," she said, making herself relax, "let's pretend we're not getting divorced, okay?"

"Sounds good to me," Teague replied, sliding a hand up under her sweatshirt to caress her breast.

Joanna was instantly hot. She swallowed a groan as Teague leaned forward to nibble at her neck, her earlobe, the base of her throat.

An image of Teague's next wife invaded her mind.

Pretend, Joanna told herself silently, *pretend.*

He began, very slowly, to undress her, and soon she was straddling him in the chair, her body already moving to the age-old rhythm, straining to take him inside her.

But Teague would not be rushed.

He took his time, fondling her breasts.

He tongued her nipples, but only sucked them when she begged.

He cupped her buttocks, squeezing them firmly.

And then she felt his right hand sweep around, find the core of her, and part her to ply her clitoris between his fingers. Joanna was instantly transported back to college days; they'd made love like this then, in the backseat of Teague's rattletrap car, in her dorm-room closet during a wild party, once on his parents' bed, while they were downstairs, playing bridge with neighbors.

In their first apartment, after they were married.

Teague slid a finger inside Joanna and worked her G-spot until she was half frantic with the need to come. But he always withdrew, just at the crucial moment; he loved to make her wait.

Once, he'd loved *her.*

"Teague," she murmured, throwing her head back, abandoning herself to his hands, his mouth, his damnably infinite patience. "Teague, oh, please—"

"Not yet," he told her.

She began to buck against his hand, desperate for release.

"*Please—*"

"Too soon," he said, taking most of her right breast into his mouth, then pulling back to tease her with his tongue.

"*Teague—*"

"Shh." He worked his fingers faster inside her, then slowed.

She rode his hand, felt his palm making slow circles against her clitoris even as his fingers worked her G-spot.

And she shattered, broke apart into a million flaming pieces.

It was over, then, she thought. Over so soon.

But it wasn't over.

Teague shifted, opened his jeans, and she felt him, hard and hot, ready to take her.

She sagged against him, her body still convulsing with soft climaxes.

He eased into her, but the size of him made her draw in a sharp breath and push back from his chest, beginning another ascent even as she trembled with the last sweet, sharp climax.

There was a difference, though. Joanna was in control now, even as she climbed inexorably toward another orgasm, one she knew would be brutal in its sheer force.

Gripping Teague's bare shoulders, she straightened so she could watch his face change in the dying light of the fire. Slowly, he raised and lowered his powerful hips in long, deep strokes, determined to set the pace.

Joanna took over.

She moved faster along his length, took him deeper, twisted her torso slightly every time his shaft was sheathed inside her.

He groaned, tried to slow her pace with his hands, but Joanna would not be turned from her purpose. She pumped harder, faster, deeper, with a primitive grace that soon had *Teague* pleading, just as she had earlier.

"Joanna," he rasped, the muscles of his neck cording as he threw back his head, beginning to lose control. "*Joanna—*"

She rode him ruthlessly.

He came with a low shout and a stiffening of his whole

body, nearly throwing her off with the upward thrust of his hips. She felt his warmth spilling into her and savored his unqualified surrender.

I love you, she almost said.

He settled slowly back into himself, his breathing still quick and shallow, his chest and thighs damp with sweat against her own slick skin. He pulled her close, held her against him.

And they slept.

When Joanna awakened, she was still straddling Teague. The sun was up and the furnace was running, chugging dusty heat through the vents.

The power was back on.

Joanna sat back, blinking, and was chagrined to find Teague wide-awake, watching her with a tender, puzzled little smile.

In the night, she'd been reckless, passionate, even wanton.

In the daylight, she was forty-one.

A grandmother-to-be.

And the dog was whining at the front door, needing to go outside.

She shifted to get to her feet, but Teague stopped her. Tightened his strong hands on her bare buttocks.

"Joanna," Teague said.

"Don't," she whispered.

He let her up and propelled her in the direction of the bathroom.

By the time she'd finished her shower, squirmed into a pair of jeans that reminded her of the five pounds she'd gained, and added a bra and a T-shirt, Teague and Sammy were back from their walk.

Teague was in the kitchen, whistling.

Coffee was brewing.

"Let's have breakfast out," he said as she entered. "Unless you want kibble or leftover salad."

"I'm not hungry," Joanna lied. Didn't he know she was fat?

"Well, I am," Teague said.

Sammy munched happily on his kibble.

And the telephone rang.

"Mom?"

"Hello, Caitlin," Joanna said, feeling oddly embarrassed.

"I guess the storm must be over, huh?" Caitlin asked.

Joanna glanced at Teague and found him watching her. The expression in his eyes was not grandfatherly in the least. "Yes," she said. "The storm is over."

"I was pretty hysterical last night," Caitlin said softly.

"You're allowed," Joanna replied.

Teague made a face.

Joanna made one back.

"But you and Dad are at the cottage. Together."

"Caitlin—"

"There's hope, then." A frown entered Caitlin's voice. "Isn't there?"

"We're here to—talk."

Teague waggled his eyebrows suggestively.

"To decide things," Joanna said, blushing. She turned her back to him.

"What things?"

"Caitlin."

"Okay, okay, I'll let you off the hook. For now. But I still think it's intriguing that you and Dad are—"

"We got stuck here," Joanna answered.

"Poor choice of words," Teague whispered, suddenly behind her, his breath warm against her nape, causing her skin to tingle.

"Maybe if you just—talked. You know, communicated?"

"I've heard of it, yes," Joanna replied dryly. "Are you feeling better today, Cait?"

"Lots better," Caitlin said. "It was probably just hormones."

"Yes," Joanna agreed, turning to glare at Teague because he was trying to turn her on and she was talking to *their daughter.* "It was probably just hormones."

Teague pulled an invisible dart from his chest. "Sammy and I are going to the store for breakfast-type food," he said. "Tell Caitlin I love her and congratulations."

With that, he took the keys to his sports car from the countertop and whistled for Sammy, and the two of them left the kitchen, headed for the front door.

Joanna relayed the message, adding that Sammy and Teague had gone to the supermarket.

"Good," Caitlin said. "Then you can talk."

"Caitlin, we *are* talking."

"About you and Dad, and your marriage. You know, the sex part." A silent *eew* shrilled beneath Caitlin's words.

"Caitlin Marie, do not go there. You are my daughter and I adore you. But your father's and my marriage is off-limits. *Especially* the 'sex part.' "

"So you're admitting you do have sex?"

"I'm not admitting anything of the sort. Your father and I are getting a divorce, Caitlin. I know that's hard for you to accept, but it wasn't a spur-of-the-moment decision. We made it very deliberately and gave it a lot of thought first. We're both going to be a lot happier in the long run."

Maybe the *very* long run, Joanna reflected.

"Is there another man in your life, Mom?"

Joanna nearly choked. "*No!*"

"Does Dad have a girl on the side?"

"He says he doesn't, and I have no reason not to believe him." *Except for the sports car.* "Caitlin, why are we having this conversation when I made it perfectly clear about five seconds ago that what goes on in your father's and my private lives is patently none of your business?"

"I don't understand why you're doing this," Caitlin said, sounding hurt. "That's all. You don't have another man. Dad doesn't have another woman. What is so terribly wrong that you can't work it out?"

"We've grown apart," Joanna said. "Your father wants to build a sailboat. I want to write a novel."

"And those things are mutually exclusive?"

For a moment, Joanna was stumped for an answer. She could say they'd tried to save their marriage, she and Teague, but it wouldn't be true. They *hadn't* really tried. One day, one of them—she couldn't remember which—had said, "Maybe we should just call it quits." And the other had replied, "Maybe so."

Things had escalated from there.

A tear slipped down Joanna's right cheek, but she managed to keep her tone normal. Bright, perky, everything's-fine ordinary.

"Okay," Caitlin said, "just tell me one thing, and I'll leave you alone. I promise."

"Okay," Joanna agreed, a split second before she realized she'd just taken the bait.

"Do you love Dad or not?"

An enormous, painful lump formed in Joanna's throat. She tried to swallow, but it wouldn't go down.

"Mom? Are you still there?"

"I'm—here," Joanna managed.

"That's what I thought. You still love Dad, don't you?"

Joanna realized she loved the man Teague used to be, but he'd become someone else over the past few years. As for last night, well, that had been—what? A time warp? Some kind of primitive reaction to being stranded together in a storm?

"Mom?"

"Caitlin, not now. Please."

"I'm coming up there," Caitlin said decisively. "Someone has to talk sense into the two of you."

Joanna drew a deep breath and let it out slowly, silently reminding herself that she loved her daughter. Caitlin was only trying to help. "You're expecting a baby, sweetheart," she said gently. "You have a husband and a nice apartment and a very demanding job. You can't just pick up and leave."

"Peter and I talked it over last night," Caitlin said. "We want to take Sammy."

"Take Sammy?"

"You know, give him a home."

"He *has* a home."

"A *broken* one." Caitlin gave a small, stifled sob.

Again, Joanna's eyes stung. "Yes," she admitted, suddenly imagining all of them—herself, Teague, Caitlin and Sammy—picking their way around the storm-tossed wreckage of some once-great ship, unable to reach each other. "A broken one."

"I guess Sammy wouldn't be happy in this little apartment," Caitlin admitted.

Suddenly needing to move, Joanna wandered out of the kitchen and into the living room to stand with one bent knee resting on the window seat cushion. Sunlight danced, dazzling on the water—it was as if there'd been no storm in the night, as if she'd dreamed it.

While Caitlin talked on, Joanna, only half listening, stared out at the sandy, stony beach in front of the cottage and remembered Teague and Sammy playing there. Teague throwing sticks, Sammy chasing them, bringing them back.

"Sammy needs your father," Joanna said.

And deep in her heart, a silent voice added, *And so do I.*

Three

By the time Sammy and Teague returned from their supermarket mission, Joanna had brought the bumpy conversation with Caitlin in for a safe landing, gathered up the quilts from the living-room floor, and opened several windows to the warmth of the day.

"He's jonesing for a walk," Teague said with a nod toward Sammy as Joanna stepped outside to help carry in the bags of groceries stuffed into the tiny trunk of the sports car. "Think breakfast could wait?"

Joanna smiled even as her heart splintered inside her. Why couldn't life always be like this—simple, easy, glazed in sunlight? "Sure," she said.

So they left the groceries, and Teague caught hold of her hand, and they went across the dirt road and down the bank to the beach, Sammy gamboling joyfully ahead of them.

Joanna bit her lower lip, watching him, trying to stay another spate of tears. They would have this one last glorious weekend together, she and Teague and Sammy. She envied the dog because he couldn't know just how short the time would be.

"What?" Teague asked, noticing what she was trying so hard to hide.

"I was just wondering—do you think we tried hard enough?"

Teague looked puzzled.

"To save our marriage, Teague," Joanna prompted.

"No," Teague said. He bent, still holding Joanna's hand firmly, and picked up a stick. He tossed it a little ways for Sammy, who shot after it, a streak of happy, golden dog catapulting down the beach.

"What could we have done differently?"

"Talked, maybe. Instead of always assuming we already knew what the other was thinking or feeling and proceeding from there."

"Talked," Joanna mused. "Tell me about your boat, Teague. The one you want to build."

"You hate boats. They make you claustrophobic and seasick," Teague reminded her.

She smiled. "True," she said. "But talking about them is not the same thing as spending weeks at sea."

"Weeks at sea?" Teague echoed, confused.

"Aren't you planning to sail around the Horn or something?"

He chuckled, though whether it was because her question had amused him or because Sammy was nudging him in the knees with the stick, wanting him to toss it again, Joanna had no way of knowing.

So she waited, strangely breathless.

"No," Teague finally said after throwing the stick, a little farther this time, and watching as Sammy raced after it. "I just want to go fishing."

"Then why not simply *buy* a boat?" Joanna asked. "Why go to all the trouble of building one?"

"For the experience, Joanna," Teague answered. "I'm used to building things. Caitlin's backyard playhouse. The dog steps in there by the window seat. The company."

"Oh," Joanna said. "I guess I pictured you sailing the high seas."

Sammy came back with the stick, but he was tiring. He wasn't used to running along beaches anymore.

Teague spotted a fallen log a little way down the beach and led Joanna there to sit. Sammy lay down gratefully in the sand, panting but still holding on to his treasured stick.

"You pictured me sailing the high seas," Teague said, gazing out over the waters of the sound, so tranquil now, so dangerously stormy the night before. He looked sadly amused. "No doubt with a long-legged blonde for a first mate?"

Joanna hesitated, then let her head rest against the side of Teague's shoulder for a long moment. "And the whole time, you were imagining a dinghy a hundred yards from shore?"

"Pretty much," Teague said.

"I should have asked you."

"I should have told you, whether you asked or not." Teague slipped an arm around Joanna and held her close for a moment. "Are we still pretending right now, Joanna," he asked, "or is this real?"

"I'm not sure," Joanna said softly.

"Me, either," Teague admitted. He leaned to stroke Sammy's mist-dampened back. "I'm not sure of much of anything right now."

"Neither am I."

"Tell me about the novel."

"It would be about a marriage. A young couple falling in love, having a child, building a wonderful life together—and growing apart in ordinary ways. Becoming strangers to each other."

"You forgot about the golden retriever they adopted at the pound," Teague said, with an attempt at a grin that pierced Joanna's heart again.

"Oh, I didn't forget that," Joanna answered.

"Will they break up, these people in your book? Or will they work things out?" He was looking deep into her eyes now, peeling back the layers of her very soul. "Stay together for the sake of the dog, maybe?"

Joanna chuckled, but it came out sounding more like a sob. "I don't know," she said. "Maybe it's too late for them. Maybe it would be better—kinder—to just cut their losses and run."

Sammy had recovered after his brief rest and got to his feet, eager to chase the stick again.

Teague let his arm fall slowly from around Joanna's shoulders and stood, Sammy's stick in his hand. "Time to head back," he told the dog. "You don't want to overdo it, boy."

Joanna rose, too, reluctantly. She'd wanted so much to hold on to the moment she and Teague had shared, but it was already gone.

So the three of them walked back to the cottage, one buoyant with faith in a good world, two doing their best to pretend things weren't falling apart.

Joanna needed to be busy, so she constructed an elaborate omelet from the contents of Teague's grocery bags. While she cooked, he plugged his cell phone in to charge, in case of another power outage, and carried in more wood from the shed out back. The transistor radio burbled news from the kitchen counter.

Some of the ferry docks had been damaged in the storm, so only a few routes were still being run, and while the weather was good now, there was another system brewing off the coast, one that might get ugly. She switched off the radio, set the table, poured juice, and waited while Teague washed up at the kitchen sink.

"I guess we couldn't get back to Seattle today even if we wanted to," she said lightly, wondering all the time she was speaking why she was practically holding her breath for Teague's reaction.

"Oh?" Teague asked without turning around.

"Maybe not tomorrow, either. According to the news, we're likely to have another storm."

"That's terrible," Teague said, but when he faced Joanna at

last, he was grinning. "Absolutely the worst thing that could possibly happen."

Confused, Joanna blinked, momentarily speechless.

"No wonder everybody was buying up all the bottled water and propane when Sammy and I were at the market," Teague said.

Sammy, lying on a nearby rug, lifted his head at the sound of his name, then rested it on his forelegs again when he realized no stick was going to be thrown.

"You're being awfully casual about this," Joanna said.

Teague rounded the table, stood behind Joanna, placed his hands on her shoulders, and gently but firmly pressed her into her chair. "Have you got a better idea?"

"Well, maybe *we* should stock up on bottled water and propane."

"Eat, Joanna," Teague said, sitting down across from her and helping himself to half the omelet. "I bought some already. Madge Potter will drop it off later, in her truck."

Madge, who had lived on Firefly Island all her life, was a local institution. She published the small weekly newspaper, dug clams when the tides were right and sold them door to door—and delivered groceries.

"You're *enjoying* this," Joanna accused, but she was smiling.

"The omelet? Definitely. This is first-rate, Joanna. No wonder your cookbooks sell like—"

"Hotcakes?" Joanna teased.

He grinned. "Does the woman in your book write cookbooks?"

"No," Joanna said. She hadn't written a word of the novel yet, but Teague spoke as though she were halfway through. "She's a chef and owns an elegant restaurant."

Teague paused, swallowed, and frowned thoughtfully. "Oh," he said. When he met Joanna's gaze, his blue eyes were solemn, even grave. "Do you wish you'd become a chef? Started that restaurant you used to talk about?"

Joanna considered. "No," she said. "It would have taken

too much time. Raising Caitlin and being your wife pretty much filled my dance card."

" 'Pretty much'?"

"I was happy, Teague."

"Emphasis on the 'was'?"

"I didn't say that."

"Joanna, if you were happy, we wouldn't be dividing everything we own—including the dog."

"If *you* were happy, you wouldn't have worked eighteen-hour days long after the company was up and running," Joanna said. "You wouldn't have bought a sports car."

"That again? It's a *car*, Joanna. Not an effort to recapture my youth."

Joanna lowered her fork to the table and stared down at her portion of the omelet, as yet untouched.

"Look," Teague said, making an obvious effort to hold on to his temper, "if the car bothers you so much, I'll sell it."

She looked up. "You'd do that?"

Before he could answer, a vehicle rattled into the driveway alongside the house, backfired a couple of times, and clunked its way to a reverberating silence.

"Madge is here," Teague said. And he smiled.

In the next moment, a knock sounded at the back door.

Sammy gave an uncertain woof and slowly raised himself to all four feet.

Teague went to the door.

"Got your water and propane and all that camping stuff," Madge boomed out. "It's an extra ten bucks over and above what you already paid me if I gotta unload it."

Teague chuckled. "Come in and have coffee with Joanna," he told Madge. "I'll unload the truck."

"Don't mind if I do," Madge thundered as Teague stepped back to let her pass. She was a tall, burly-looking woman, well into her sixties and clad in her usual bib overalls, flannel shirt, and rubber fishing boots. Her broad face was weathered by years of wind and salt-water spray, her gray hair stood out around her head, thick and unruly, and her smile was warm and full of genuine interest. She leaned to pat Sammy on the head once before he followed Teague outside.

"Hello, Madge," Joanna said, already filling a mug from the coffeemaker. "Have you eaten?"

"Hours ago," Madge proclaimed. "Not a bit hungry. That was some storm we had last night, wasn't it? Nils and me, we thought it would take the roof right off our cabin."

Nils was Madge's live-in boyfriend. He worked on the fishing boats in Alaska in season and ran the printing press when he was home. He was a good twenty years younger than Madge and was known to write her long, poetic letters when he was away.

"Sit down," Joanna invited, handing Madge the steaming mug.

"Best stand," Madge said. "Sit down too much, and these old bones might just rust enough so's I can't get up again."

Joanna chuckled. As colloquial and homey as Madge's speech was, she wrote like the seasoned journalist she was. Joanna particularly enjoyed her column, which contained everything from political diatribes to recipes to local gossip. "Not likely," she said.

"Good to see you and Teague out here together," Madge went on, narrowing her eyes speculatively. "The way I heard it, you two were on the outs. On the verge of divorce."

"Madge Potter," Joanna said, as a disturbing possibility dawned, "don't you *dare* write about us in that column of yours!"

"Well, I wouldn't name names or anything like that," Madge promised before taking a noisy slurp of her coffee. " 'Course, if I said anything about that sports car, everybody'd figure it out. Stirred up a lot of interest around here, I can tell you, when Teague showed up driving that flashy rig with that redhead—"

Madge gulped back the remainder of the sentence, but it was too late.

"Redhead?" Joanna asked, mortified, furious, and totally blindsided, all at once.

"Oops," Madge said.

Teague appeared in the open doorway at just that moment, a propane jug under each arm. He looked from Madge to Joanna, connecting the dots, and the color drained out of his face.

"I guess I'd best be going," Madge announced and hastened out. Seconds later, her old truck roared to life and rumbled away.

"You were here—on the island—with a redhead?" Joanna asked, her voice deceptively mild.

Slowly, Teague set the propane tanks down. Sammy slithered between Teague and the door frame and headed for the living room, ears lowered and tail tucked, like a canine soldier hearing the whistle of approaching mortar fire.

"It wasn't what you think," Teague said.

"Wasn't it?" Joanna retorted, folding her arms. "Teague, you and Caitlin and Sammy and I came here as a family for years. Everybody knows us. And *you brought a redhead to this cottage?*"

"Joanna—"

"Shut the door."

Teague reached behind him and closed the door with a soft click.

"You *rotten liar!*" Joanna accused.

Teague reddened, and his jaw took on a familiar hardness. He was shutting down, backing away. In another moment, he'd turn his back on her and refuse to—refuse to what? Explain? Tell more lies?

To Joanna's surprise, relief, and outrage, Teague stood his ground. "You're not going to like the truth a whole lot better than what you *think* happened," he said. "Ava isn't my lover. She's a real estate agent, specializing in vacation properties. I should have talked to you about it first, I admit that, but you were so busy doing interviews to promote your cookbook—"

Joanna dragged one of the chairs back from the kitchen table and fell into it. "A real estate agent?" she murmured. "You were going to put the cottage on the market—without even telling me?"

"Of course I would have told you," Teague insisted. "Eventually."

"Like when I came out here to start my novel and found a For Sale sign posted in the front yard?"

"Joanna, I didn't sign anything. I was just doing—research."

The sun must have gone behind a cloud, because suddenly the bright kitchen seemed dark, full of shadows.

"And naturally you needed the *sports car* so the whole island would see you zipping around with a hot redhead."

Teague's jaw tightened again, but he didn't speak.

And the room got darker.

Thunder crashed somewhere in the distance.

"I'd better bring the rest of that stuff inside," Teague said.

"Go for it," Joanna said coldly.

Teague went out.

She sat there for a few moments, absorbing the aftershocks. Then, because it was too painful to sit still, she got up, cleared the table, scraped the remains of the celebrated omelet into the garbage, filled the sink with scalding hot water, and banged dishes around until they were clean.

Rain spattered the roof.

Teague returned several times, lugging gallon bottles of water, a case of wine, a small portable camp stove that could be used outside, a couple of battery-operated lamps.

"Were you expecting a siege?" Joanna asked, keeping her back to him.

"More like an arctic chill," Teague replied, but the joke fell flat between them, plopping like an overfilled water balloon.

She turned, leaning back against the sink, gripping the counter edge with one hand. "What else haven't you told me, Teague? What does the whole island—the whole city of Seattle—know that *I* don't?"

"Nothing, Joanna."

" 'Nothing, Joanna,' " she mimicked. And suddenly, she was crying. She threw her hands out wide from her sides. "We spent vacations in this cottage, Teague. We brought our daughter here. We decorated Christmas trees and set off Fourth of July fireworks and carved Thanksgiving turkeys. And you had the *nerve* to bring a real estate agent here to put a price on all that? Without even mentioning it to me?"

"You were busy," he repeated.

She launched herself at him, colliding with his rock-hard chest when he didn't give ground. She jabbed at his breastbone with a furious finger. "How much is it worth, Teague? How much for the dreams, and the laughter, the lovemaking, and the checker-playing in front of the fire? *How much is it worth?*"

He caught her wrists in his hands. "Too much," he said hoarsely. "Way, way too much."

Joanna blinked. Staring up at him, she was fairly strangled by anger and heartbreak. It almost would have been better if he'd confessed to an affair with what's-her-name, the red-headed, red-hot real estate agent. Almost.

She squeezed her eyes shut, but the tears flowed anyway. Teague didn't let go of her wrists, and she didn't have the strength to pull free.

So they just stood that way while the rain pattered over their heads and the room darkened and all the dreams Joanna hadn't realized she still cherished drained away into hopeless reality.

All the pretending in the world wasn't going to change the fact that she truly *didn't* know Teague Darby anymore. The man she'd married, the man she'd loved so fiercely for so long wouldn't have dreamed of selling this cottage. For all their success, they'd always agreed that, if everything suddenly went to hell in the proverbial handbasket, they could sell the business and the mansion, empty their bank accounts, and liquidate all their investments—but the *cottage,* the cottage was sacred ground.

A sob tore itself out of Joanna's throat.

Teague pulled her close again and held her tightly. "I didn't mean to hurt you, Joanna," he said. "Honest to God, I didn't. I just wasn't thinking straight. I—ever since we started planning this divorce—"

She drew back, though his arms were still around her, and looked up into his taut, drawn face. He needed a shave, and there were deep shadows under his eyes.

"Who are you, Teague?" she whispered. "Who *are* you?"

"Joanna, I'm sorry—"

She shook her head and pulled back, and this time, he let her go.

"I don't want to talk to you right now," she said. "I don't want to look at you. I'm—I'm going out for a walk."

"Are you out of your mind? It's *raining!*"

She tried to smile but fell short. "A little rain never hurt anybody." It was standard Seattle vernacular. Most of the natives didn't even carry umbrellas; they simply expected to get wet and eventually dry off.

"Will you listen to me? It's cold, and the wind is rising, and—"

Joanna moved past him, into the living room, and opened the front door.

"At least wear a coat!" Teague said.

Sammy came to her and nuzzled at the knees of her too-tight jeans.

Joanna stepped outside like a sleepwalker, shutting the door behind her. She heard Sammy whimper and scratch on the other side, but she didn't turn back. She ran over the rain-slickened grass through the downpour. She ran until her hair was dripping and her clothes were soaked. She ran until she was breathless, knowing all the while that she was behaving like an idiot, and completely unable to do anything else *but* run.

She was well down the road when her stamina finally gave out and she had to stop, bent double, gasping, shrieking silently with a grief as profound as if everyone she loved had suddenly died.

And then Teague was there, as wet as she was, wrapping a yellow rain slicker around her, raising the hood to cover her head.

"I hate you!" she screamed. "Teague Darby, *I hate you* for turning into somebody else when I wasn't looking!"

Teague stared down at her for a few moments, oblivious to the rain, unspeaking. Then he lifted her into his arms, turned, and started back toward the cottage.

Inside, he kicked the door shut with one foot, but he didn't set her down. He carried her through the house, both of them dripping, Sammy following fretfully behind.

In the bathroom, Teague set Joanna down hard on the lid of the toilet seat and started hot water running in the huge claw-foot tub they'd bought at an estate sale and had refurbished.

"What are you doing?" Joanna asked before sneezing.

Teague crouched in front of her, and pulled off her wet shoes, peeled away her socks. "Trying to keep you from catching pneumonia," he said, "and I'd appreciate a little cooperation!" He stood and stepped back. "Get naked, get in the tub, and soak until you feel warm. I'm heading for the kitchen."

Joanna sniffled. She felt like a first-class fool, sitting there on a toilet, soaked to the skin. What had she been thinking, running in the rain like that?

But that was just it. She *hadn't* been thinking. She'd been *feeling*, and it had hurt too much. She'd tried to outrun the pain, foolishly, desperately. And it was still with her.

Better get used to it, she thought. This is your life, Joanna Darby. From now on.

Teague was gone before she got around to wondering what he intended to do in the kitchen. She undressed and stepped into the steaming tub, wincing at the heat of the water, welcome as it was.

Maybe, she reflected with grim amusement, sinking to her chin, she ought to drown herself.

Teague returned a few minutes later, carrying a cup of something hot. "Drink this," he said, shoving it at her.

It was a hot toddy, stout on the brandy side.

Joanna sipped.

Teague plopped down on the toilet-seat lid. He was soaked and shivering a little, but he appeared not to have noticed.

"That was a stupid trick," he said.

"Thank you for that insight," Joanna replied thickly. Oh, great. Her sinuses were already clogging up.

The lights flickered, went out, and came on again, but tentatively.

"You'd better get into this tub while we still have hot water," Joanna said. She'd always been the practical one.

The bathroom door was open a crack, and Sammy stuck his snout in, whining.

"At least *he's* dry," Teague said, stripping.

Sammy retreated, padding off down the hall again.

Joanna sat up a little straighter, pulling her legs back and crossing them so Teague could fit in the other end of the tub, facing her. His lips were blue, and his teeth were chattering slightly.

Joanna extended the cup to him, and he took a sip, but grudgingly.

"Why didn't you make one for yourself?" she asked.

"Somebody has to stay sober around here," he grumbled. "Not to mention sane."

She giggled, and the sound was a congested snort.

"I don't want to sell this cottage," she said, lifting the mug in a sort of defiant toast.

"Yes," Teague said, "I gathered that."

"The water's getting cold," Joanna remarked thickly. "Turn the spigot marked *H*, please."

"Thanks for the highly technical instructions," Teague said, but he turned, his fine butt making a scooching sound on the bottom of the big tub, and hot water flowed. "Does it bother you that my ass is getting scalded?" he inquired.

"Not at all," Joanna said.

Grumbling, he shifted so he was sitting with his back to Joanna. He slid back against her and she had to straighten her legs to keep her kneecaps from snapping.

"You're squashing me," she complained.

"Too bad. I'm not going to parboil my butt by turning around."

Joanna laughed. "How much brandy did you put in this toddy?" she asked.

"Enough," Teague answered with a sigh.

She set the cup on the wide brim of the tub, where they used to burn candles, back when bathing together meant having aqua-sex. Then, a little drunk, she slid her hands around to the front of his chest and played with his nipples.

He groaned.

She stroked his taut belly.

He sat up a little straighter, the muscles in his back and shoulders hard with tension.

She took hold of his cock.

He gasped. "I think I should—shut off the water—"

"But then I'd have to let go of you," she said sweetly.

"As much as I hate that idea—your letting go of me, I mean," Teague choked out, "the tub is going to overflow."

Reluctantly, she released him.

He shut off the flow of hot water and turned, facing her, kneeling now. He was huge, rigid.

Magnificent.

Joanna sat up. She took Teague into her hands, then into her mouth, savoring him, teasing him with the tip of her tongue.

He clasped the edge of the tub with one hand, burying the other in Joanna's hair.

And he murmured her name.

She worked him harder.

He groaned again, struggling to hold himself still, to hold himself back.

Joanna was taking no prisoners. She nipped him lightly, and he tensed and gave a ragged, raspy cry. When she began to suck again, he suddenly grasped her head in both hands and drew out of her mouth.

"Teague?"

"If you keep doing that, I'm going to come."

She kept doing that.

And he came.

She stayed with him until he stilled, dropped to his haunches in the cooling bathwater, breathing almost as hard as before his orgasm.

He sagged forward onto her, and they lay still in the big tub, Joanna's hands stroking his shoulders.

In the distance, the telephone began to ring.

"Ignore it," Teague pleaded.

"It might be Caitlin," Joanna said. "What if something's wrong?"

Teague got up, stepped out of the tub, wrapped a towel around his waist, and tossed another towel to Joanna.

By the time she caught up to him in their bedroom, he was just hanging up the phone.

"Is Caitlin all right?" Joanna asked anxiously.

Teague grinned. "As far as I know," he said. "That was somebody selling vinyl siding. We qualify for the V.I.P. rate. At least, that's what I think he said. He was calling from Pakistan, so I'm not really sure."

Joanna stood still in the doorway, barely covered by her towel.

In the living room, Sammy gave a loud snore.

"Come here," Teague said, his gaze smoldering as he dragged it from her feet to her face.

And before she knew she'd moved, Joanna was standing in front of Teague and he was relieving her of the towel.

Four

"Sex," Joanna said sagely, when she recovered her power of speech, "is not the solution to our dilemma."

Teague, lying beside her in the tangle of bedding, hauled her on top of him and chuckled. "You couldn't prove it by me," he said. "Right now, I'm wondering what 'our dilemma' *is,* exactly."

Outside, the wind howled around the edges of the cottage and rattled the glass in the windows.

Joanna knew she ought to withdraw from him, get out of bed, get dressed, but there was a disconnect between her mind and the corresponding muscles. She'd melted, that was the problem. "We don't talk when we're having sex," she said, idly winding a finger in a strand of Teague's hair.

"Maybe that's a good thing," Teague suggested. "Maybe words get in the way of what we're really trying to say to each other."

"I don't see how we can settle anything if we don't talk," Joanna replied. "But I'm intrigued by the theory." She reached under the covers and closed her hand around him, pleased that he was getting hard again.

Teague gave a low moan.

Joanna slipped beneath the covers, kissing her way down Teague's chest and belly.

But he drew her up before she reached her intended destination. And then, in a rolling motion of his body, he turned both himself and Joanna so that she was on her hands and knees in the middle of the mattress and he was behind her.

Joanna closed her eyes as heat surged through her, and instinctively gripped the rails in the headboard with her fingers.

Teague, already pressing against her, began caressing her breasts, one and then the other, delicately rolling her nipples between his fingers.

Now *she* was the one moaning.

He teased her with the moist tip of his cock even as he eased her thighs apart.

"Do it," she whispered.

He bent, kissed her nape, the bones in her spine. "Do what?"

Joanna groaned out a long, needy "Ooh—"

"Do what?" Teague repeated, tracing the lines of her shoulder blades with the tip of his tongue.

"*Fuck* me," she said.

"Don't you want to—*talk*?"

"*Fuck me*," she repeated, grinding against him, shameless in her need.

He found the entrance to her vagina and slammed into her in a low, hard thrust that made her throw back her head and give a guttural cry.

"Harder," she pleaded. "Oh, Teague—harder—"

He toyed with her clitoris, still inside her, filling her.

She reached the first sharp orgasm, and Teague's control shattered. He gripped her hips to steady her and fucked her in earnest, hard and fast and deep.

She gloried in the furious friction as he pounded into her, possessing her, ravishing her, like a wild storm that would not be stilled until it had spent itself.

They met in the whirlwind, their bodies fully joined in one final, shuddering collision of consuming fire.

Joanna came repeatedly, softly, all during the deliciously slow descent, Teague still grasping her hips, still moving in and out of her, though more gently now. He knew, damn him, how to extract the last, quivering release from her, how to melt the very marrow of her bones.

She sagged, exhausted, to the mattress.

He rested on top of her, his forearms braced on either side of her shoulders.

A long, long time passed before either of them spoke.

"Joanna," Teague said, "I don't think this divorce is working out."

She giggled, crying at the same time, crushed flat beneath him.

He raised himself, turned her over, and looked deep into her eyes.

She crooned and stretched, limp with satisfaction. "I could sleep for a month," she murmured.

"If I planned to let you," Teague said. And he slid down a little to suck idly at her breasts. "Which I don't."

"All this sex—it's—"

"Good," Teague finished for her, taking her nipple into his warm mouth and drawing upon it until she groaned.

There was no denying that. But then, sex had *always* been good with Teague. In recent years, though, it had been mechanical—both of them climaxed because they knew each other's bodies so well, but it was as if a part of them remained untouched. Though satisfying, the whole experience was oddly detached—clean, safe, dignified.

Or, at least, it *had* been that way—until this weekend.

Normally, Joanna despised the word "fuck"—it was crude. She preferred the term "lovemaking," because it was more sedate, more acceptable. The intimate version of a handshake.

But this time, in this bed, she hadn't wanted Teague to

make love to her. She'd wanted him to *fuck* her, full out, no holds barred, and he surely had.

She'd missed that.

She'd missed Teague.

The old Teague. The one who'd come home sometimes, in the middle of the day, while Caitlin was in school and the housekeeper was off on some errand, and had Joanna wherever he happened to find her: bending her over the washing machine, the back of the couch, even the dining-room table. It hadn't been lovemaking—it had been good old-fashioned *fucking,* and she'd reveled in it. Reveled in orgasms so intense she shouted and howled and begged.

Tears seeped between her lashes.

Teague raised his head from her breasts, sensing the change in her mood. Kissing the wetness off her cheeks.

"What is it?" he asked hoarsely.

Joanna wrapped her arms around his neck and allowed herself to do something she'd sworn off long ago, for the sake of dignity, because they were grownups, with a child to raise and a business to manage. She clung. "Why can't it always be like this?" she whispered.

Teague chuckled. "Well, primarily because it would probably kill both of us," he said. He wriggled against her. "Eventually."

"Can we just stay here? Not go back to Seattle at all?"

Teague blinked, confused.

"I mean it," Joanna said. "Why does this have to end?"

He kissed her, with his eyes open and full of puzzlement.

More tears came, tickling Joanna's temples, rolling into her ears. "Do we have to divide things up and go our separate ways?" she asked. "Do we really have to?"

Teague swallowed hard. "Are you just saying that," he asked gruffly, "because you want my body?"

"I'm saying it because I want *you,* Teague." She smiled, squirming a little to tease him. "Although your study body is a definite plus."

His eyes were wet. "God, Joanna, I love you. I always have. I guess I just forgot how to tell you, how to show you—"

"Shh," she said, lifting her head to kiss him. "You're not the only one who forgot. I did, too. Do you think we could try again?"

Teague laughed hoarsely. "That depends. If you're talking about another session like the one we just had, I need a little time. I'm almost a grandfather, you know. If you're talking about the marriage, it's an unequivocal yes."

"Think we can get it right?"

"I think we'll make a lot of mistakes, and get it right *most* of the time."

"Sounds sensible," Joanna said softly, stroking the side of his wonderful face with a slow motion of one index finger. "I'd like to suggest one ground rule, though."

"What's that?"

"If one of us decides to leave, the other one gets the dog."

Teague grinned. "Deal," he said.

And then he kissed her in a very ungrandfatherly way.

One month later

Joanna looked up from her computer, watching through the front window as Teague and Sammy came up from the beach, Sammy as spry as a pup now that he was getting a lot of fresh air, attention, and exercise, Teague relaxed and happy, with sawdust on his jeans. He spent mornings in the garage behind the cottage, working on his boat, while Joanna worked on her novel.

Today, she had a surprise for him.

"Hello, Gramps," she said as he and Sammy came in, bringing a pleasant summer breeze with them.

Teague crossed to bend and kiss her.

"What do you say I fuck your socks off while Sammy takes his nap?" he asked.

She grinned. "Bend me over something," she said. "I'm all yours."

His eyes glowed with anticipation and mischievous plans as he pulled her to her feet.

"But first," she said, "there's something I have to tell you."

He frowned. "Caitlin's all right?"

"Caitlin's fine—I talked to her an hour ago. She's over the morning sickness, and she and Peter are coming for a visit in a couple of weeks."

"That's good news," Teague said, sliding a hand up under Joanna's T-shirt and bra to cup her breast.

"There's more," Joanna said, tugging his hand from her breast—much as she'd loved being fondled—and gripping it in her own. "Come with me."

"The bedroom?" Teague murmured. "Not very imaginative."

"The bathroom," Joanna said, pulling him along behind her.

"Not very *romantic*."

"You seemed to like it well enough yesterday when I gave you a blow job while you were trying to shave," Joanna reminded him sweetly.

A slow grin spread across his face. "Oh—yeah."

"Forget it, Gramps," Joanna said. "This isn't about getting you off."

"Damn," Teague said, disappointed.

They'd reached the bathroom doorway, and the kit Joanna had bought at the supermarket a week before but been afraid to use lay on the counter next to the sink.

"What—?" Teague murmured, clearly confused.

Joanna picked up the stick and showed him the little plus sign in the window.

His expression was priceless as it went from bafflement to possibility to realization.

"We always said we wanted more kids," Joanna said.

He stared at her. "But I'm—you're—we're—"

"Almost grandparents," Joanna supplied.

"A *baby*, Joanna?" His eyes were alight with joy, with hope, with ecstatic amazement.

All the things she'd hoped for.

"A baby," she confirmed.

He threw back his head and shouted. Then he lifted Joanna off her feet, squeezing her so tightly she couldn't get her breath for a moment. His face was a study in fatherly concern as he loosened his grip.

"A *baby*?" he marveled. "After all this time?"

"After all this time," Joanna said softly.

"How did—?"

"I suppose it was the fucking," she answered.

He laughed.

"But it was also fate, probably," she added. Spending these weeks virtually alone with Teague, she'd begun to see that there was something *beyond* the things they said to each other, ordinary or incendiary. There was a space, a magical silence, almost meditative and certainly sacred, where words simply could not reach.

And there, with not only their bodies but their souls joined, this new baby had been conceived.

Teague looked worried. "Have you told Caitlin?"

"Of course I haven't," Joanna said. "I wanted you to be the first to know."

"We'd better get you to a doctor."

"Right now, this instant? I feel *fine*, Teague. Better than fine."

"But you need to be on special vitamins and have sonograms and stuff. Joanna, we have to do this right."

She stood on tiptoe, wrapped her arms around his neck, and kissed him. "I've already called our doctor, and she referred us to an OB-GYN guy. My appointment is tomorrow morning at ten."

Teague huffed out a relieved breath, but his eyes were troubled. "Joanna, you're—*we're*—not young. There could be problems."

"There can always be problems, Teague. And these days, a lot of people are having healthy babies in their forties."

"How do you think Caitlin will react?"

"She'll be shocked at first," Joanna said. "We're her parents, and this is proof positive that *we have sex*." She grinned, waggling her eyebrows.

"*Sex*?" Teague gasped, pretending to be horrified.

"Old and decrepit as we are," Joanna replied. She moved to pick up the test stick and drop it into the trash.

"Wait," Teague protested. "Shouldn't we keep that? Put it in a frame or a scrapbook or something?"

"Teague," Joanna pointed out, "I *peed* on it."

"Oh," he said. "Right."

She disposed of the stick and washed her hands at the sink.

"What do we do now?" Teague asked. "I guess the red-hot sex is out for a while."

"Only if the doctor says so," Joanna said. "As for what we do now—well, I'd like to see what progress you've made on that boat of yours. Then we could have lunch and take Sammy for a walk."

Teague made a grand gesture, indicating that she should precede him through the bathroom doorway. "Your barge awaits, Cleopatra," he said.

She laughed, dried her hands, and stepped into the corridor.

The "barge," really a sleek twelve-foot rowboat, rested on a special arrangement of sawhorses in the garage behind the cottage. Teague had been as secretive about it as Joanna was about her novel, and probably for the same reasons.

Both the boat and the book were creations of the heart and mind, fragile in their beginnings.

Joanna drew in her breath. The craft was far from finished, still rough slats in need of endless sanding, not to mention varnishing—not unlike her novel, she thought—but the intent was there.

"Oh, Teague," Joanna said, marveling. "It's beautiful."

Teague caught her face in his hands—the palms felt work

roughened and strong against her skin. "*You're* beautiful," he said.

She drew in the Teague scents of sawdust, sun-dried cotton sheets, toothpaste, and soap. "I love you so much," she told him.

He kissed her, long and deep. When he lifted his mouth from hers, he opened his eyes and said, "And I love you, Joanna. I have, always. Even when I didn't know how to show it."

She swallowed hard and nodded. It felt dangerous to be so happy, but delicious, too. "I don't suppose you'd like to take a look at my novel, after lunch and Sammy's walk?"

"I've been waiting for you to ask," he said.

An hour later, with lunch over and Sammy sleeping off a happy trot down the beach, Teague settled into one of the armchairs in the living room, the sixty-odd pages Joanna had written in his hand.

His expression was solemn with concentration as he read.

Joanna tried not to watch his face, but she couldn't help it. Every nuance either plunged her into despair or sent her rocketing skyward.

When he'd finished, he set the pages aside and stared thoughtfully through Joanna for a long time.

"Well?" she finally demanded. "What do you think, Teague?"

"I think you're amazing," he said.

"The *book*, Teague!"

He stood, crossed to her, and took her shoulders in his gentle boat builder's hands. "It's so good it makes me scared," he told her.

"Scared?"

"Scared it won't be enough for you, living here on the island, in this cottage, with Sammy and the baby and me. Scared you won't want this simple life anymore."

She touched his cheek. "Never gonna happen. I'm *thriving* here, Teague." She laid her hands against her still-flat belly, and tears of joyous wonder sprang instantly to her eyes. "Are you? Are you happy here? Do you miss the mansion and the business and all those meetings?"

He placed his hands over hers. "I'm happy, Joanna." A grin lit his face; he looked inspired. "And I can prove it."

"How?"

Teague went to the coffee table, picked up that week's issue of the *Island Tattletale,* Madge's modest but interesting sheet, opened it, folded it, and brought it to Joanna.

"The classified ads?" she asked, confused.

Teague tapped one of the little squares.

Joanna beamed as she read the bold print.

It said: **For sale cheap, one sports car.**

You Give
Love a Good
Name

Jennifer Apodaca

One

Four months earlier

Lexie backed up as the bride threw the bouquet, trying to stay out of range.

She stopped short when her shoulders hit a hard male chest. She jerked in reaction and nearly lost her balance. Large, warm hands settled on her bare arms to steady her. From behind her, a low voice chuckled and said, "Ducking the bouquet? I thought you women were supposed to fight for it?"

Recognizing the voice of the bride's brother, Nick Vardolous, she enjoyed the feel of his hands on her arms for a few seconds. It was just a little indulgence, perfectly innocent, she told herself. Then she turned, sliding out of his touch, and smiled up at him. "The wedding planner doesn't catch the bouquet." He stood beneath one of the crystal chandeliers in his dark suit and Lexie was struck by how good-looking he was. He had that hot Greek thing going on from his wavy black hair all the way down his six-foot frame. Strong bone structure showed off his incredible eyes, so light green that they sometimes took on a gold hue. Every time she looked into his eyes, she felt a little shock of lust jolt her system.

"You deserve more than a bouquet for putting up with my sister and mom."

She laughed. "It's my job. I get paid to handle the problems in weddings." The truth was she hated it, but she was stuck until her mom fully recovered from her heart attack and came back to work. She tore her gaze from Nick to look around and make sure everything was in order. "The bride and groom are leaving. I need to—"

He touched her hand. Lexie felt the sensation run up her arm and down her spine. They'd flirted for days. She really liked Nick, but he was the client's brother, not a date.

His gaze turned intense. "We'll talk later." He gently squeezed her hand, then strode away to hug his sister and shake hands with his new brother-in-law.

Lexie watched for a moment, thinking that in just a few days Nick had stirred a longing in her. Then she shook it off. She had work to do.

An hour later she picked up the last box off the table, turned, and almost yelped. "Hey, Nick, I didn't hear you." She'd seen him talking to his family as they were all leaving, but she hadn't really thought he'd stay behind. What did he want to talk to her about?

Nick reached out and took the heavy box from her. "You finished in here?"

She headed out the door to the parking lot. "Yep. Your sister is officially married and off on her honeymoon, the hall is cleaned up, and everyone lived through the experience." She stopped at her light blue Explorer and opened the rear door.

Nick slid the box in.

She smiled at him. "Thanks. I guess you're heading back to . . . wherever you came from?" Nick had told her his job kept him traveling, but he hadn't been specific about what his job was.

He shut the rear door and turned to look at her beneath the parking lot lights. "Leaving in the morning."

Nodding, she said, "It's been nice to see you these last couple days. And thanks for carrying the box." She wondered if he really wanted to talk to her or if he had just used her as an excuse to avoid his family.

"Lexie."

His voice was soft and low, the kind of tone that made a woman pay attention. "Yes?"

"Spend the night with me."

She knew her eyes widened. "Uh, the night?" *Stupid!* She knew what he meant. But she didn't do stuff like that.

Nick stood a couple feet away, watching her. "You're a sexy woman and I'm interested in you. I'm leaving early in the morning, but I can promise you an unforgettable night."

He was so incredibly honest, and he stayed a respectful distance away. She liked that. She liked him. She wanted him, but she didn't do one-night stands. She was so tempted, but no. "I can't, but thanks for, uh . . ." She felt like an idiot and looked down at the black pavement. *Thanks? Thanks for wanting to have sex with me?* God.

"Lexie."

That was some voice he had. Repressing a sigh, she looked up. "No." She hurried around him to the driver's side door, fumbling with her key to unlock the door.

Nick reached around her and took the keys from her, then beeped the door unlocked.

Hot embarrassment crawled up her neck, but she forced herself to turn and face him. "I'm sorry, I just . . ."

He smiled down at her. "I know what the word *no* means. Relax. I'm just going to make sure you get in your car and lock the door. It's a habit from having a baby sister."

God, she wanted to be someone else, the kind of woman who went home with a sexy man who made her feel desired and safe. He probably got women to go home with him all the time. That thought made her feel even worse somehow. She blurted out, "I'm not impulsive."

He opened the driver's side door.

She slipped past him and hoped the flush crawling up her

neck and face didn't show. Holding her skirt, she climbed up to the driver's seat, bringing her eye to eye with Nick.

He handed her the keys.

"Thanks."

"Lexie."

He had to stop saying her name like that. It was seductive and made her want to crawl into his arms. She tried to keep her gaze focused out the front window of the SUV, but against her will she turned to look at him. "Nick."

"If I were another guy . . ."

He was trying to make her feel better. "But you're not."

"No, I don't hang around in relationships. I'm a loner. But if I were looking for a relationship, I'd work hard to get you interested in me."

He was seducing her with what if's, or maybe it was his honesty. "And if I were an impulsive woman . . ."

His smile reached his eyes. "I'd be a lucky son of a bitch."

She laughed. Nick was sexy, so easy to be around.

Something flared in his green-gold gaze. Then he leaned forward and said, "Ah, damn, Lexie. I'm not going to be able to close this door until I kiss you." He put his hand on her shoulder, then slid his fingers up to cup the back of her head.

Warm excitement pooled in her stomach, and her muscles softened in reaction. Nick leaned forward and kissed her. The touch of his mouth sent sensual shivers down her spine to curl deep inside of her. His hot breath tasted like wine from all the toasts. Putting her hand on his arm, she felt the hard ridges of his muscles.

Felt the pulse of both their excitement.

Nick shifted just enough and she opened her mouth, wanting him inside of her. Wanting to feel the rush as his tongue touched hers.

Nick pulled back, breathing hard, and his green eyes warmed to a light-gold tone. "Time for you to go home, wedding planner."

"But . . ."

He shook his head. Determination hardened his features and his mouth lost the curve of amusement. "I'm not the sticking kind, and you're not a one-nighter. Go." He stepped back and shut the door.

He was still standing there when she drove away.

Present day

She had to find a way to keep the hostages alive . . .

Lexie Rollins stopped typing. How was she going to get her heroine and the hostages out alive? Her laptop was getting warm on her bare thighs. She shut it down and stood up on the patio off her room that overlooked the ocean.

She'd recommended this place for months as a perfect honeymoon for the clients of My Perfect Wedding. Sand Castle Resort in San Diego, California, lived up to its reputation.

It was beautiful with lush tropical plants and very private Mediterranean-style rooms right on the beach. The walls of the rooms were done in textured layers of paint in a color scheme of either blue, green, or rustic browns. The rooms also had beautiful mosaic tile to match, exquisite wrought-iron beds and tables, and ceiling fans to complement the air-conditioning.

Perfect for honeymoons and hiding from stalkers.

Since just the idea of a wedding made Lexie nauseous, she was there to hide from her stalker. And the media. And her lawyer. And her family.

In short, her life sucked.

But the good news was . . . hell, there was no good news. No, that wasn't true. She still had the memory of the face of the groom—William Harry Livingston's face when he had cornered her at the lovely garden wedding rehearsal dinner, drunker than a seaman on leave, and tried to seduce her. He had unzipped his pants and revealed Mr. Pathetic Penis to her.

Ugh. For the first time in Lexie's entire life, she'd lost it. Truly lost it. She'd grabbed up the staple gun she'd used to secure the decorations and stapled Harry's pants closed. Then she stapled his pants to his waist to prevent any further viewings of Mr. Pathetic. She told him to save it for his bride.

He cried, actually *cried*.

Lexie had chalked it up to a stressed and drunk groom and forgotten all about it.

Until she was arrested for assault and battery. With a staple gun.

Wedding Planner Goes Ballistic with Staple Gun was just one headline that resulted from the stapled groom giving interviews. Her family tried to stage an intervention to get her help. They were sure she was cracking up. And they needed her to get over it real quick and get back to work as a wedding planner.

They told her to forget all this stalker business. No one was sneaking into her apartment and booting up her laptop, she just forgot to shut it down. And everyone lost underwear at those Laundromats, no one was stealing them. In short, no one was stalking her, she was just imagining it. Like one of her plots for the thriller she was never going to write. Lexie needed to *get real* and *face reality* and *be reasonable* and *realize wedding planning is a good career*.

Even her lawyer didn't believe her.

She had no one to blame but herself. She was the one who had let family treat her like this her entire life. Determined to solve her own problems, she hired a PI to watch her apartment and catch the creep stalking her. Then she'd go back and fight these ridiculous charges.

Hopefully, her PI would catch the stalker in the next few days. And with a little luck, a few more days away from home would help her to get some perspective on her life. Standing at the balcony in the light afternoon breeze was a good way to start. The briny scent of the ocean was sharp, while the bright sun made her squint. Couples were spread out on the white sand, some sheltered by blue and white cabanas while others soaked up the sun in lounge chairs. A few people swam in the waves. Waiters moved effortlessly as they served cold drinks.

One man walking out of the waves caught her attention. Even from the distance she could see he was tall. And buff. He wore white board shorts with blue and black trim. The water made his hair look slicked back and dark.

A jolt of familiarity raced through her and she leaned forward with her hands on the railing of her balcony. His confident walk . . .

It was the involuntary tingle of her mouth that pried the name loose in her brain.

Nick Vardolous. The hot Greek one-kiss wonder. He'd kissed her and walked away.

What the hell was Nick doing here? She didn't believe in coincidences. Her world was too crazy, too out of control for Nick to have just shown up at the same exclusive beach resort where she was. Especially a resort that catered to couples like honeymooners. He'd made it perfectly clear that he wasn't interested in couplehood.

A disturbing thought rushed through her—what if he was another reporter tracking her? He'd said he traveled a lot for work, but she didn't know what that work was.

An even darker thought occurred to her. What if Nick was her stalker?

She didn't believe it. A man who asked straight out for what he wanted? Why would he stalk her? Nick was handsome and had good social skills; he didn't need to stalk women.

But what if he was the stalker? Wasn't Ted Bundy handsome and socially adept? Fear skittered up her spine, and she shivered in the warm afternoon breeze. The loneliness pressed down on her.

She had to find out what Nick Vardolous was doing at the resort.

* * *

After discovering that Lexie wasn't in her room, Nick charmed a maid into letting him in. This was an easy bond recovery, one that probably didn't require him to do a room search. Hell, he wasn't even hiding his presence at the resort. Lexie had no reason to be afraid of him, and he was sure she would cooperate. She had signed the bond agreement that pretty much signed away her civil rights and gave him the authority to arrest her and take her back to Santa Barbara. Since the maid assumed he got locked out and that he was knocking to get his wife to let him in, Nick seized the opportunity.

But he didn't think Lexie was running from the law. Her room didn't look like she was on the run—no hair dye in the bathroom or other telltale signs. She had left her cell phone in the room, turned off. Her lawyer had already told him she wasn't answering her cell. She had a laptop, which he supposed she could use to look for a map to Mexico or book a flight, but he doubted it. Looking at the two paperback novels on her bedside table, the shorts, bikinis, and sundresses in the closet and dresser, he thought she'd just gone on vacation. Her lawyer admitted that he hadn't reminded her about the court date she missed.

Her lawyer and family seemed to think she had snapped. Nick doubted it. In the four days he'd seen Lexie at his sister's wedding, nothing made her lose her composure. His sister and mother had spent a lot of time with her to arrange the wedding, and both of them insisted Lexie was calm and reasonable. She herself said she wasn't impulsive. Nick suspected she just thought the whole arrest was stupid.

He sure did. Any man who claimed a woman assaulted him with a staple gun was a hard man to take seriously. Hell, Nick felt like buying the man a staple remover and telling him to get over it.

Usually he didn't take these pissant cases, but he was doing it as a favor to her lawyer, and because he didn't want some other unprofessional bounty hunter getting a hold of Lexie.

He didn't like the idea of another man touching Lexie at all. That woman had gotten under his skin. His best bet was to talk to her tonight, then pack her up first thing in the morning and get her back to Santa Barbara. Her lawyer had turned out to have some balls and probably a little guilt at not making sure she knew about the missed court date, and he'd negotiated with a sympathetic judge to get Lexie a plea agreement of anger management classes and her solemn promise to stay away from staple guns. The agreement stipulated that Lexie show up in court in five days, and if she didn't, then she would face a trial and wait it out in jail.

He'd get her there and he'd walk away. That's what Nick did best. There was nothing that caused him any concern in her room, so he left, letting the automatic lock do its job when he pulled the door closed. He walked on the brick path beneath the lush foliage toward his room. The ocean roared not far away. He thought about getting in some surfing before heading back with Lexie. He rounded the corner of the terra cotta building that held his room and stopped.

The door was propped open a sliver by something wedged in at the bottom. From the green color, he thought it might be the room-service book. He could hear tapping sound of sandals on the tile inside of his room, and the shuffling of papers. The maid didn't usually wear sandals or shuffle through paperwork.

He sighed, having a pretty good idea who it was in his room. The question was, why? He did a visual sweep of the area, but he didn't spot anyone. No lookout or any reason to think that someone he'd apprehended in the past had tracked him down for a little revenge. Quietly he walked to the door, which was set back in an arched doorway. He eased it open and stepped inside.

Lexie Rollins stood by his bed, holding the mug shot of herself. She looked up, glared at him, and demanded, "Just what the hell are you and why do you have pictures of me?"

Two

Nick went into his room and shut the door. Lexie wore a light blue sundress dress short enough to show off her long, tanned legs. Jerking his gaze back up her slender, five-foot-seven-inch frame, he focused on her furious chocolate brown eyes. Her silky long brunette hair was pulled back in a ponytail, making her cheekbones more prominent. She might have lost a few pounds, but she was even more pretty and enticing then he remembered. It almost made him forget that he was there as a fugitive recovery agent, not a lover.

He shook it off and moved toward her. Then he saw her hand holding the picture tremble. That brought him to a stop halfway to the bed where she had the stuff spread out. He knew she was angry, but scared? Was she scared of him? "Lexie, I can explain."

She dropped her gaze to the mug shot the police took the night they'd arrested her. Then she looked up. "Is it you?"

"What?" He didn't have a clue as to what she was talking about.

She took a breath, forcibly calming herself. "Why are you here? And don't lie."

It bothered him that she didn't trust him. "I've never lied to you."

"Yeah, well, you didn't tell me a whole hell of a lot about yourself, either."

True. He didn't talk about his job with women he was interested in. He kept his life separate. What bothered him was the edge in Lexie's voice, the fear. He decided the best thing to do was to be straight. Now that Lexie was a job, sex was out of the question. So he told her the truth. "I'm a bounty hunter. Your lawyer pulled some strings and got me hired to bring you back to appear in court in five days. He's negotiated a good deal for you."

She stilled like a statue. "A bounty hunter? They are paying you to bring me in? I'm a *job*?"

What did she expect? Nick couldn't help but look at her full mouth and remember that kiss. It had taken all the will he had to send her home that night. He'd wanted her, but that kiss was too hot, the chemistry between them too volatile; there was just too much emotion there. And Lexie was too much of a one-man woman. If he'd taken her back to his hotel, then walked out in the morning, she'd have been left hurt.

And he'd have been left feeling like a jerk. So he did the right thing.

Now she looked hurt anyway. Or was that skeptical? Maybe she didn't believe him. "I'm doing you a favor," he said gruffly. "Another bounty hunter might be rough, or . . . hell." He ran his hand through his hair.

"A favor? By following me, having pictures of me . . ." She trailed off.

He didn't know what the hell she was thinking, so he took a guess. "Look, you don't have to go to jail. We'll leave in the morning, get to Santa Barbara in a few hours, and clean this mess up. You'll be fine."

"And you'll get paid for doing me a favor." She turned away from him and dropped the picture on the bed.

Her voice was thin, her bare shoulders tight. There was something else going on here. A dark idea settled in his chest.

"That man that you attacked with the staple gun, did he hurt you?"

"No." He watched her back expand as she took a breath. Then she turned, her face grim. "I'll be back in time for the court hearing. Your job is over; you can leave." She walked, making a wide arc around him to head for the door.

Her sandals clicked on the tile and sent echoes of unease into the base of his skull. What was he missing? He couldn't let her go. He moved fast, getting to the door before she could open it. "Lexie, stop." He leaned over her, putting his hand on the door. The scent of a flowery lotion, warmed by her body, assaulted him. He had to think. "What are you doing in my room? How did you get in?"

She stared at the door, her fingers around the handle. "I saw you here and didn't think it was a coincidence. Let me go."

"My room was locked."

"I'm resourceful."

He nodded to himself, thinking she'd done the same thing he had and gotten a maid to let her in. But why? What made her worried enough to sneak into his room to find out why he was there? "Why didn't you just ask me? I planned to find you and talk to you tonight anyway." He didn't remember her being this paranoid or suspicious.

Her shoulders dropped. "Just cautious. Let me out of the room, Nick."

The fear in her voice cut him. Jesus. "Not until you tell me what the hell you're afraid of. Now."

"Nothing. But I'm not going back yet."

He was done talking to her ponytail. Taking his hand off the door, he reached for her arm.

She jerked, whirling around with her eyes wide. "Let go!"

Startled, he dropped her arm. "What the hell? I'm not going to hurt you. I—"

"Don't touch me." Her voice quavered.

Nick took a breath to calm down. It was clear to him that

Lexie Rollins was on her last nerve. Scared, maybe even terrified. He'd seen her handle four long days of temper tantrums, wedding-dress disasters, last-minute changes, all the dramas that went with weddings, and she hadn't even broken a sweat.

Right now she looked at him like he might be a monster. What the hell had scared her? He didn't believe for a second she'd had a breakdown, but she was scared. Stepping to the side, he said quietly, "Go sit down. I won't touch you."

"I'm leaving."

He sighed. "Then I'll touch you. I won't hurt you, but I will stop you from leaving."

She leaned back against the door. "It's not you stalking me, is it?"

Nick blinked. "Stalking you? Like following your trail because I'm a bounty hunter and that's my job, kind of stalking you?"

"Like getting into my apartment, leaving my laptop on, opening my mail, taking underwear . . ." She clenched her jaw, then added, "Making countless phone calls from different phone numbers and hanging up. Coming into my apartment while I'm in the shower and dumping all my underwear all over my bedroom . . . I heard someone in my apartment, but by the time I got out of the shower and dressed, they were gone. Just the underwear all over . . ." She shivered and crossed her arms tightly. "The last straw was finding a note on my car that said, 'Die, bitch.' "

Shit, now her fear made sense. "Jesus," he swore and strode to the bed, then quickly sorted through the paperwork he had on her until he came up with the bond piece. Going back, he handed it to her. "I'm not stalking you. This is what the bond company issues to give me the authority to find you and bring you in."

She took the paper and read it, her mouth thinning in more frustration.

He asked, "If you're being stalked, why haven't you gone to the police?"

Handing the paper back, she leveled her tired gaze on him. "I told them, but it was after the assault charge and they seemed to think I was inventing stories to get the charges dropped. I told them one thing had nothing to do with the other, but they seemed to think I was building some kind of stress defense. Especially since the note on my car was written on my own stationery from my apartment."

"So you saw me here and—" He didn't need to finish. He got the picture. She was scared but no one believed her. Her own lawyer had told Nick she was unstable. To keep from touching her, he moved to the bed to drop the bond piece onto the pile of papers and photos. "Your family?"

"They think I'm trying to get out of work." She pushed off the door and stood up straight. "But I'm handling it. I've hired a PI to watch my apartment while I'm gone. He'll catch the stalker and then I'll go back to Santa Barbara for my court date. You'll get your money. Good night." She turned and reached for the door.

"You should have called me." As soon as he said it, he knew it was stupid. But he was feeling very protective, although he was baffled as to why.

She looked back at him. "For what? A night of sex? And how would I call you, Nick? Look you up under one-night stands in the phone book?"

He winced. Since all he'd ever offered her was sex, and no details about his career, she'd had no reason to think he would or could help her—although as resourceful as she obviously was, she could have gotten his number from his sister. "I deserved that. But I'm here now and I'm going to help you."

Anger narrowed her gaze. She dropped the door handle and turned. "Are you worried I'm going to disappear and you'll be out your bounty hunting fee?"

He crossed his arms over his chest. "Honey, I hate to break it to you, but you're not worth enough money to bother with."

"Then stop bothering!" She turned again, heading back for the door.

Damn, she had to be getting dizzy with the rushing back and forth. He understood her stress, but she needed to trust him—he wasn't the enemy. Nor could he let her walk out. "I'm not going to let you leave my room. If you open that door, I'm going to assume you want my hands on you." He had no idea how she would react.

She halted a foot from the door and turned, her brown gaze meeting his. In a soft voice, she said, "Maybe I do."

Unfolding his arms, he frowned and wondered what the hell she meant. "Do what?"

She shook her head, looking like she'd do anything to take back her words.

She looked beautiful and . . . raw. Needy. Yet so alone it made him mad, frustrated, and determined. "Don't lie to me now." He advanced on her, and he was going to be ticked if she dared to be afraid of him. He'd understood it when she didn't know why he was there, but now she did know.

She leaned back slightly. "I guess I haven't forgotten that kiss."

He smiled then. "Good to know I'm not the only one."

"But you weren't interested after you kissed me."

That surprised the hell out of him. "What gave you that idea?"

"You told me to go home."

Women. Christ. "You told me no. One kiss and you were reconsidering—we both know you would have regretted that."

She leaned the back of her head against the door and smiled. "Ha. I scared you."

That made him grin. "Yeah. I think you did. You're not an easy woman to walk away from."

She shrugged. "Okay, bounty hunter, what now? If you won't let me leave, and I won't go back to Santa Barbara with you, we seem to be at a stand-off."

He put his hand on the door over her head and leaned close to her face. "You're in my custody now. That'll get the lawyers and bail bondsmen to shut up for a few days. Together we'll figure out how to deal with your stalker."

Lexie's fingers tapped out a steady rhythm on the keyboard of her laptop. The night was quiet, and through the closed door she could hear the waves crashing against the shore. She considered opening the sliding glass door to let in the sea breeze, but that didn't seem wise at one A.M.

Every sentence she typed increased her sense of accomplishment. She was heading into the home stretch of her book. Her heroine's life hung in the balance, as did those of the hostages. Even she was on edge, and she knew the outcome—she knew the heroine would live.

Unfortunately one or two of the hostages would die, but . . .

A squeak and click startled the bejeebers out of her. Jerking her head up from staring at the screen, she tried to place the noise. Her heart banged against her chest wall. What was that?

She didn't hear anything else. She wasn't even sure what direction the noise came from. The door to the room was on the left of where she sat on the bed, propped up by pillows. The sliding glass door covered with blackout drapes was on her right. The room was large, with the walls done in a hand-troweled texture of green and white. There was mosaic tile on the floor, with colorful rugs. The tile could make the room echo, especially in the quiet of the night.

Her heart rate calmed down.

With her attention diverted from her book, her mind wandered to Nick.

Nick Vardolous. Here. At Sand Castle Resort. And he was hotter than she remembered. Those eyes . . . oh hell, all of him. He'd been her fantasy man since that kiss. A safe man to fantasize about, but she hadn't expected to meet up with him again.

It rankled that she was nothing more than a job to him. Which she knew was ridiculous. They hadn't had a relationship; they hadn't even had sex.

At least he had believed her when she told him about her stalker. Then he'd checked out her private investigator, Tate Zuckerman, and told her she'd made an excellent choice. He treated her like an intelligent woman, although he had insisted on checking out her room for any danger, then confiscated her car keys before he agreed to leave her in her room.

Nick. He did something to her, made her feel safe and sexy. That kind of charm should be . . .

A tapping noise scared the hell out of her. She shoved her laptop off her legs and leaped off the bed.

What was it? It came from the patio sliding glass door. Was someone out there?

Her heart pounded in her ears, her blood rushing so fast she was dizzy. Standing on the cold tile floor, she sucked in a breath. *Think.*

Thunk, thunk, thunk.

Oh God! Someone was out there! Nine-one-one was the first thing she thought.

Then Nick. He was closer. She grabbed the phone and dialed his room number.

He answered on the first ring. "Vardolous."

"Nick! It's Lexie. Someone is pounding on my sliding glass door. I don't . . ."

"On my way." He hung up.

The sliding glass door rattled. Someone was trying to open it, but it was locked. Then a voice called out, "I know you're awake! I see the light on!"

She didn't recognize the voice. She shivered, wrapping her arms around herself and backing up until she felt the solid wall behind her. Was it her stalker? Maybe a random killer?

He yelled again, "I just want to talk to—oomph!"

Lexie blinked and leaned forward. All she could hear was shuffling and a thump. Nick?

Her phone rang. The shrill sound arrowed right through her. Grabbing it, she said, "What?"

Nick answered, "Lexie, it's me. I have the guy. He has press credentials."

"A reporter?" Her voice climbed as the adrenaline spiked in her bloodstream.

"Drunk reporter." Nick's voice was knife edged with disgust. "Security is taking him away."

"Oh. Okay. Thank you, I—"

"Open your door."

"My door?"

"I'm right outside your door. Not the slider, the door. Check the peephole, then open it."

She was standing by the door and did as he instructed. Nick stood there with his cell phone to his ear. She hung up the phone, undid the locks, and opened it.

He closed his phone, walked in, and shut the door behind him.

Lexie backed up and stared. Nick took up a lot of room. He was half naked, only wearing a pair of loose-fit jeans hanging low on his hips. His black hair was tousled and his jaw shadowed with a dark beard that set off his green bedroom eyes. In the glow of her bedside lamp, his gold-toned skin stretched over some serious muscle in his shoulders and chest. He looked hot and tasty. It had to be some kind of adrenaline high channeling her thoughts to naked skin and sizzling sex. She forced herself to get under control.

"You okay?" His voice was low and tight.

No. She wasn't okay. Stalkers, getting arrested, a ticked-off family, drunk reporters, and a way-too-sexy bounty hunter were ripping away control over her own life. She was tired, scared, lonely, and stunned that Nick came to her rescue. She couldn't remember anyone ever doing that for her. It was always Lexie who fixed things.

"Lexie?"

She had to pull herself together. "Sure. I'm fine. I'm always fine. It's a family rule . . ." Jeez, that made no freaking sense.

Closing her eyes, she leaned back against the wall and brought her hand up to rub her eyes. "Sorry, I'm a little rattled, but fine. Thank you for dealing with this for me. I realize now I could have just called security myself. Sorry I bothered you."

"Now you're pissing me off."

No big surprise there. She dropped her hand and opened her eyes. "You're going to have to get in line."

Nick drew his eyebrows together in a thunderous expression. "Say what?"

"There's a line of people mad at me." Why didn't she just shut up? And why did Nick have to look so hot? She dropped her gaze to his seriously ripped chest. He had sinewy muscles, not the gym kind, but the lean muscle of an active man. The deep urge to lean on some of that muscle was an unexpected weakness. A new weakness, that's great, just what she needed—a bad case of Man Hungry on top of everything else. It'd been almost a year since she'd felt a man wrap his body around hers, slide inside her, make her feel valuable and real.

The silence stretched out, then he said, "Look at me."

She looked up. His darkly stubbled jaw emphasized the liquid gold floating in his light green eyes. "While we're here, if you're in trouble, you are going to call me first."

Just nod, she told herself, desperate and tired of being alone. She knew she was too vulnerable, feeling too impulsive to trust her mouth. She tried to nod, but she blurted out, "Even for sex?"

Three

Nick took a step toward her before his brain kicked in. It was the damned pink panties. When she'd opened the door and he'd seen her wearing a thin pink tank top, she'd taken his breath away.

Then he'd seen the panties and his blood went south. He'd hardened so fast it was a wonder he didn't get dizzy.

Clenching his fists, he knew his hard-on strained against his pants. "Lexie—"

She stepped up to him and put her hand on his chest. "I'm tired of being cautious and worrying about tomorrow. I want to try impulsive."

He caught her hand and inhaled. Damn, she smelled like that flower, night jasmine or whatever, mixed with warm skin. His whole body throbbed with hard-core lust. They were both on adrenaline overload. He could control this, he would control it. "No. No sex." He barely got the words out.

Her body deflated, and her hand slid from his grasp. "Okay. Thanks again, Nick. I'll call you if I'm in trouble, but not for sex. Good night." She reached for the door.

She was making him crazy, infuriating him. He wanted her naked and under him, looking up with unfocused eyes while he drove himself into her. He wanted her breath to hitch and pant as she lost control, her body shivering and spasming with pleasure while he watched.

Then she had the nerve to pull open her door, put a hand on her hip, and stare at him expectantly.

He had to shock them both back to reality. "If anyone walks by, they are going to see you in your panties."

She looked down. The expression on her face was priceless— total shock.

Nick reached over, closed the door, and locked it. Then he turned to see Lexie walking quickly to her dresser. Away from him. Her tight ass covered by the sheer pink panties twitching in her rush. He was going to burst into flames. Before he realized it, he was moving. He scooped her up in his arms.

"Nick! What are you doing!"

"Putting you in your bed and covering you up before I do something stupid." He all but dropped her on the bed and wrenched the covers up over her.

She sat up, leaning back against the pillows. "I'm not going to attack you!"

He stared down at her.

Her gaze moved to his crotch. Then her gaze slid up. "Oh."

"I don't get emotionally or sexually involved with my work. Ever." He'd learned that the hard way, and he never forgot the lesson.

She blinked, her mouth tightening as she seemed to battle with herself, then she lowered her gaze back to his crotch. She jerked her head, looking everywhere but at him. "Okay. Got it. You should leave now."

Nick leaned down, putting a hand on either side of her hips so he was nose to nose with her. "I'm not leaving you alone so another lunatic can break in here. I'm staying. And if you don't stop talking, or wiggling that prime ass of yours in front of me, I'm going to strip you down to your skin and fuck you until you are screaming my name in pleasure, over and over. And then when I regain my senses and realize that I screwed up, I will be forced to take you back to Santa Barbara immediately and insist that you be locked up in a cell where you're safe until we find your stalker. Your choice."

"I'll stop talking."

The phone woke her up. "Hello?"

"It's nine in the morning! And you're sleeping!"

At the sound of her brother's irritated voice, Lexie snapped awake. "Larry? How'd you find me?" She sat up in bed and looked around. The patio lounge chair had a pillow and rumpled blanket on it . . .

The night came back to her, the memory of Nick sleeping in her room. Where was he?

"By calling all the hotels in your honeymoon file. What the hell is the matter with you, Lexie? How can you be so selfish? Mom is having chest pains. She had to do two weddings and you know she's not up to it after her heart attack! Amber is hysterical. Dad is threatening to cut you out of the will. Clients are screaming. You have to get your ass back to work!"

She shoved her heavy hair out of her face, heard the shower turn off, and assumed Nick was in there. Throwing her legs over the side of the bed, she forced herself to deal with her brother. "Mom is fine. The doctor said she could go back to work months ago." Her sister, Amber, had been hysterical from the day she was born; that was nothing new.

"You were always selfish, Lexie, but I never thought you'd pull something like this. One of the cakes for a wedding this weekend was wrong. *Wrong!* The Pattersons screamed at me for a whole hour. I don't have time to fix your screwups! I'm running a business, and you know Patricia and I are buying a house and selling our condo. How could you just run away and leave us all to clean up your mess?"

She knew damn well it wasn't her screwup, but Larry's. Her brother was lazy and she had to double-check every cake order he did, just as her mom had done. Fatigue weighed down her shoulders as she dropped her gaze to the green mosaic pattern in the white tile. "I didn't run away . . ."

"Yes, you did. You left us all in a bind. Mom is afraid to book any weddings. She's afraid! She had a heart attack, remember? And just how am I going to make a living, huh, Lexie? We have a potential buyer for the condo, which means I have to worry about a bigger mortgage on the new house. Does it always have to be about you?"

Shame pressed down on her chest. She really thought her mom had been taking advantage of her. That she'd had her first taste of real freedom after being a workaholic for decades. But maybe she was wrong, maybe the heart attack had damaged her mom's confidence. "Is Mom all right?"

"No! What have I been telling you! And I need more cake orders. You have to come back."

Her stomach cramped with real fear. "I can't, not yet. Larry, someone has been getting into my apartment. If you know anything . . ."

He cut her off with a rude noise. "Don't start that shit again. You are ruining my life, trying to blame me because you can't remember using your laptop or keep track of your clothes! I was in your apartment once, once! It was a mistake. I'm under a lot of pressure here, Lexie."

Right, and screwing a woman who wasn't his wife in Lexie's apartment was the obvious way of relieving pressure. She wouldn't have found out if her dumb brother hadn't left the condom wrapper on her nightstand. It hadn't taken Lexie long to figure out he'd swiped her house key from their mom. "I'm not trying to ruin you. I just need to figure out who is getting into . . ."

"For God's sake, stop thinking about yourself! We're all sick of it. Especially Harry. He doesn't even come around anymore. He's too humiliated after you attacked him and caused his fiancée to dump him right before the wedding."

A noise made her look up.

Nick stood there. His hair was shower wet, his skin still damp, and his expression was ice cold. "Who are you talking to?"

She put her hand over the mouthpiece. "My brother."

He reached over and took the phone from her. "Your sister is being threatened by a stalker. Any idea who it might be?"

Lexie was stunned. No one took control from her like that. She stood up to grab the phone back.

Nick slung his arm around her shoulders and held her to his side.

She heard her brother bellowing that Lexie was just trying to get out of work when her family needed her, and something about her making wild accusations. It was easier to concentrate on the feel of Nick's chest expanding as he breathed, along with his warm, damp skin scented with the soap from his shower. She sank into the pleasure of having his arm around her and wondered when she had become this pathetic.

"Now I know why she ran." He leaned over and slammed the phone down.

Lexie took the opportunity to put some distance between them. It was one thing to think about seducing Nick in the middle of the night. Before he knew that she'd run out on her family. That her own family didn't believe her. Shame and embarrassment rolled around her gut. But she faced Nick. Better to just get it over with.

He turned on her. "You're not going back there until it's safe. You sure as hell can't count on your asshole brother to help you."

She bristled. Only she could call her brother an asshole. "Don't talk about my brother like that. It's a lot of work to own a bakery, plus he's selling his condo and he's worried about our mom. He depends on wedding cake orders from My Perfect Wedding."

He stepped toward her. "Then he's a leech and an asshole.

Let him get his own damned cake orders. If you were my sister, I'd have looked into this stalker situation the first time you told me."

He was close enough to kiss her. And it hit her that she only had on her sleep shirt and panties. She felt her face heat at the memory of his reaction to her panties last night. She needed distance, now. She couldn't risk him dragging her back to Santa Barbara. "Your sister is lucky. I'm going to take a shower. There's no reason for you to stay here, I'm perfectly safe." She escaped into the bathroom and closed the door.

Once she finished showering, she decided on her black bikini. She'd brought two with her and kept them in the bathroom to dry out. Brushing out her wet hair, she looked into the fogged mirror. She decided against blow-drying and left her hair down. Opening the door, she walked into the cool room.

"You're trying to kill me."

She jumped, her heart slamming in her chest. And yet, part of her was pleased. Nick sat at the table by the sliding glass door, drinking a cup of coffee from the in-room coffeemaker and reading the complimentary newspaper.

"I thought you'd left."

He ran his gaze down her length and back up to her face. "I should have and saved myself. Jesus, Lexie."

Was that a compliment or insult? And since he'd made his position on sex with her clear, why did she care? "It's just a bathing suit." She went to the closet, pulled out the wrap-around dress she used as a cover-up, and shoved her arms in it. Concentrating on tying the strings to secure the dress, she added, "No one's stopping you from leaving now."

Nick stood up and approached her. "I'm not an asshole like your brother. That's what is stopping me."

She knew he was close behind her, too close. Shoving her feet into her flip-flops, she said, "Stop calling my brother that."

"Stop defending him."

She turned to him. The room was flooded with daylight,

and Nick looked even more gorgeous. His hair was dry, black as night, and had a slight wave. His green eyes focused on her. There was no more hiding. "My mom had a heart attack. I took over running My Perfect Wedding for her. For a year, I hated every single minute of it. I begged my mom to come back, but she kept putting me off. Then the groom, William Harry Livingston, got drunk at the rehearsal dinner and flashed me. I lost it and stapled his pants to his waist. Then the arrest, the stories in the tabloids, my stalker . . . I just left. I went to my parents' house, dumped all the open files for upcoming weddings on my mom's table, told her it was her business, not mine, and left." She stopped talking. What else was there to say?

"Back up. Livingston exposed himself and that's why you stapled him?"

She looked at his chest. "Yes."

"Then why the hell were you arrested?"

Startled, she backed up a step. "Because I didn't report it. I figured he was just drunk and stressed. I was arrested the next day when he filed a complaint against me. I told everyone . . ." She took a breath. "This isn't getting us anywhere. The point is that my brother—"

"Is an asshole."

"Will you stop—"

He reached out and tugged her to him, close enough that she could see the icy anger in his green eyes. "Did I miss the part where your brother found Livingston and beat the shit out of him? How about your dad? Did anyone in your family take your side? Back you up?"

His eyes bored into her like green ice.

"It's not like that—"

"No? It sounds like they blame you and side with Livingston."

Embarrassed, she wasn't going to tell him that Larry took Harry's side because Harry brought him business from his real estate connections. Instead, she blurted out, "I can take care of myself. I could have handled Harry better, he was just drunk and stupid." A pocket of air caught in her chest. In order for her family to love her, she had to be the good girl. Part of her had thought when she dropped everything and left, they'd realize that she was in trouble. That she needed them for a change. It didn't happen.

He let her go.

She glared at him, desperate to get away. "You have my car keys, Nick, I'm not going anywhere. All I'm going to do is get something to eat, go to the beach, and work on my laptop. Alone."

He opened his mouth.

She was at the edge. "Please, just leave me alone!"

Nick drank his beer and stretched out his legs. People were milling around the balcony bar overlooking the ocean. The cool breeze did nothing to calm his lust.

Damn Lexie and that bikini. He'd managed to keep tabs on her all day, and she'd done just as she said she would. She'd spent time sitting on the beach working on her laptop. After lunch, she'd stowed her laptop and swum in the pool. Then she'd disappeared into her room, probably to sleep.

Nick had talked to her PI, Tate Zuckerman. Tate was an ex-cop, and it turned out that he and Nick had some mutual friends with the Santa Barbara Sheriff's Department. Those friends had vouched for Tate and evidently told Tate that Nick was an okay guy. Lexie had given the PI permission to tell him anything related to her stalker, but unfortunately, Tate had nothing, not a single sign of her stalker hanging around the apartment. The PI was worried and said he was going to talk to people in Lexie's life to see if something popped. Nick swore under his breath. Her stalker should be agitated by now, hanging around, looking for any sign of Lexie.

It was Monday. They had four more days until Lexie had to be back for court at 9:00 A.M. on Friday.

He couldn't take one more day of watching her and wanting her. She was getting under his skin, threatening his self-control. He couldn't help but admire her resiliency in spite of her family's lack of support. She had found a very good PI and hired him, then removed herself from the situation. Smart, resourceful, and so damned sexy his dick wasn't listening to his brain.

But he couldn't take her back to Santa Barbara if they didn't know who or where her stalker was.

A man dropped into the chair next to him, jarring him out of his thoughts.

"Rough night, Vardolous?"

Nick nodded to Mac Koontz, head of security at Sand Castle Resort. They went way back. Koontz wore slacks and a blue and white polo shirt with a Sand Castle logo on the pocket. "Lounge-chair sleeping sucks."

Koontz laughed. "Your questionable charm didn't get you into her bed, huh?"

He turned his gaze to Koontz. "I don't mix sex and work."

Mac's face tightened. "I thought you were putting it behind you. It's been eight years. Let Ellen go."

Nick stared at him. "I watched her die, I let her go. But I haven't forgotten that I screwed up and got her killed."

Mac stared back with his intense blue eyes. "The fact is that no amount of martial arts will win against a gun." He took a deep breath. "We both learned that. You walked away, Nick, but you never stopped training or teaching. You're making the right decision getting back in now. All you have to do is sign those papers and we're partners once again."

He forced his clenched hands to relax. "You're awfully sure I'll sign the partnership papers." He loved karate, and through those long dark days after Ellen's death, karate kept him sane. He taught some classes at a friend's studio. He had done what he could as a bounty hunter to put the past behind him. More and more, he wanted to get back into teaching karate full time in his own place.

Sighing, Mac said, "We sold our studio because neither one

of us could deal with what had happened. But we're older now, and it's time to get back to it." Looking at Nick, he added, "Share a little of our life experience. Give students a foundation for the shit life throws at them, you know?"

He knew. And it was too close to the truth for Nick, so he grinned. "Marriage is making you old and soft."

Mac raised his eyebrows. "Maybe, but I'm getting it every night too."

Nick let the dark memories slide away. "You're damned lucky. Shelly's too good for you."

"I'm off duty now. Come over, we'll barbecue, make margaritas."

He shook his head. "Can't. Got a skip in my custody." Cozy domestic scenes weren't his thing.

"Bring her. Lexie is a nice woman. I've gotten to know her a little bit while she's been here, and everyone here loves her. She's friendly to all the staff, making her an instant favorite guest. She can't really be a fugitive." Mac shook his head.

"It's a bogus charge." Nick stared at the cold bottle. Lexie was doing something to him. To his guts. She was reaching into him and finding the man he'd once wanted to be.

Before he'd let his emotions make a decision that caused a woman he loved to suffer a brutal death.

That man was gone, dead, and it ticked him off that Lexie made him remember. Made him want to be the kind of man worthy of a woman like her.

Of her.

And the worst part was, nobody stood up for Lexie. She'd been doing it all herself, and when her world crumbled, her asshole brother yelled at her.

He realized Koontz was talking and tore his gaze from the bottle. "What?"

Dark eyes locked in on him. "Oh shit, Vardolous. You're falling for her."

"No. I'm doing my job." As a courtesy to his old friend,

Nick had gone to see Koontz first thing, declared why he was at the resort and that the apprehension would be low key. Mac had been surprised by the idea of Lexie being a fugitive. "There's a complication. Lexie has had some trouble with a stalker back in Santa Barbara. We're hoping a PI she hired can catch him before I take her back."

Mac studied him. "Think he'll track her?"

Who knew with these freaks? "She was easy to find."

He nodded. "I'll tell the staff to be on the lookout."

"Thanks." Wouldn't hurt to have another layer of protection.

Mac settled his dark blue eyes on him. "I can help with security. Can't do anything about your feelings for Lexie."

Nick kept himself under tight control. She was in trouble, and he had to stay clearheaded to help her while doing his job. Sex and intimacy clouded judgment. "I don't have feelings for her. She's a job, nothing more. The sooner I get Lexie Rollins off my hands, the better."

Mac lifted his gaze behind Nick and winced.

The hair on the back of Nick's neck stood up. "Shit." He turned around to see Lexie standing there. She had on a pretty sundress, her hair flowing in soft waves in a sharp contrast to her tight mouth and wide eyes. Before he could react, she turned around to walk away. Jumping up, Nick said, "Lexie, I just meant that—"

She turned and the skirt of her sundress whirled around her legs. Color rushed into her cheeks while her eyes shimmered with either anger or unshed tears. "I know what you meant. I'm going to get some dinner. I came to let you know in case you were hungry, but now I think eating together is a bad idea." She walked away.

Mac hurried past him. "Lexie, hey!" He caught her arm.

Nick watched her shoulders tighten, then relax when she saw it was Mac.

"Lexie, come have dinner with my wife and me. We have

plenty of food. Shelly was hoping Nick would come over, but he turned me down. Besides, she'll like you much better than she likes Nick."

Furious, Nick closed the space between them. "She's not going anywhere."

Lexie ignored him. "Would you mind giving me a ride? Nick confiscated my car keys. I can grab a taxi to come back."

Like hell she would. "I'll drive you. I'm not letting you leave the resort without me."

She frowned at Mac. "I thought Nick wasn't going? I've changed my mind, I'll stay here and eat."

It was slowly sinking into his head that Lexie had dressed up a little bit. She had on a bit of make-up, had brushed out her long hair, and wore high-heeled sandals. She'd come looking for him, planning to ask him to have dinner. Then he'd gone and hurt her feelings. Damn it. He walked over and shoulder-bumped Mac out of his way. "Lexie, I just meant that I will feel better when you're safe."

"You'll feel better when you get your money." She barely spared a glance for him. "Thanks for the invitation, Mac. Maybe another time when I'm free of my current situation."

Him? Was she talking about *him?*

Mac didn't give him a chance to ask. "Lexie, please reconsider. Shelly would love to meet you. Nick can come if he wants to, but I'll make sure he doesn't bother you."

Now he *bothered* her? Frowning, Nick crossed his arms over his chest. "I go where she goes."

Both of them ignored him. Lexie said, "Are you sure your wife won't mind?"

Mac's face split in a grin. "No, and I'll bring you back tonight and make sure you get in your room safely."

Damn it, when did he disappear? "I will bring her back!"

"Thanks, Mac." Lexie walked off with him toward the employee parking lot.

Nick stood there by himself. "What the hell just happened?"

Four

"Another margarita?"

Lexie grinned up at Mac as he poured the chilled drink into her glass. "I'm not driving, why not?" Two margaritas and she felt no pain.

Well, less pain, anyway.

Nick's comment about getting her off his hands had hurt. She had put on a dress and some make-up and thought maybe they could go to dinner and at least be friends.

She'd been wrong. He couldn't wait to get rid of her and pick up his money.

Sipping her margarita, she felt Nick's gaze on her from where he sat on her left. They were sitting in Mac and Shelly's lush backyard, eating crab legs. Three of them were having a good time.

Nick appeared to be brooding. He'd been brooding since he'd shown up at the house one minute after Mac and Lexie had arrived in Mac's car. At least she hadn't had to ride with Nick and feel his urgency to get rid of her.

From across the table, Shelly said, "So tell us about yourself, Lexie. How did you manage to get the Super Bounty Hunter on your trail?"

"Ha. Funny," Nick said as he picked up his iced tea and drank it.

Lexie considered suggesting that one or two margaritas might restore his sense of humor, but she decided to ignore him. She was having fun in spite of him. Shelly was one of those beautiful women you couldn't hate because she was nice with a quirky sense of humor. Mac had a tendency to touch her every few minutes in the unconscious way of lovers. As much as Lexie hated the wedding planning business, she had seen real love occasionally, and these two had it.

Shelly shot Nick a frown, then said to Lexie, "I shouldn't have asked, maybe you don't want to tell us."

Shrugging, Lexie explained about William Harry Livingston and the staple gun.

Shelly burst out laughing while Mac looked bemused. He said, "You can't be serious. They are charging you with assault and battery for that?" He looked over at Nick. "I'm thinking we need to pay this guy a visit."

"Hell, yeah. But it'll have to wait until this stalker problem is resolved."

Lexie swiveled her gaze between Mac and Nick. Then she looked at Shelly. "What are they talking about?"

"Defending your honor or whatever the enlightened Neanderthals are calling it this year." Shelly shrugged and picked up her drink.

"That's ridiculous." Even though she was on her third drink and a little looped, Lexie still couldn't believe Nick and Mac were serious. Mac hardly knew her, and Nick couldn't wait to get rid of her.

Shelly set her glass down. "They don't get that women can take care of themselves. Just ignore them."

Nick snorted. "Ask Lexie what her asshole brother did about the groom exposing himself, then filing charges against her."

"Nick!" She turned to glare at him. "Don't call my brother that. I told you . . ."

He stared right back at her. "That he leeches off your mom, and now you. I remember. Any other leeching siblings?"

"Amber is not a leech! She's young, and she's just getting her photography business going. You don't know anything about my family."

"They all use you and leech off you. Don't want to know any more than that."

Loneliness wrapped around her, making her suddenly feel separated from the three of them. For a couple hours, she'd been part of the group. Until Nick opened his big mouth and told Mac and Shelly that her own family didn't support her. Anger roiled inside of her, fueled by the margaritas. "What makes you so different from them? I'm no more than a bounty to you." Crap, too late she realized she was practically yelling. She looked at Shelly and Mac, who'd been so nice to her. "Sorry."

Nick grabbed her shoulders, forcing her to look at him. His green eyes burned into her. "The difference is that I believe you. I won't let anyone hurt you. If anyone tries, I'll hurt them. Does that clear it up for you?"

Stunned stupid, she sat there like a lump. Why? Why would he do that? Until she finally remembered. "Because I'm your job?"

He let go of her, turned back to look into his glass. "Yes."

Shelly blew out a long breath. "Nick, you're an idiot. I've never seen you act like this."

Lexie took control. "It's okay, Shelly. He's being honest. It's not a big deal." It was to her, but she could keep that to herself. She drained her margarita.

Shelly smiled encouragingly. "So you don't like wedding planning. What do you want to do?"

Looking up into Shelly's pretty dark eyes, Lexie surprised herself by saying, "I want to write. Um, books. Thrillers."

Shelly perked up. "Really? I love to read! Are you writing something now?"

Lexie told herself not to think about Nick sitting beside her and judging her. "I was in the UCLA writing program but when my mom had her heart attack I dropped out to take over My Perfect Wedding."

Nick snorted. "Right."

That did it. Hadn't she heard it all her life? That she wasn't ever going to make it as a writer, so she needed to be realistic and take over My Perfect Wedding? That her dream was selfish and stupid? That she was the plain ordinary sibling, not the creative type like Larry and Amber? Tears burned at the back of her eyes and clogged her throat, but she would not let Nick Vardolous make her cry. She wouldn't let anyone make her cry. Anger was easier. "I don't care what you or my family think. I *am* writing my book. I'm almost done. And I'm not doing it to prove anything to you or them. I'm doing it for me." She stood up and realized her head was a little fuzzy from the drinks. Carefully she turned her back on Nick and asked Mac and Shelly, "May I use your phone to call a cab?"

Mac met her gaze. "I'll take you back, Lexie."

Nick said, "I'll take her."

She shook her head, then got dizzy and had to grab the edge of the table. It was hard to hold on to her dignity and the table while everyone stared at her, but she did her best. "I'll just get a cab. Thank you for dinner." She escaped inside the house before anyone could stop her. Finding a phone in the kitchen, she picked it up to dial information.

Nick came in and said, "Put the phone down."

Lexie shook her head. She leaned over to the kitchen window to look out and saw that Mac and Shelly were still sitting outside.

Nick took the phone from her hand and set it down. He trapped her between his body and the counter. "Shelly's right. You're turning me into an idiot. I can't think around you."

Frowning, she wondered just how drunk she was.

He moved his hands up her bare arms. "I believe you, Lexie. You can tell me anything and I believe you."

She wanted to look away, but his gaze held her captive. "You didn't. Not about my book."

He threaded his fingers into her hair. "I did. And I believe you left school to rescue your family. It just pisses me off that you did. They don't deserve you. And you deserve much better than them."

Why was he being nice to her? He stood so close that she could smell the scent of his soap mixed with his body heat. He made her feel small and protected, and it confused her. "I must be drunk. I never drink more than one drink." She closed her eyes to escape his stare. "I just want to be impulsive and free for once."

"You're not drunk. You're feeling loose and you were feeling happy until I ruined it for you." He lowered his head. "I can't do this." He said the words and pressed his mouth to hers.

She was drunk, she had to be, because she put her arms around him. Nick slid one hand to her bare upper back, pressing her closer to him. Then he said against her lips, "More, Lexie."

She opened her mouth, feeling the slide of his tongue fill her. Heat washed over her, and raw need to fill the gaping loneliness inside of her. Running her hands over him, she felt the hard ridge of muscles. Everything else drained from her thoughts but Nick.

Until he made a noise and lifted his head. His green eyes were almost all gold. "We can't. I can't risk it."

Cold dread mixed with embarrassment. "Right. I'm your job."

He wrapped his hand around a length of her hair, gently tilting her head back. "Because you matter. I won't screw up and let you get hurt or dead just because I'm horny. I did that once, and Ellen died." He dragged in a breath. "She was murdered right in front of me."

* * *

Nick had the TV on and tried desperately not to think of Lexie in the bed a few feet away. She had her laptop opened, he presumed to work on her book, but the typing had stalled. She had to be tired. Propped up on the uncomfortable lounge chair wearing only his pants, he flipped channels and hoped something would catch his attention.

"You live here, in San Diego, don't you? You knew exactly where Mac and Shelly lived. You and Mac seem to have a history together, like you've been friends a long time."

He could practically hear her thinking. "Yes." Before he could stop himself, he added, "I'm not home much." But that was going to change.

"Ellen's murder happened here, in San Diego?"

He stared hard at the TV. "I'm not going to talk about it."

"I'll give you the bed if you'll tell me."

"Go to sleep, Lexie."

In his peripheral vision, he saw her set the laptop aside and scoot to the end of the bed. "You can't sleep in that chair, you're too big. I'll trade you even if you won't tell me."

She was probably tormenting him on purpose. She had on panties, a tank top, and way too much skin showing. Gritting his teeth, he said, "Get back in that bed."

"Tell me about Ellen."

He looked over at her. Her eyes were heavy from the alcohol and fatigue. She sat cross-legged. Dropping his eyes, he saw her nipples pebbled against the thin shirt, her slightly rounded belly, her thighs spread, and . . . the powder blue panties barely covering her.

His dick snapped to attention. He threw his arm over his eyes and said, "You're making me pay for hurting your feelings."

"I . . . uh . . . no. I just thought you'd feel better if you talked about Ellen."

He lifted his arm off his face and looked at her sincere face. "Why?"

She met his gaze. "Because I saw the pain in your eyes when you told me tonight. I don't want you to hurt so much, Nick."

Shit. "Trying to fix me, Lexie? With your family out of reach, am I your project?"

He heard the movement on the bed. Maybe she'd leave him the hell alone. Then her warm hand touched his chest.

His balls seized up with raw lust.

She said, "Go take the bed. I'll leave you alone."

He grabbed her hand and pulled her down on top of him. To his surprise, she went boneless, letting him catch her weight on top of him. The contact warmed him and inflamed his lust. "You are stubborn." He put his hand over her head, holding her face to his chest. He just wanted to hold her. Was that so wrong?

Softly, she said, "Be glad I don't have my staple gun."

He laughed. Damn, she was funny. His cock throbbed, but having her on top of him, feeling her take each breath, eased the old pain in him.

She moved her hand, laying her spread fingers and palm on his chest. "Nick, how long ago did she die?"

"Eight years." Hell, she'd slipped that answer out of him by distracting him.

"What happened?"

"If I tell you, will you promise to go to sleep?"

She took a breath, expanding her breasts against him. "I'll promise to shut up. Best offer."

He stroked her hair, enjoying the soft feel of it. "Eight years ago I owned a karate studio with Mac." He felt her start to talk and said, "Let me tell it all or I won't do it."

She nodded.

"I had a student, Ellen. She was learning straight self-defense. I moved her to Mac's class and started dating her. Eventually I learned that her ex-husband had been arrested for drugs and got out on bond. Ellen was going to testify against him. He was calling her, threatening her, and she was scared. I was convinced that Mac and I could protect her. After all, we were both black belts, young, and we thought we were invincible." He stopped talking, the memories bitter.

She lay quietly on top of him. Just her hand moved, stroking his chest in gentle circles.

Nick ran his hand down the length of her hair, and farther to the small of her back. She felt warm and solid and made the memory bearable. He went on. "We hadn't made love because her ex had been a brute. We were going slow. One night, at her place, we both got hot and horny. I never gave her safety a thought. I just got us both naked and was deep inside her when her ex-husband broke in." His body involuntarily tightened at the memory.

Lexie kept touching him with her hands. The feel of her hands trying to soothe him reached deep inside him, and his muscles relaxed. But she didn't say anything. Not a word.

He took a breath and forced the words out. "I jumped off her, sure I could handle anything. He had a gun and shot Ellen before I could get to him. I still remember her ragged scream of pain as I slammed into him. I knocked him unconscious. I would have killed him." His whole body tightened and strained against the vivid memory. "But Ellen was bleeding. I had to try to stop it."

Lexie lifted her head, looking up into his eyes.

He was stunned to see her eyes were bright with unshed tears. He heard his voice say, "She was dead by the time the paramedics got there."

"Nick—"

The memory gnawed at him, but worse was the fear that it could happen to Lexie. She was so vital, so alive, and she deserved a good life. He shifted her off him, and when she stood up, he looked into her face and told her the brutal truth. "You wanted to know, now you know. I keep my emotions in check, and I don't mix sex and work."

Five

Nick woke up to an empty room. Leaping off the lounge chair, he checked the bathroom.

No Lexie.

Where the hell did she go? His heart pounding, he grabbed the phone and dialed Mac's cell phone.

"Koontz."

"Lexie's not in the room. I woke up and she's gone." How the hell did she get out without him hearing her? But he knew. Lexie had fallen asleep with her computer on. Nick had gotten up, moved the computer, and damned if he didn't start reading.

He'd read for hours.

Lexie could write. It'd been two A.M. when he finally fell into a dead sleep.

"She's with Shelly."

"Where?" he demanded, a sick feeling washing over him.

"Surfing. Shelly and Lexie had breakfast and decided to sign up for the surfing lessons. Perfectly safe."

His heart rate slowed. Nick sank down on the bed. "She could have left a note or something." Christ, he sounded like her mother.

Mac snorted. "She wants to have fun, be impulsive before

she has to go back and face the charges against her. Not worry about being *your job*." He hung up.

Nick slammed the phone down. Before he could stop it, he remembered the feel of Lexie stretched out on top of him. How she'd coaxed him into telling her about Ellen. That was all the more reason to keep his distance from her—just as soon as he made sure for himself that she was safe.

He hauled ass to his room, grabbed a shower, yanked on his board shorts, and hit the beach. To do a visual check. Lexie was in his custody, and he had to keep tabs on her.

Walking over the cool, slightly damp sand, he caught a few women watching him. Once he freed himself of Lexie, maybe he should come back and check out the scenery. Hole up for a day or two with a nice, willing woman.

Maybe he was just horny.

Once he finished this job, he'd go back to his hit-and-run sex—that would cure his Lexie-lust. Sex with no emotions, and keep it separate from work. It had worked for him for years, and no one got hurt. He wasn't going to let Lexie screw it up.

Where the hell was she? He scanned the sand but didn't see her, although the cabanas blocked much of his view. Mac had said she was surfing, so she was probably with a group. Shielding his eyes, he looked out to the waves. A group of about five women straddled surfboards while two men helped them.

Nick spotted Lexie. She was in a red bikini, and a man had his hand on her lower back, explaining something.

Anger surged inside of him. Was she out of her mind? She didn't know that man. He could be dangerous. Without thinking, Nick stormed out into the water.

A wave came up behind the women. They all lay flat on their boards, pushing up on their palms to position themselves to try and catch the wave.

Nick's gut tightened. He surfed all the time and he knew the dangers. Lexie was a novice! She could get hurt. Helplessly, he stood in knee-high water and watched as the wave caught under her board. She got her feet under her and stood up.

Her face lit up in joy. Even from a distance, he could see her huge smile right up until she lost her balance and fell off the board.

Nick swam toward her, grabbing her arm and jerking her toward him. She sputtered. "What . . . oh. Nick. Did you see me? I was surfing! I did it! I got up!"

Her tiny top barely contained her breasts as she panted with excitement. Looking down into her face, he said, "Yes. And I saw that man with his hands all over you, too. Is that what you left the room for? To go find some guy to feel you up?" What the fuck was he saying? He was out of his mind.

The happiness in her eyes dimmed. "Let go of me."

"Nick? What are you doing here?" Shelly pushed her board over to them.

He glared at her. "This is your fault. You put her up to this."

Shelly widened her brown eyes. "Up to what? Learning to surf? Or pissing you off?"

He turned back to Lexie and realized he was making a colossal ass out of himself. Dropping Lexie's arm, he said, "I'm just saying that you don't know that man. He had his hands all over you. You're supposed to be in my custody."

Lexie's face tightened. "He's just teaching me to surf."

"Why didn't you ask me? I can teach you to surf." God, he was just mad. So damned mad. Why the hell did she let that man touch her like that?

"It's not your job to teach me," she said calmly. She turned and headed back to the instructor, who was holding her board for her.

Nick stormed back to the shore. He was not going to stand there and watch another man pawing Lexie.

He went to the gym.

* * *

Lexie and Shelly had spent the day together, doing the spa and a little shopping at the resort boutique. She really couldn't afford all this, but Shelly had a discount and what the hell.

Okay, she wanted to look hot.

She slid the slinky black dress over a lacy thong, then she brushed out her hair to soft waves. With all the sun, she only needed a touch of make-up. After putting on her shoes, she looked at the time. Six-thirty, time to check in with her PI. She sat on the bed, turned on her cell phone, and ignored the voice mail messages that were most likely from her family trying to make her call them.

Tate answered, "Hi, Lexie, no news."

He sounded frustrated. "Maybe he's given up, Tate." She'd liked Tate right away when she hired him. He was about her dad's age, a retired cop, and thorough.

"Maybe, but I'm worried. He should be frantic by now since he hasn't seen you. He should be making mistakes."

Her stomach clenched and tension shot up her spine, tightening her neck muscles. "He could have given up."

"I don't like the way this feels. Let me talk to your family. We need to clear up just how often your brother was in your apartment. He's not going in now, or I'd see him on the cameras I have set up."

She hesitated, not really wanting more trouble with her family. She knew Tate wanted to rule her brother out or see if he'd copied her house key, maybe given it to someone, but Lexie didn't think Larry would do that. Larry was about the opportunity—he wanted to have sex with a woman and obviously couldn't do it at home where his wife might catch him, so hey, why not use his sister's apartment. In his mind, that didn't hurt anyone. But giving out a copy of her house key would be dangerous; even Larry would know that.

Tate interrupted her thoughts. "This is your *life* we're talking about."

He was right. She cleared her throat and said, "Fine, do it."

She gave him all the information he needed, all the while deciding that she had to move. She couldn't live in that apartment anymore. Just the idea of going back made her queasy. There was a knock on her door, so she said, "I'll call you tomorrow."

"Be careful."

She turned off her cell, checked the peephole, then answered the door. Shelly had on the silver dress she'd bought and looked fabulous.

"That dress ought to make Nick drool," Shelly said.

The black dress was fitted, low cut, and had a flared skirt for dancing. But between the phone call with her PI and thinking about Nick, her stomach was knotted and uneasy. "Maybe this isn't a good idea." Much as she liked Shelly, Lexie suspected that she and Mac were playing their own twisted version of matchmaker. She should stay out of it. Nick had his reasons and she should respect that.

But she'd given her impulsive streak a little freedom, and now that streak was taking over. She was tired of being ignored . . . by her family and now by Nick. One second he acted like he cared, the next he told her she was just a job. It hurt more than it should, and she was lashing back by teasing him.

God, what did that make her?

Shelly snapped her fingers to get her attention. "Let's go, Lexie. I'm not letting you back out."

Lexie grabbed her purse and key card. "Okay," she agreed, because her only other option was to sit in her room and wonder where Nick was and worry about the stalker. They went across the resort to the Bayside Restaurant and Bar. As soon as they opened the door, they were blasted by the vibrant music with a salsa beat. Already five or six women were dancing with the hired male teachers, who were all yummy looking. They appeared to have a sultry Cuban or Spanish heritage. She looked around the bar, seeing several couples watching. There were a few stray men, either belonging to the women learning to dance, or perhaps hoping to score.

But no Nick. She told herself it was for the best.

An hour later, Lexie was hot and having fun. She'd danced with three of the male teachers and she totally sucked. She knew it, but she didn't care. The music was upbeat, the men were nice, the woman all laughed, and no one minded. No one judged; the whole point was just to have fun.

What a concept, no one judging her.

Raoul pulled her back against his chest and said, "Try to follow me. It's supposed to be sexy."

She laughed. "I'm more comical than sexy."

"Not true." He settled his hands on her waist. "You're just self-conscious. Relax, let the music talk to your body."

Lexie closed her eyes to try, but the hair stood up on her arms.

"Having fun?"

Snapping her eyes open, she saw Nick. He towered over the other men. Wearing dark slacks, a cream-colored shirt rolled up his forearms, and a serious frown. "What are you doing here?"

Nick narrowed his eyes. "Came here to get a drink with Mac, and what do I find? You with another man's hands all over you." He moved in a step closer. "She's dancing with me." He glared over her shoulder at her dance partner.

Raoul lifted his hands off her waist. "Sure. Whatever."

"Nick!"

He looked down at her.

"Why are you doing this?" She was trying to keep her distance.

His jaw flexed hard enough to crack nuts.

Frustrated, she said, "Weren't you the one pushing me away?"

"I can't stop myself. Damn it, Lexie, you are turning me inside out." He leaned down. "You're making it impossible to do my job."

Her chest tightened. She was his job. He was pissed that he was sexually attracted to her when she was nothing more than a job. He was being forced into close proximity with her because she was in trouble.

A burden.

If she didn't do exactly as she was supposed to, then she was a burden. An inconvenience. A problem. She knew Nick had thought she'd be easy money. He'd counted on his charm to talk her into going back to Santa Barbara and he could collect his money. Now he knew the truth: Lexie never did what she was supposed to. She always screwed things up.

The salsa music pulsed around her, escalating her anger until her fragile hold on her self-control shattered. Without a word, she dragged her arm away and slid past him. As soon as she reached the edge of the dance floor, she ran.

Out of the restaurant. Away from Nick. Away from the feelings he roused in her until she couldn't breathe. But she couldn't outrun her attraction to Nick—the man who didn't want to be attracted to her. She'd lain on top of him and felt his erection last night. Then he'd just pushed her away.

She hurried along the stone pathways, wondering where to go. Back to her room? Nick could find a way to get in there. And he had her car keys, damn it.

Where?

She kept going, winding around the stone paths down to the area called Palm Park. Swaying palm trees decorated with colored lights enclosed the small park. It had wrought-iron tables and chairs with bright cushions surrounding a graceful dolphin fountain. Lexie followed the sound of the water. Colored lights shone up on the dolphin, illuminating the creature as he appeared to arch toward the sea. She could smell the ocean just yards away, but the little park was quiet. People had picnic lunches here and just sat and talked. Sometimes the park was rented out for weddings or parties.

Tonight the empty park echoed her loneliness. Sliding off her shoes, she set them on a bench and stepped into the water to ease the pain of dancing for an hour in high-heeled sandals.

She could probably strike dancer off her list of possible career choices.

"Lexie."

His tone was low, with an undertone of silky steel. It pissed her off that just his voice made her belly quiver. Holding out a hand to the gentle fall of water, she didn't look at him. "Take me back, Nick. Tonight. Get your money and we're done."

"Still being a martyr?"

She turned around, uncaring that the waterfall splashed her. "No. I'm being realistic. I'm done running. I'm going back." Her throat thickened as she stared at him. The blue, green, red, and yellow lights highlighted his inky black hair, the dark shadow on his clenched jaw, the breadth of his shoulders. He looked tense, ready to pounce. She forced herself to add, "Away from you. Either you take me and collect your money or I'll get there another way."

He stood as still as the statue except for his breathing, then he broke free, striding toward her. He stopped at the edge of the fountain to kick off his shoes and pull off his socks. Then he stepped in and came face-to-face with her in two steps. "The hell you will. I'm not letting you go back when you're in danger!"

It was all she could do not to back up. He was in her face, not touching her but in her face. "It doesn't matter if I'm in danger. I'm just a job to you. Nothing more. No emotion involved. Do your job." She couldn't do it, couldn't stay with him one more minute constantly craving something from him he couldn't give her. She'd rather deal with her stalker. She'd find a way to ensure her safety. She could stay in a hotel if the cops didn't put her in jail.

He flexed his hands at his sides. "Be reasonable, Lexie!"

Her control snapped. None of it mattered anymore. "I'm so damned tired of being reasonable! I ran away thinking my family would finally get it. They'd understand that I needed them for a change! Did that happen? No! And now I need you . . . and . . ." She shuddered and tears burned her eyes, ran down her face. Hot embarrassment flooded her. "I'm going back." She tried to turn, to get out of the water.

Nick caught her by the shoulders, his hands firm. He pushed her back a step, flush against the statue. His green eyes caught the lights, flickering with a raw need. "I never let my lust get out of control. But you, Christ, you smash my willpower and make me ache for your touch. I'm done fighting. Hell with the consequences." He pressed his body into hers, his erection into her belly. "I'll worry about your safety tomorrow; tonight you're mine."

More tears brimmed over and ran hot down her face. "Nick." She put her arms around his neck.

He slammed his mouth down on hers, one hand sliding into her hair to hold her.

She inhaled the scent of him—soap and hot skin mixed with the water trickling over them. He made an impatient noise in his chest and invaded her mouth. Or she invaded his. She didn't know, and she didn't care, she just wanted Nick. Needed him, needed him to wrap himself around her and make her feel real and substantial. She slid her tongue along his and dug her fingers into his shoulders. Hot desire ripped through her.

Nick slid his hand off her shoulder and cupped her breast, squeezing just enough. She moved against him. He ran the pad of his thumb over her pebbled nipple through the thin dress, making her shiver. She stroked her hand over the soft material of his shirt, down to the front of his pants, and pressed her palm against his dick.

He groaned deep in his chest. Lifting his head, he said, "What are you wearing under the dress?"

Her voice was raspy. "Panties. Thong."

He slid both his hands down the sides of her body, dropping to his knees. "Show me."

She looked at him on his knees, in the water, his pants getting wet, his head tilted as he stared up at her with those eyes.

He put his hands on the outside of her knees. "Now."

Lexie pulled up her dress until she felt the cool air and wet droplets of water from the waterfall.

Nick dropped his gaze. "Damn." He stroked his hands up her thighs, over the thong, then grasped the edge and eased it down and off. Then he reached up and pressed her legs apart. The cool mist touched her sex and she shivered.

"God. I've wanted this." He touched her with his thumbs sliding along her seam, then spreading her. Touched her clitoris, stroking his thumb in circles.

Lexie fell back against the statue, her back wet, the dress sticking to her while she held up the skirt. "Nick . . ."

"I'm not stopping. Not now."

She saw his dark head lean into her thighs, then his tongue touched her, sliding over her clit and deeper to taste all of her. A deep shudder wracked her.

Nick reached up one hand to hold her against the statue.

He centered his tongue on her clit, wet, lapping circles until Lexie thought she'd cry. She ground against him, desperate. "Oh!" She held the dress with one hand.

He increased his licks and slid his hand deep between her legs, one finger easing inside of her.

Panting, she knew she was making noise. Probably begging. Nothing had ever felt like this. Free. Sexy. Just her and Nick. The cold water on her skin, her dress wet against her sensitive breasts, and Nick sucking her, thrusting his finger in her.

Then he added a second finger. Lexie shattered, her entire body rocking with deep spasms of pleasure. Nick pushed her further, tonguing her, thrusting his fingers inside of her to keep her orgasm going until she was breathless.

He rose up, his eyes so light with gold, they were intense. "Keep holding that dress." He undid his pants and pulled his cock out.

In the colored lights, his penis looked deep in color, thick and long. She had never wanted to be filled up like she did now.

Tonight. By Nick. She might have whimpered.

"Every time you make that noise, it makes me hornier." He reached around her, lifted her up, and held her against the wet column of the statue. "Take me, Lexie."

"Are you sure? It slippery in here and—" Suddenly her eyes widened. "Condoms."

"Shit." He eased her down to her feet.

Six

Nick inserted the keycard, opened the door, and looked at Lexie.

The flush of her orgasm was fading from her face. Her dress was wet and clinging to her breasts and legs. He had her panties in his hand with his shoes and socks. She shivered as she walked into the air-conditioned room.

No way was he letting her think too much. He was light-years past thinking and one hundred percent into Lexie, just Lexie. Shutting the door, he tossed the stuff he carried, took the shoes from her hand, and rubbed her shoulders and bare arms. He felt her tremble, felt the rise of gooseflesh beneath his palms. "I only want you wet where I make you wet. And shivering when I make you shiver." He moved behind her and found the zipper of her dress. Dropping a kiss on her shoulder, he slid the zipper down her long back, then pushed the tiny straps down her arms. The material whispered down her body, revealing her tan lines, the white swells of her ass, her legs. He reached to gather her in his arms and remembered his wet clothes.

Nick stripped his clothes off. Then he pulled her against him. Her skin against his, her curves pressing against him. He leaned down to her neck, inhaling the scent of her, the lingering sunscreen, slight chlorine of the waterfall water, and just pure Lexie. He could still taste her on his tongue. Unable to stop from touching her, he skimmed his hands over her nipples, feeling the tremor go through her. Cupping her breasts, he brushed his thumbs back and forth across her nipples. His cock strained against her back. "I want you, the real you. Raw, honest, riding my cock, Lexie. Taking the pleasure you crave. The pleasure you denied yourself trying to be good and perfect for everyone else."

She leaned back into him. "Yes."

It ripped through him, the untainted trust in her. She'd been riding the edge of wild since he'd met her, reaching for a chance to throw off the shackles but always pulling back. No pulling back tonight. Not with him. He'd known in that first kiss, when she'd melted into him with trust, that she'd let go for him.

It had scared him to death.

Now his cock thickened and his pulse pounded. He glided his hand down her belly, sensitive to the quivers in her stomach muscles. Dipping between her legs, he separated her gently. She was soft and wet, her body opening to him. Male pride swelled and drove him to give her pleasure, to push her to be free with him. He stroked her, and she writhed against him, her skin sliding over his while his fingers sank into her wet heat. She arched against him, forcing his fingers deeper into her body.

He groaned. "Condom," he told her. Taking his hands off her body, he went to his dresser and found the condoms. Grabbing one, he turned and holy God, he stopped. Lexie's hair was wild, her face flushed, her eyes sparkling. Her breasts were tightly nubbed, and between her legs, her curls were wet. Her clit peeked out.

She came to him, taking the condom, opening it, and sliding it on him.

He grabbed her shoulders, pushed her back to the bed, and

went down on top of her. Nick opened his mouth over hers, sucking her tongue. He was so hard, so goddamned desperate to be inside her, he worried he'd hurt her. Grabbing her waist, he rolled her over him. "Let me watch you."

She rose up on her knees and straddled him, her hair sliding over her shoulders and brushing over her tits. Taking hold of his cock, she pressed the tip against her sleek hot entry. She was looking down, watching as he slid partway into her. Then she looked up at him.

He reached over his head, hooking his fingers around the wrought-iron headboard. "More, Lexie. Jesus, you're killing me." Her walls were hot and slick and sucking him in. Sweat coated him. But he watched her face. The flare in her brown eyes. She wanted him, she wanted something . . . "Take it, Lexie. You want it, take it!"

She took him all.

Nick squeezed his fingers around the wrought iron over his head. The feel of her body taking him in deep slammed him with a truth—this wasn't just sex, but an all-consuming passion.

Lexie began to move, sliding him in and out, torturing the hell out of him. The need to possess her, fill her, grew, but he fought to let her set the pace. Color rose in her face and chest, and she began to undulate in a frantic way.

Nick got it, realized what she was trying for. He let go of the headboard, reaching down to separate her folds and expose her clit better.

She stopped moving, startled.

He looked into her face, desperate to reassure her. To teach her to take what she needed from him. "I want to feel you rubbing your pussy on me while my cock is deep inside you." He took hold of her hips, showing her how to rock herself on him.

Then she did it on her own. God. He arched up under her, grabbing the headboard as she rode him. Her breasts bounced, her face softened, and she arched as she found it . . . her orgasm.

She made sexy noises, bearing down on him, rubbing her pleasure on him. Her face flooded with color, and Jesus, she was so fucking beautiful.

He lost it. He reared up to put his arm around her shoulders and pulled her into his chest. He had to feel her, hold her. Putting his free hand on her lower back, he dug his heels into the bed and thrust up high and hard. Her body was soft and pliant and he couldn't get enough of her. He thrust harder, deeper.

A small voice warned, *Don't hurt her.*

But he went deeper and came holding Lexie against his chest, feeling her hot skin against his and inhaling her scent.

As soon as he could breathe, he said, "Did I hurt you?"

A small tremor went through her, wrapping around his cock. "No."

He knew it was true. Her body was spread out, still soft and supple, with little aftertremors. He hadn't hurt her. He'd just lost control.

And his mind.

Lexie watched the cold gray dawn, barely able to see the ocean. She could just make out the white caps of the waves. Fog chilled her and she wrapped both hands around her mug of coffee. The noise of the crashing waves somehow sounded like freedom to her. Like the powerful sense of freedom she'd felt last night.

She hoped the sound of the waves would always remind her of that precious feeling. And of Nick.

She knew last night cost him, blurred lines that he couldn't emotionally afford to blur. Ellen's murder haunted him, and he coped by keeping sex and duty separate. Who was she to judge that? Hadn't she been judged enough? She wouldn't do that to Nick. One day, he would find a woman he could care about again. A woman who came without trouble that brought out the memories for him.

Hearing the slide of the door behind her, she tried not to tense up.

Nick moved up behind her. "What are you doing out here? Can't you sleep?"

"I didn't mean to wake you."

He reached around her, sliding the cup from her hands to take a drink, then settling the warm mug between her palms. He put his arms around her. "You're cold. Come back to bed."

She had put on his shirt because it was easier than her dress. His warmth penetrated the material. She could feel his hard-on pressing against her lower back. Desire rose, thick and desperate. But with the morning came the consequences. "No. We should get going. It's a long drive."

His arms tightened around her. "Lexie."

She turned, stepping out of his arms and putting a little distance between them. "I'm not going to let you bend your rules because of some kind of twisted logic that you have to protect me. You don't. I'll handle this situation with the stalker. I'll go back and fix things."

"You mean cave in to your family?"

There was enough light now for her to see Nick wearing only his boxers. She intimately knew the curve of his shoulders, the feel of his muscles covered by skin that smelled like Nick—bold and determined. He was powerful and overwhelming as a lover, and yet, she'd touched a part of him last night that was vulnerable. He handled his vulnerability by keeping barriers in place; she wasn't going to cross those barriers and cause him more pain.

"I'll deal with it, Nick. They are my family, they're all I have. I shouldn't have run."

He returned her stare. "Running was the first smart thing you did do." Dragging a hand through his hair, he added, "I read some of your book. You are good. It's only Wednesday. We have until Friday morning. Keep working on your book."

Her chest hollowed, and her hands tingled like they were falling asleep. She set the coffee cup down on the small table. "You looked at my book? On my laptop?" It was hers. Her book. Just hers. The only thing she had that was hers. Emotions welled up, burned. Anger? Nerves? Did he like it? She didn't know what she felt.

"Yes. You fell asleep while working on it the night we went to Mac and Shelly's. I was making sure the file was saved to shut down your computer . . . and I ended up reading. I'm not sorry, Lex. I read for hours. I didn't want to stop. Hell, I've been trying to work up the courage to ask you to read the rest of it."

She stepped farther back, hit the edge of the chair, and fought for her balance. Something was moving inside of her, shifting, swelling.

Nick closed his hand around her arm. "I know it was wrong to invade your privacy. But where you're concerned, I have no self-control. None." He voice dropped to a caress as he added, "I like you in my shirt."

She shivered and couldn't resist asking, "You liked it? The book?"

He smiled. "Yes." He pulled her against him, leaned down, and kissed her.

She couldn't sort it all out, but Nick wrapped one arm around her waist, lifted her up, and carried her inside. Taking her mouth from his, she tried to keep the boundaries in place. "Sex? This is about vacation sex, right?"

His grin turned wicked. "Sun, sand, and sex. Mostly sex." He tossed her on the bed.

She had to be out of her mind. He had the ability to keep his emotions separate, but she knew it was too late for her anyway. She cared for Nick, cared so much she couldn't leave him and yet was desperate to ease his worries and conscience. Did two more days really matter? Bouncing on the bed where he tossed her, she watched him strip off his boxers. He was hard, his dick thick and twitching. Still wearing his shirt, she got to her knees on the mattress and touched him.

He thrust his hips and groaned at her touch. Sinking his hand in her hair, he tilted her head up to him and said, "I intended to go slow, drive you crazy—"

She cut him off. "Nick?" He closed his eyes as she stroked his cock and cupped his balls.

"What?" He groaned.

"Shut up and get down to business."

He snapped his eyes open. Then he grinned. He reached out and slid his shirt halfway down her arms, then he picked her up and put her on her back.

Lexie realized he'd bared her body to him, but trapped her arms to her sides. She could roll over and free herself, but why the heck would she do that? She pretended, though. "No fair."

He laughed, then he bent her legs, spread her knees, and looked his fill. He touched her clit, stroked her. She writhed, spreading her thighs for him. He took his hand away.

"Nick, don't stop!"

He went to the dresser and got a condom. "Lexie?"

She watched him roll the condom onto himself. "Hmm?"

"Shut up, sweetheart." He moved on top of her and slid his cock inside of her. "Unless you're whimpering." He thrust hard, reaching the spot that fired her nerves. A spot that only he knew.

She whimpered, wrapped her legs around him, and arched up to take more of him.

"Or panting." He thrust again.

Her breath rushed out of her.

Nick rose up, placing his arms on either side of her head. He looked down at her, his eyes golden. "Or you come . . ." He slammed into her, over and over, deeper. "Come hard, Lexie, squeeze me."

She cried out, her release pulsing and squeezing even as he shoved her halfway up the bed, burying his cock in her and groaning his release.

Nick rolled her over on top of him and stripped the shirt off her, throwing it to the side. Then his arms wrapped around her, holding her. He drew one hand down her back to spread his fingers over her butt cheek. "How about you spend the day writing in bed while naked?"

Lexie sank into the warmth, hearing the slam of her heart, feeling the sting of his sweat against her face. Her whole body throbbed. "I think you tricked me into staying under false pretenses, bounty hunter." She took a breath and asked, "Will you be naked too?"

He tightened his arm around her. "Oh, yeah."

Seven

Lexie's stomach rumbled loudly.

Nick walked out of the bathroom with a towel slung around his hips. "Is that your subtle way of telling me to feed you?"

She laughed. "A body can't exist on sex alone." Although she was happy enough to try. He looked good in a towel. It was a shame to watch him pull on board shorts.

The room phone rang, startling her.

Nick walked over and grabbed it. "Vardolous." A pause, then, "Yes, she's here." He handed her the phone.

"It's for me?" Who could possibly know she was in Nick's room?

Nick grinned. "It's Mac."

She took the phone, a little bemused. "Hi, Mac, is something wrong?"

"Evidently not, if you're in Nick's room."

She blushed, remembering breakfast with Mac and Shelly yesterday morning. Lexie had known they were doing some creative matchmaking. "Uh, what can I do for you?"

"Can you come up to the lobby for a few minutes?"

"Why?" She had no idea why he'd want to see her.

"Nothing to worry about. The resort manager would just like a quick minute."

Was something wrong with her credit card? She wasn't anywhere near her limit. "Uh, okay. I'll be there in a few minutes."

"See you then." Mac hung up.

Lexie set the phone down and stared at it.

Nick walked up behind her, put his hands on her arms, and rubbed up and down. "What's up?"

She turned. "The resort manager wants to see me. I don't know why. I'm sure my credit card is fine. I haven't done anything wrong."

He laughed. "Why don't we stop by your room so you can get your swimsuit and laptop, then we'll go see what terrible crime you've committed. If you aren't arrested, then we can get some breakfast, and I was thinking that maybe you'd like to try surfing again before you get to work."

"You mean the class?" She'd had fun in the class except when Nick got all bent out of shape.

His dark eyebrows drew together in a frown. "Not a chance. It'll be my hands all over you this morning." Drawing himself up, he added, "I'll teach you."

She didn't get it. "Why?"

He reached out and touched her face, sliding his fingers along her jaw. "Because when you stood up on the surfboard yesterday, I could see your smile even from a distance. I want to see it again. You were doing pretty good. Come on, it'll be fun."

He wanted her to have fun. With him. She was just digging herself in deeper and deeper. "Well, uh—"

He leaned down, brushing his mouth over hers. "Or we can come back to my room and you can try to work naked."

Shivers danced in her stomach, but she tried to look stern. "Try? I'm very serious about my book, I'll have you know."

"Hmm. I might have to test the level of your commitment."

He dropped a hand to the bare skin of her thigh and slid it under her dress.

God, she was too easy. With Nick. She wanted to strip off her dress, strip off his board shorts, and . . . she shoved him away. "Hands off, bounty hunter. Mac is expecting me soon."

Nick grinned. "I could kill him and solve the problem."

"Nick!" Her horror somehow turned into laughter. There was nothing sexier than a man making her feel desired. Nick had that way about him. *With all women?* she wondered. That thought hurt, but Lexie was determined to accept that this was just vacation sex, nothing more. "Let's go."

Since she had showered in Nick's room, it didn't take her long to put on her bathing suit and cover-up, then grab her beach bag. They left their laptops in her room for now and walked to the lobby. It was cool inside with the lazy ceiling fans, mosaic tiles, and an indoor waterfall. Mac strode toward them with two women, both wearing the blue and white resort colors.

Mac grinned at her. "Lexie, I'd like you to meet the resort manager, Rose, and our event coordinator, Vivian."

Rose had short blond hair and a wide smile. "Hi, Lexie, Mac's told us a lot about you. So has the staff that has worked with you to book rooms for your clients' honeymoons."

At a loss for what to do, Lexie smiled and said, "It's a pleasure to meet both of you. What can I do for you?" The professional tone was automatic, although she felt awkward in her bikini and flip-flops. What did they want? She was pretty sure it had nothing to do with My Perfect Wedding.

Rose said, "I'll make this quick so you can make the most of a beautiful day here at our resort. Vivian will be leaving Sand Castle Resort in a month. I understand that you are an excellent wedding planner but you are considering a career change. I've talked to two of your clients this morning, and they raved about you. I'd like you to consider a job as an event coordinator here at Sand Castle."

She turned and looked at Mac.

His blue eyes glittered. "I recommended you, and the staff backed me up."

A vein of possibility opened up, spilling out excitement. She could move to San Diego, work at the resort, and write in her spare time. It'd be a fresh start, put some distance between her and her demanding family. She'd have to plan some weddings, but she'd also be planning events for businesses. It'd be different and challenging. She already had friends—Shelly and Mac. Her mind spun, trying to break it down and grasp it.

Nick checked her thoughts when he said, "She can't work here. She lives in Santa Barbara."

The excitement drained out like her lifeblood. San Diego was Nick's home. Mac and Shelly were his friends. Lexie didn't belong here, she was just . . . vacation sex. She turned back to Rose and Vivian. "Thank you. I'm pleased that you would consider me. But I won't be able to accept."

Rose's sharp gaze drifted over all of them, then settled on Lexie. "I'm sure the offer is a surprise. Why don't you take some time to think it over? We can talk later." She reached out her hand.

Lexie shook it and turned to shake Vivian's hand. To be polite, she said, "That's very generous of you. I'll be in touch with you soon."

Nick watched Lexie ride her third wave of the morning, his chest swelling with pride in her. She was a great student, willing to listen to direction, yet trusting her own body. She didn't try to fight the waves, she let them carry her and the board. When she fell off the last wave, he swam to her. She popped up with a proud smile.

He pulled her into his arms and kissed her.

She leaned back, still grinning. "That was so cool!"

"You're a natural."

She smiled at him. "Thanks, Nick. I really had fun, and

you're a good teacher. I'm ready to go in, though. I want to work for a while."

He grabbed the board. "Let's go." They made their way to the shore and their cabana. While Lexie settled in, Nick went to the room and collected both their laptops. He could get a little work done too.

They both booted up their machines and focused on their projects.

A few minutes later, Nick was reading an e-mail from his lawyer about the partnership papers with Mac when Lexie said, "Nick, I copied my book, if, you know, you still want to read it. Here."

He looked up to see her holding out a CD.

"I mean, if you don't want to read it, fine. I just thought . . ."

Her brown eyes had such hope and fear it made him forget to breathe. He reached out and took the CD. "I can read it? I know I didn't ask the first time, but I'm asking now."

She shrugged. "If you want to. Or not. Doesn't matter to me."

It mattered. He could see it in the lines of her tense arms, raised shoulder, and strained neck. "I want to." He shifted his laptop and got up, then he leaned over and kissed her. "Thank you. I know how much this book means to you."

She stared at him with wide eyes, all kinds of emotion shifting through the brown depths. Then she said, "I'm not being that brave. By next week, I'll never see you again. Even if you hate it, what do I have to lose?"

He kissed her again to shut her up, but the thought of her being gone from his life lingered. And he didn't like it, not one damned bit.

But he'd get used to it. He always did. Nick loaded the CD and started reading.

It was past lunchtime when Lexie got up and said, "I'm going to cool off in the water." He waved her away, then watched her walk down the sand toward the waves. Her black bikini cupped her ass in a way that made his hands curl with the need to feel her butt in his palms. He dragged his gaze from her and back to reading.

Until Mac's voice intruded. "What's the word, Vardolous?"

"Scram." He didn't look up, but kept reading.

"Who's that man Lexie is talking to?"

Nick looked up.

Mac laughed. "You're so predictable."

Turning his attention to Mac, he said, "Why haven't I killed you?"

Mac's gaze grew serious. "Because I'm your business partner."

Nick rubbed his eyes with his thumb and forefinger. He and Mac already had picked out a building for the karate studio and leased it. Nick wasn't backing out, but he liked screwing with Mac's abundant confidence. "I haven't signed the papers yet."

"You will. You're tired of the nomad life and you know it."

Nick didn't like being analyzed. Turning, he glared at Mac. "I know you and Shelly were goading Lexie into driving me crazy."

"Good times, huh?"

Leaning his head back, he stared out at the waves where Lexie stood waist deep in the water. "You went too far with the job offer. You're sticking your nose where it doesn't belong." It would be hard enough when he left Lexie in Santa Barbara. But having her in San Diego? Close by? How would he stay away from her?

"I know this will come as a shock to your enormous ego, but the job offer isn't about you. It's about Lexie. Shelly and I like her."

Nick narrowed his gaze. "You never chummed up with the other women I slept with."

"You didn't bring them around."

He hadn't wanted to bring them around. They were nice women, but he hadn't been interested in introducing them to his friends or family. Lexie had met his mom and sister, and his friends. He was losing control of this situation. "I didn't bring them around because you obviously fancy yourself a matchmaker."

"Nah. Don't have time since I'm going into partnership with you. And I plan to kick your ass regularly. In front of students."

Nick considered that. "Yeah? How about I kick your ass right now in front of all the people at the beach?"

Mac snorted. "It's not snowing in hell, so it's not happening."

He laughed. Nick had taken down vicious animals many times as a bounty hunter, but Mac was formidable as a sparring opponent. He had a fourth-degree black belt in karate, and that was only one of his disciplines. There was no one he'd rather have at his back. Mac was fast.

Nick was power. And a sixth-degree black belt.

Mac stood up. "Just checking in. Want to have dinner with us tonight? Maybe take the girls dancing?"

His gut twisted. "Girls? I'm not dating Lexie, we're just having sex. She's not *my girl*." It sounded like high school, for Christ's sake, not a mature decision to slake their lust.

"Well, I am a girl. Sheesh. Hi, Mac." Lexie lifted up her laptop and dropped into the chair.

Christ, his timing sucked. "Sorry, I just meant—"

She waved her hand at him. "Guy talk, I know. Go with Mac and Shelly tonight. Have fun." Lexie shoved her wet hair out of her face and opened her computer like he wasn't even there.

What the hell? He sat up. "What's that supposed to mean?"

"Uh, I have to go . . . work or something." Mac turned and strolled off, whistling.

Nick ignored him to stare at Lexie.

She met his gaze. "Mac's just messing with you. I know that. Don't worry about it. I'll see you when you get back."

"Back from where?" What the hell was wrong with her? She was acting irrational.

She widened her eyes. "Dinner, dancing, whatever you're doing. I thought that's what Mac said."

He ran his hand over the back of his neck, feeling the bulge of his muscles, and snarled, "If you want to go dancing, we'll go."

Her brown eyes dropped to her laptop. "Don't be ridiculous. I never said I wanted to go dancing with you."

God, she was pissing him off. If she wanted to go dancing, all she had to do was say so. He'd take her dancing, damn it. "You were happy enough to dance with all those men last night. Now you don't want to dance with me? What's wrong with me?"

"Maybe you've been out in the sun too long?"

He leaned back in his chair and looked down at the laptop. "I'm not the one who's being unreasonable." He started reading and ignored her. He didn't want to think about this . . . anger churning inside of him. He couldn't concentrate because he kept seeing the days ahead without Lexie. And he didn't like the view. Staring at the words, he said, "It's just that we aren't in a relationship. We only have a couple days."

She resumed typing on her book. "Sun, sand, and sex. I know. Not a problem."

Good. He read a sentence, but it didn't make any sense. This was her fault. Did she have to be so damned cheerful about it? Didn't the sex mean anything? How many men made her come like he did?

He didn't want to know.

He needed a beer. An ice-cold beer. Standing up, he said, "Want anything from the bar?"

"Iced tea or anything cold. Thanks."

He stood there staring down at her, watching her gnaw at her lower lip as she thought about something while staring at the computer. Her hair was drying into a stringy mess, her face was free of all make-up, and yet, she looked pretty. Real.

She looked up, then flushed. "Oh, sorry. I know I have my room key here somewhere to pay for the drink."

Swear to God, she was just trying to piss him off. "I'll buy the damned drinks." He turned and stalked off. He got the drinks and returned to the cabana. Setting the drinks on the table, he picked up the computer and settled in to read the book.

"I'll buy the next round."

He refused to let her bait him. No woman had ever turned him into a stark raving butthead before. Not even Ellen. Ellen had made him feel needed, powerful, strong. Lexie made him crazy. The kind of crazy that drove him to act like a Neanderthal, just as Shelly had accused him of being. He wanted to claim her as his and kill anyone else who looked at her.

Sunstroke was a distinct possibility.

The best thing to do was just shut the hell up. Let her think anything she liked, but he was not taking money from her. He would not leech off her like her family.

After reading the same sentence six more times, it finally dawned on him why it wasn't making sense. It didn't fit. And it was in bold print. His heart sped up, and he sat forward to read.

You have a secret life writing your book. I have a secret life, a life THEY will never control. We're meant to be together, in spite of THEM. Together in our secret love. Wait for me, I'll fulfill your craving for adventure.

Nick went back over what Lexie had told him in his head. She thought the stalker had left her laptop on. Jesus Christ. "Lexie."

"Hmm." She kept typing.

"Do you reread your work? Or do you just keep going forward?"

"Depends, why?" Frowning, she looked up at him. Her eyes were shadowed, but he saw her shoulders tense. "I told you it was rough. Typos and—"

He softened. "This isn't about typos. Please, Lex, just answer me. Have you gone back and read through your book?"

"No. Not since about the halfway point. I want to get to the end, then rewrite. Why? What's the problem?"

He looked around and could have kicked his own ass. It was midafternoon and there were tons of people milling around. "I don't want you to get upset, but I found something that doesn't seem to belong in your book."

She stared at him. "Like an unnecessary scene?"

"No." He got up and walked around to her with his computer.

She pushed her computer down her thighs to make room for his machine.

Nick set it down and pointed with his finger to the passage he'd found buried in her work.

Lexie quietly read it, then said, "Oh God. Nick, I didn't write that."

He hunkered down by her chair and put his hand on her shoulder. "No, I didn't think so." He felt a tremor go through her. Rubbing her shoulder, he looked into her eyes. "Let's pack up and go to the room. We'll talk there."

Lexie found a second note embedded in the manuscript, in bold print.

Danger is an aphrodisiac. You feel it, Lexie, the danger of never knowing when I'll show up. What will I do to you? Maybe you'll be in the shower . . . maybe you'll be in your bed . . . just make sure you're alone. You belong to me, only me.

A dirty, greasy feeling rolled in her stomach. She'd poured her heart into the book, into a thriller with a heroine who had to rise to incredible challenges, and yeah, there was sex, but . . . "Oh God, he's making it disgusting, he's . . ."

"A twisted prick." Nick put his arm around her shoulders. "It's not your book. It's him twisting things in his perverted head."

She copied and pasted the passage for the file they were going to send to her PI, Tate. Nick had talked to him on the phone, so he was waiting.

She kept searching. It looked like the stalker had put his comments in bold so she could find them. The ring of the room phone interrupted her. "Maybe it's Tate." She got up, walking over the cold tile to circle the bed and grab the phone. "Hello."

Silence, then, "So Larry was right. While your mother is working herself into another heart attack, you're on vacation."

"Dad?" She started to shake, needing her father. She stared at the textured green walls of her room, struggling for control. "Is Mom okay? Did she have another heart attack?"

"You've had your fun. Get back here and help your mother. Larry and Amber are making her nuts, she's screaming at everyone. You know she's sick. Stop acting like a child."

Her eyes filled with tears, and the green walls blurred. "Dad—"

Nick stomped over and grabbed the phone from her startled hand. "Mr. Rollins—"

Lexie felt a second of sheer relief, a second where she could just breathe. Then she got a hold of herself. This was her father. She reached over and snatched the phone back, determined to take control. "Dad—"

"You're with a man? While your mother—"

"Stop it, Dad!" It felt surprisingly good to fight back. "Stop trying to guilt me into fixing everything. Mom is fine, the doctor assured us that she's fine. If you want Amber and Larry to back off, tell them yourself. You and Mom allowed them to leech off you, so you can put a stop to it." She would not cry anymore, damn it. She refused to look at Nick, although she could feel him staring at her. She kept her gaze on the green mosaic tile.

Her dad said, "Of all the selfish—"

Nick put his arm around her and pulled her into his side,

but he didn't try to take the phone from her again. He just stood next to her like an anchor. It gave Lexie strength. Calmly, she said, "No, I'm not being selfish. I'm scared, Dad. More scared than I've ever been. I needed you, but you wouldn't listen to me."

"Is this that stalker thing again? Look, Larry admitted that he was in your apartment with a girl. He knows it was wrong. You have no business sending that private investigator to talk to him. What if his wife had found out?"

She leaned against Nick. "Good to know where your priorities are, Dad." She bent over and set the phone down. Emotion welled up and tightened her throat, but she wasn't going to fall apart. She was a woman, not a child. She would take care of herself and be fine.

The phone rang.

She ignored it and went to the computer. "Don't answer it. I have nothing else to say to him."

"Your decision." Nick sat next to her. "Want to talk about that shit with your brother?"

She assumed he had been able to hear her dad on the phone. "He screwed his girlfriend in my apartment. In the beginning I assumed the stuff I found was Larry's doing. We had a huge fight. He had stolen the key to my apartment from my mom. I made him give it back. It was ugly. He told my parents that he made a mistake and was trying to fix his marriage. He also claimed that I was trying to ruin his marriage because I was jealous." She paged down the manuscript, looking for the next note from the stalker.

Nick said, "Your brother is an asshole."

"I know. But he's the son my dad always wanted. Whatever." She stopped paging down and read.

Each time I check and see that you've been working on your book, I know you're staying home at night, waiting. Being a good girl and waiting for me. When I'm here in your apartment, I am too hard to wait. Have to

take the edge off. You have such pretty underwear . . .
Today I left the bed unmade for you. Lie there and know
I was there . . .
  And I'll be back.

She was going to throw up. She'd slept in her bed after . . .

Nick shoved his chair back and turned Lexie so she was facing the bed. He reached up behind her and forced her head down toward her knees. "Breathe. In and out."

She did what he told her, fighting to force the refrigerated air in and out of her lungs. The black spots dancing in front of her eyes started to fade and her nausea eased up. Finally she said, "I'm okay."

He took his hand off the back of her neck.

Sitting up, she looked at Nick. His face was pulled tight to reveal his prominent cheekbones and blazing eyes. He said, "There might be more."

She shook her head. "There's not."

"Lexie . . ."

"There's not. I came home from work one day and saw my laptop opened on my unmade bed. From then on, I took it with me to work." She forced herself to breathe and fight not to let the nausea rise. "I thought it was Larry. Bringing his girl-friend to my apartment, then checking his e-mail. Or that they were reading my book and making fun of me." She hadn't been able to believe some unknown person was getting into her apartment. It hadn't seemed real or possible.

Nick took her hand. "Okay, let's send all this to Tate. Maybe he can get a lead. But first I need to ask one thing."

She knew what he was going to ask. "I don't know who it is, Nick. Nothing rings a bell. I haven't dated in months. I just don't know." Damn it, she would not cry. What was next? "Do we go back now?"

"Hell no. Tate's an ex-cop, and he and I know some of the same cops in Santa Barbara. We'll ask Tate to file a report with them and get the process started. But we don't know who the stalker is, Lexie. All the police will do is open a file. We need some kind of break to point the police in the right direction."

She fought hard to control herself. She didn't ever want to go back to Santa Barbara. She wanted to stay here in the room with Nick. Forever. But that wasn't reality. She had to go back. She had to face the charges against her, and she had to deal with the stalker.

And Nick had his own life to get back to.

Eight

"Do you think it could be your brother behind this?" Tate asked over the speakerphone.

Lexie felt both Nick and Mac look at her. They were using Mac's office. Mac sat behind his desk across from them, while Nick sat on her right. She had her laptop on the desk in case Tate needed anything else off it. She wasn't sure how to answer.

Did she think it could be Larry?

She felt ill just considering it. "That's not really Larry's style. He's not likely to put so much effort into something like this. Plus he relies on me to fix his screwups."

Tate said, "He seems really angry at you. He denied making a copy of your mom's key to your apartment before giving it back, but I think he's lying."

"Probably," she agreed, done with pretending about her family. "That's just like Larry. Tuck a key away in case another opportunity for a little adultery comes up."

Tate asked, "Could he be trying to discredit you so that his wife and your parents don't believe you?"

Her stomach tightened painfully. "About using my apartment for an affair?"

"Yes."

"He might, except that Larry's brain doesn't work that way. He's reactive, not proactive. He doesn't think ahead, that's why I have to double-check every cake order, remind him where and when the cakes need to be delivered. I could see where he might write one note, but . . ." She shook her head while keeping her gaze fixed on her computer screen. "Copying my mom's key to my apartment is about as far ahead as he thinks. He simply had the opportunity—saw my key at Mom's and swiped it. Then he had it, so why not copy it? But coming up with and following through on a plan to discredit me is too involved for him."

Tate said, "Okay. Anyone else? I've checked out the two men you gave me who were odd. Both of them seem to be in the clear."

Nick looked over at her.

She shrugged. "One was the father of a bride, the other a best man. I thought they were long shots."

Tate explained, "I told Lexie to tell me anyone who seemed interested in her, no matter how remote a possibility it seemed."

Mac surprised her by jumping in with, "What about the guy you stapled?"

Lexie lifted her head. "William Harry Livingston?" She frowned. "The cops told me he's a respectable guy, never been in any trouble."

Nick sat up next to her. "You suspected him? Lexie?"

She twisted her fingers. "After the note on my car, I was scared. I probably jumped to conclusions."

"Don't forget the underwear. That kind of behavior is a sign of a dangerous stalker."

"What underwear?" Nick said.

She winced at his harsh tone. "I told you some underwear was missing. Well, it turned up with that note."

Tate added, "The underwear had been hacked up into little pieces and stuffed in a Ziploc bag. It was left with the note on her car."

"Jesus Christ!" Nick exploded to his feet and glared down at her. "Why didn't you tell me?"

"Because the police found my fingerprints on the Ziploc bag and the stationery." She would never forget the visit from the detective. They thought she was a whack job looking for attention or trying to get out of the assault charge. She crossed her arms over her stomach, trying to just hold on. Or shield herself from Nick if he didn't believe her.

"Nick, calm down," Mac said.

He ignored Mac to stare at her. "You should have told me."

A throbbing started behind her eyes. "I didn't want you to take me back to Santa Barbara."

He snorted. "I'm not your asshole brother, Lexie. I believe you. Obviously the stalker took one of your Ziploc bags and your stationery when he was in your apartment."

Stunned, she lifted her gaze to him. He just believed her? No explanations, no battle? He just believed her. The thing that had been shifting and moving inside of her for days slid and locked into place.

She was in love with Nick.

And she was so screwed.

Nick turned from her and said to the speakerphone, "Tate, we need to find out who is powerful enough to make the cops believe Lexie is doing this to herself. Cops aren't stupid, they wouldn't just believe anyone."

Tate answered, "Right there with you. I'm going to start running more in-depth backgrounds on everyone Lexie gave me. So far I haven't found any trail, but I just haven't picked at the right thread yet."

Lexie took a deep breath. "William Harry Livingston, Tate. Start with him."

"Why?" Nick and Tate said it at the same time.

"Because his mother is a judge." She had completely forgotten. "Harry is a mild man, about five foot eight, maybe one hundred and fifty pounds. He's a real estate agent. I only met his mother at the rehearsal dinner. Otherwise, she had nothing to do with the wedding arrangements. The bride and her mother did it all and dragged Harry along with them. The only time Harry perked up was when he met my brother to discuss the cake. He and Larry became casual friends. But overall Harry did as he was told until he got drunk. Then he . . ." She shrugged. "He was aggressive, and I didn't respond well."

Nick reached out, took her hand, and squeezed her fingers. "I'm proud of you, Lexie. You're a woman who won't let people abuse her."

Heat flooded her body and flamed her face. "Harry started crying, and everyone came running. He told his bride and mother that he was taking a leak and I attacked him like a crazed woman."

Mac said, "They believed him?"

"The wedding was called off the next day. I don't really know if they believed him. Probably his bride didn't believe him, or she didn't want to marry a man who urinates in public."

"Underachieving son of a powerful mother who was publicly humiliated. That could very well be your stalker," Tate said. "I'm going to get to work now and track him down. Lexie?"

"What?"

"If it's Harry, how did he get a key to your apartment?"

Nick sat on the arm of Lexie's chair and said, "Didn't you tell me that your brother is selling his condo and Livingston is a real estate agent?"

"Oh." The creepiness skittered down her spine and spread a greasy cold in her stomach. "But Harry's not Larry's real estate agent."

Tate took over. "He'd have a key to the lockbox to your brother's house. He could get in there and find your key. It wouldn't be hard to get it copied and return it before your brother knew it was gone."

"He went to that much trouble?" She tried to understand. "Every time I met with Harry, he just seemed like . . . Harry.

Ruled by the women in his life, and a little pathetic. I tried to be nice to him because I felt sorry for him."

"Delusional stalker," Tate said. "If it's him, he fixated on you because you were nice and he turned it into obsessive love. That kind of delusion will drive the stalker to extremes. I'm going to try and find William Harry Livingston right away. And I'm going to see what my police contacts have on him. In the meantime, Lexie, you be very careful." Tate hung up.

Mac said, "Why don't we pick Shelly up and the four of us get some dinner? I know Shelly wants to talk to you about taking the job here in San Diego. She'd love to have you close by."

Nick stood from the arm of her chair. "Sorry, we have plans."

She looked up at him. "We do? What?"

He looked down at her. "I'm taking you to dinner. Just us."

He was? "Oh." He didn't want Shelly talking her into the job. "Nick, I'm not taking the job. Shelly won't—"

He reached down and pulled her to her feet and put his arm around her shoulders. "I want to take you to dinner and spend some time with you."

"Nick's at the Beach?"

Nick watched her look around the two-story restaurant with its ocean view. "The name is a coincidence, although maybe I should tell you I own the place to impress you. Let's eat downstairs where it's a little quieter. Upstairs is more of a sports bar. But we could play a little pool up there after dinner." He wouldn't mind seeing her lean over a pool table in that short denim skirt. What color panties did she have on? Maybe green ones to match the halter top she wore? He put a stop to his thoughts before he ended up sporting a massive hard-on.

The waitress asked if they wanted to start off with drinks. Lexie ordered a Coke.

He reached out and took her hand. "They have a really good wine list here."

"I'm not a big drinker."

He never thought she was. "Have some wine." He had ruined her fun the other night at Mac and Shelly's, then yesterday when she was surfing. The last thing Lexie needed was anyone else judging her. He knew how much she wanted to break free of the bonds on her. She could do that with him and be safe. He smiled to encourage her.

"Okay, then I'll have Chardonnay."

Nick ordered the same, although he would limit himself to one glass. He was uneasy with the stalker situation and wanted to keep his reflexes sharp. He wore his gun in a shoulder holster under a lightweight jacket. Shredded panties with a death threat was the sign of a really pissed-off, delusional stalker. But he didn't want to talk about that tonight. He wanted this evening to be about Lexie.

Keeping hold of her hand, he said, "I wanted to talk to you about the job offer. If you're interested, I think you should—"

She slid her hand from his and fiddled with the silverware. "I'm not going to take it. I have to settle my life first before I think about a new job. I still have the court date Friday, and no matter how nice a deal my lawyer has negotiated, I will have some obligations. And I doubt that Mac mentioned that I've been accused of assault and battery. That's not going to look good on my record. Besides—"

The waitress came, set down their drinks, and they ordered dinner. Lexie chose the artichoke pasta while he had the tortilla-crusted mahi mahi.

It struck Nick that she'd been thinking about that job a lot. Did it mean that much to her? After tasting his wine, he said, "Finish your thought. Besides what?"

Setting her wineglass down, she squared her shoulders. "I may fight the charges."

He leaned back in surprise. She didn't look away, but he caught the way she compressed her mouth, probably thinking he didn't agree with her decision. He reached across the table, took the fork she was turning over and over from her hand,

and wrapped his fingers around hers. "Good. I hope you do. You can win, Lexie. There's probably someone else who saw William Harry Livingston expose himself."

"I'm sure there is. I don't know why I didn't think of it before." She looked away. "This is a nice place. One of your favorites?"

"I come here sometimes when I'm home. The food is good, the bar upstairs is fun, and I play a mean game of pool."

She surprised him by turning her hand over and rubbing her thumb over his wrist and palm. "I guess I really don't know much about you. You like pool." She lifted her gaze from his hand and added, "Do you miss karate? You must have been good."

Shit, her touch was stirring his desire to sizzling. But he didn't want to hurt her feelings by stopping her from touching him. He tried to concentrate on her question. "I'm still good, sweetheart. I'm damned good. I train whenever I can at a nearby studio."

She grinned. "Modest, too." Her face sobered. "You must love it, karate, I mean. I thought you left it all behind. Became a bounty hunter to avenge Ellen, I guess."

He couldn't even think about Ellen when Lexie's feathery touch was traveling through him, heating his blood and sending it all to his dick. He just shrugged as an answer.

Lexie's face stiffened slightly, but she went on. "Sorry, I didn't mean to pry. We'll talk about something else. When do you want to leave for Santa Barbara? I guess we have to leave tomorrow so I'll be there for my court date Friday morning. You need to get back to work. I've wondered how you can just take a whole week off, but, well, never mind. You can be back home by the end of the day and do whatever it is you do."

The waitress arrived and Lexie stopped rambling. While the waitress arranged the food, Nick felt his chest tighten and cut off his breath in a feeling of panic. As soon as the waitress left, he said, "I don't want to take you back."

She answered softly, "I have to go back. We both know that."

That wasn't making him feel any better. He knew damn well they'd end up in bed tonight, that he'd have her for the whole night, so what was eating him, making him feel like he was going to lose something vital? Whatever it was, it was his problem. He'd taken her out to spend time with her, not to brood. "How's your dinner?"

"It's great. Yours?"

"Good." The forced cheer in her voice irritated him. But he was the one talking about trivial things. She'd asked him about himself and he'd skirted the question. Yet Lexie had trusted him with the details of her life. She'd trusted him with her body, had made love with him in a way that he doubted she'd ever done before. But the thing that made his chest ache was her book. Her dream. Lexie had copied her book and handed it to him to read.

He knew what that book meant to her.

He wanted to give her as much as she gave him. As they ate, he told her about himself. "I became a bounty hunter because I could go after the bad guys without becoming involved with the victims. I loved Ellen and yet I couldn't save her. I didn't ever want to feel that again. And the fact that I was alive and she was dead really pissed me off."

"So you paid for living by catching other skips like her ex-husband? A penance?"

He'd never thought of it quite like that. "That's as good a description as any."

"And now?"

He hesitated, but it was time to let go of the past and move forward. "Now I'm tired of being on the road and dealing with scum. No matter how many I capture, more are out there." He had been thinking about it for a year. Mac and his sister were the only other two people who knew—until now. He would have to think about what that meant. Later. "Would you like dessert?"

She looked up at him with her big brown eyes. "What are you offering?"

Nick's dick twitched. "Stop that. I have to be able to get up and walk out of here."

Her smile was wicked. Teasing.

He leaned forward, unable to resist. "What are you thinking?"

"That we should enjoy the time we have left. In bed." Her grin widened. "And you don't have to feed me to get me there."

He wanted her, God he did. But he hadn't taken her out just to get her in bed. He'd wanted to spend time with her. Get to know her. Maybe he wanted to mean something to her. He'd never been like this, wondering what the woman thought about him. She was so undemanding, it was starting to make him cranky. "There are other things to life than just sex." Oh shit, had he really said that?

She leaned back, her smile slipping. "Okay. If you want dessert, go ahead. I'm not very hungry."

Of course she wasn't. Her life was a fucking nightmare and he was making it worse. She was scared. He'd felt her fear rising since the conversation with Tate. Hell, Lexie had known all along her stalker was dangerous. Thank God she was smart enough to hire a private investigator and get out of Santa Barbara. "I didn't mean that the way it sounded, sweetheart. Please believe me. Just looking at you makes me hard. I just don't want you to think I'm using you for sex." *Huh?*

Her smile was strained. "But you are, Nick. And I'm using you. Keep it simple." She broke eye contact and drained her glass of wine.

He paid for dinner, then pulled Lexie to her feet, looking into her eyes. The truth was slowly dawning on him—he couldn't hold anything back from her. No part of himself. This woman had gotten under his skin; she made him hope again. She made him want it all. "I want to show you something."

"What?"

He tugged her closer to him just to feel her body against his, uncaring of the people watching them in the restaurant. "A place that's important to me."

"Really?"

She had shown him her book; he wanted to show her this. "Really." He caught her hand and walked out with her.

Nick laughed at her endless questions as he drove through the streets. He'd sparked her curiosity, and she liked a puzzle.

"Can't be landscape because it's dark. It's not your house or apartment—"

That caught him. "How do you know that?"

She laughed. "You keep your private life out of your work. Very wise, of course, considering the dangerous felons you chase, like me. A bar maybe? Or pool hall?" She bit her lip. "But we were just at a restaurant with a bar and pool tables."

He'd never even thought of taking her to his house. It was practically empty anyway since he was rarely there. He wondered if she'd realize he was showing her more of himself where he was taking her.

She turned in the car seat. "I know! Dancing!"

Damn, he hadn't thought of that either. "Do you want to go dancing? We can go after we stop here." He turned into the parking lot of a strip mall.

"We're here?" She leaned forward against the seat belt, taking in the flower shop, small bookstore, postal annex, health food store, and upscale coffeehouse. There was an empty building between the bookstore and coffeehouse. "This is what you want to show me?"

Instinctively, he knew she'd understand. "Trust me."

She nodded and undid her seat belt, opened the door, and swung her bare legs out.

Nick watched her ass as she stood up. Then he grabbed his keys and got out. He led her to the door of the empty building, found the right key and stuck it in, and opened the door. He reached in and turned on the light. "Come on in."

Lexie walked in ahead of him.

He let the door shut and looked around. They were in the main part of the studio. Right now all that was in there was a couple of long folding tables covered in plans they were work-

ing on and some folding chairs. The studio would open in two
months.

Lexie walked in a circle, taking in the space. Then she went
through a hallway that led to a second room for smaller
classes. She headed back into the hall and found the closet, a
bathroom, and the last room at the end of the hallway.

Nick followed her, turning on lights as he went. In his head,
he could hear the grunts, the kicks, or the sound of flesh hitting boards to break them. He could smell the sweat, almost
feel the adrenaline. He could see the faces of the students as
they mastered tough techniques, or see the droop of posture
when they couldn't get it.

She stopped in the very back room, which shared a wall
with the coffeehouse. "You've already decided to give up
bounty hunting. That's why you had time to hang out all week
at the resort."

She looked so pretty standing there, the lights catching the
shimmering sun streaks in her brown hair, set off by the green
top. Her shoulders were golden tan, her face open and interested.

"Yeah, I've decided. I'm signing papers with Mac. This will
be our karate studio."

A muffled bang and scattered noises bounced in the empty
room, making Lexie jump. A burst of giggles bled through the
wall, and she laughed at herself. "That's from the coffeehouse
next door? I wonder if all the noise in here will bother them."

She was jumpy. He went to her and put his hand on her
arm. "No, this room will be the office. And we're going to add
some soundproofing to the walls of the two studio rooms."

She smiled. "You've thought a lot about this. And you have
experience since you and Mac had a studio before." She
turned and headed out the door.

He followed her down the hall, thinking he didn't blame
her for being uneasy.

Lexie went straight to the two tables shoved together. She
set her tiny purse down and pushed aside a plastic box stuffed

with office supplies to look at the plans. After a couple of minutes, she looked over her left shoulder at him. "Thanks, Nick."

He could barely breathe. "What the hell for?"

Her smile was sweet. "For sharing this with me. When you talked about karate at dinner, I could tell you loved it."

Oh hell. He reached out, put his hands on her shoulders, turned her, and drew her to him. Right now, Lexie seemed more important than karate. Or anything. Hell. To stop from thinking about that, he kissed her.

He knew he wasn't going to be able to walk away this time.

Nine

Lexie wrapped her arms around Nick, feeling the hard length of his body pressed up against hers. He'd given her a piece of himself by showing her the building that held nothing but his dreams. He made her feel special.

Right now, he was making her feel desired. A deep longing welled up in her. She wanted Nick, needed him. Pressing one hand to the back of his head, she slid her tongue into his mouth.

He groaned against her, sliding his tongue along hers. He sank both his hands into her hair, tugging her head back. "Lexie."

Every time he said her name in that growl, she nearly came. Her breath hitched and picked up speed. She just stared at him, seeing the gold spread in his light green eyes.

"You aren't a job," Nick said. "You've never been a job. And you sure as hell aren't just sex."

Oh God, she couldn't lie to him. Not like this. "It's okay, Nick. We both agreed—"

"I'm changing the agreement. I can't let you go. I can't walk away from you. I didn't ever want to feel this much again. Then I met you, and I lost control. Nothing I did helped. Even after we made love, I just wanted you more."

Her body melted into him against her will. But panic gnawed at her stomach. "Nick, maybe it's just the circumstances reminding you of Ellen." She couldn't compete with a ghost, didn't want to.

His mouth curved up. "You're nothing like her, Lexie. Nothing. You have a deep wild streak that she never had. I needed to protect her from the world. With you, it's different. I only need to stand by your side, be a team. All the responsibility doesn't fall on me." He kissed her, then added, "You gave me your book to read. You poured such power and passion into that book, and you trusted me with it."

He knew, he understood what her writing meant to her. It was more than trust, it was respect. He respected her dream, just like he'd respected her decision not to sleep with him four months ago. When he had kissed her, she'd melted into him, wanted him. But he'd sent her home, respecting that she didn't do one-night stands.

But with Nick, it wasn't a one-night stand, it was making love with a man who knew and accepted her. He'd stirred in her a wild passion that she'd fought to contain her whole life. Nick wouldn't allow her to hold back. That was what he wanted from her, the real her. She didn't regret giving it to him. She would give it to him until they parted. But they both had to be realistic. "Nick, I have to go back. Your life is here."

He dropped his hands from her hair. "Don't move." He walked across the room and locked the door. Then he returned to her. "Don't stop trusting me, Lexie. Not now. We've got something special. Trust me enough for us to see where this thing between us goes." He slid off his jacket, unhooked the shoulder harness with his gun, and laid them on the ground. Then he took off his shirt.

"What are you doing?" He had her off balance, scared to death, then she looked at his broad shoulders and his powerful chest and she didn't feel quite so frightened. He looked big enough, strong enough to lean on just a little bit. And he looked yummy enough to lick . . .

"I'm going to make love to you and show you what I feel for you. I didn't bring a condom, so we'll save that for later." He took his shoes off and stripped out of his jeans.

Right down to his navy blue boxers with his erection pressing against the soft material. His thighs were corded and tight with tension. Sexual tension. She lifted her gaze.

He watched her with raw hunger.

Swallowing her emotion, she said, "I do. I took a couple from your box." What would he think of her? She reached into her purse and pulled out a condom.

He stepped forward and took it from her. "You're not a good girl anymore, are you, Lexie?"

He was close enough to her that they could share skin, overwhelming her. "No." Setting the condom on the table, he added.

"You want to be bad, don't you? Not worry that someone will be mad? Withhold their affection because you didn't do it their way."

God, he knew her. She swallowed the feeling building in her throat. "Yes." Her voice sounded desperate, but she trusted him. He excited her, yet she felt safe. That's what he was telling her, that she could trust him to accept her for herself. She moved a step back, her butt hitting the table. Reaching behind her, she untied the bottom ends of her halter top and pulled it over her head.

Nick's gaze heated. She saw his fingers curl into his palms. His dick pulsed hard against his boxers.

The power she had over him was intoxicating. After dropping her top, she undid the zipper of her skirt and let it fall. She kicked it off, followed by her shoes.

His voice was low and rough. "Light green panties. So pale I can see through them."

She reached out, snagged the waistband of his boxers, and slid them down to his thighs. His penis sprang out, thick and long. She wrapped her fingers around him, feeling the silky hot skin of his rigid erection. It twitched with excitement in her hand. When she saw Nick reach for her, she dropped to her knees and said, "I get to do what I want." Then she did, sliding her tongue over him until he leaned forward, slapping his hands on the table to steady himself.

Then she sucked him in deep.

"I'm at your mercy." He panted the words. She felt his whole body shudder. "Watching my cock slide in and out of your mouth is making me break out in a sweat."

She slid her tongue over the sensitive head and hummed.

"Jesus." He barely breathed the word, his body jerking.

She cupped his balls and they drew up tight. Smiling, she slid him from her mouth, looked up, and teased, "Are you complaining?"

His chest heaved and his hair fell over his face. The muscles and tendons all stood out on his arms when he braced himself on the table. "Are you enjoying tormenting me, Lexie?"

Like she had to think about that. "Yes."

His grin had a pained edge to it. "Good." He pushed off the table, reached down, and pulled her to her feet. Then he slid her panties down, grasped her waist and lifted her onto the table. Putting his hands on her knees, he spread her legs and looked down at her, then back at her face. "You're so wet, and I haven't touched you yet."

She loved the hard, sensual shape of his face. She loved the way he made her feel safe and wild at the same time. "I touched you."

His gaze flared hot. Picking up the condom, he ripped it open and sheathed himself.

He leaned down, capturing a nipple and pulling it deep in his mouth.

Her thighs clenched as he fired a deep ache in her.

He stepped between her legs, keeping her thighs spread, and slid a finger along her folds, finding her swollen clit. Shifting, he sucked her other nipple and rubbed her clit.

She writhed, grabbing his shoulders for support.

Nick lifted his head, his eyes fierce. He took his hands from her, wrapped his arms around her, and said, "Lie back on the table."

She trusted him, letting him lay her on the two tables pushed together.

Leaning over her, he opened his mouth in a hot and hungry kiss. Consuming her. She opened beneath him, not holding anything back.

When he released her mouth and stood up, she felt a wave of cool air replace the heat of his body.

His gaze never left hers. He picked up her legs. "Brace your thighs against me." She felt the heat of his stomach and chest press against the backs of her thighs. It was an awkward position . . . unless she trusted him to support her. And he did, reaching down to lift her hips up. With her legs against his chest, she was wide open to him. He stared at her as he slid inside her, slow and sure. Once he was buried in her, he started stroking in and out. "I can feel every inch of you taking me in. Feel the spot that gives you so much pleasure."

She gasped, her nerves feeling singed and raw. "How do you do that?" She didn't know. No one had reached so deeply inside of her.

Holding her hips, he thrust again. "You're so damned responsive to me, all I have to do is follow your body." He looked down, watching as he thrust again. Then he closed his eyes on a groan. "You're swallowing me."

The cords on his neck stood out, his mouth was drawn tight, his whole body rigid as he kept his rhythm slow and wicked. She knew he was holding back, trying to give her as much pleasure as possible. "Nick, I want all of you."

His gaze snapped open. "Just trying to let you catch up." He drove himself in, lifting her hips to take him.

He filled her up, touching and teasing a spot inside her that made her squirm and beg. "More!"

He let go then, his fingers digging into her hips as he shoved himself into her, over and over. Harder, deeper, the craving coiling so deep inside of her, she bit her lip. "Nick . . ." He had her at his mercy, driving her higher and higher. Then the pressure released, her orgasm ripping through her. Her body opened wider as Nick drove in, arched his powerful body, and came.

He lowered her hips and slid her legs down. Bending over her, he brushed the hair off her face and said, "I think you might have killed me."

She laughed, her body so boneless and fluid it was hard to tell where she ended and he began. She opened her mouth—

But another voice intruded. "She didn't kill you, but I will."

The threatening voice behind Nick made the hairs on the back of his neck stand straight up. Guilt shoved hard at him. He realized the man had slipped inside and hidden when he and Lexie had been in the back office. That was part of the noise they heard. He should have checked, should have been more careful!

Bare-assed and buried inside Lexie, the only thing he cared about now was protecting her.

He pulled out of her, and at the same time he whirled around, shoving Lexie hard to knock her off the end of the table. "Under the table, Lexie!"

He heard the thump of her falling to the ground, along with the crash of the box of office supplies, but his attention was on the man holding the gun. He stood about five foot, eight inches, and was in his late twenties, with thinning brown hair and his face was red with anger. The vein in his temple throbbed. He glared at Nick with jealous hatred.

Nick didn't recognize him, but it had to be Lexie's stalker. "Harry! What are you doing?"

Nick's heart stopped when Lexie rose up beside him, clutching his t-shirt to her body as a shield. "Get down," he snarled at her, while reaching to his thighs to yank up his boxers.

Livingston's face got redder. "Whore. I told you to wait for me!" He waved the gun at Lexie.

A possessive rage exploded in Nick like nothing he'd ever felt. The sight of the gun moving toward Lexie made everything crystal clear.

He loved her and would kill to keep her safe.

He would die to let her live.

He sized up their chances. None of them were good. His gun was on the floor on the other side of Lexie. He tried distraction first. "Let Lexie go. You don't want to hurt her. I forced her." Delusional stalkers tended to build a story line in their heads—Nick tried to feed it.

The man bared his teeth. "I saw what that whore did to you. She liked it!" He turned his attention to her. "Bitch whore, I told you, you'll die!"

Nick knew Livingston was going to shoot her. He couldn't reach the man in time. Instead, he pivoted and threw himself on Lexie.

A gunshot exploded, the noise reverberating like a bomb.

As Nick hit the ground, he felt the searing pain dig into his left thigh, but his years of training helped him roll to keep Lexie from absorbing all his weight. As soon as he felt his back hit the floor, he tried to roll over again to get Lexie beneath him.

She shoved him off her.

His thigh screamed, a hot flash of sheer agony that ripped through every nerve in his body, then settled in the upper leg. Sweat slicked his body. "Christ."

Too late, he realized Lexie was on her knees next to him. She yelled, "You shot him!" and brought her hand back in an overhand pitch and threw something.

A wet smack and distinctive crunch sounded. "Ow! You . . ." The words trailed off, followed by a thump.

Nick rolled over, snagged the shoulder harness, and got his gun out. He used the table to pull himself to his feet.

Livingston was sprawled face first on the ground, with a gun and a plain old stapler lying next to him. Stunned, Nick said, "You hit him with a stapler?"

Lexie yanked on her panties as she ran over, scooped up the gun, and put it on the table. "He shot you. I can't believe he shot you!" She grabbed a chair and put it behind him. "Sit."

Nick did what she told him, still in shock. "You knocked him out with a stapler. Mac is not going to believe this."

When she knelt in front of Nick, she had her clothes barely on and his shirt in her free hand a cell phone pressed against her ear as she called nine-one-one. She pressed the shirt to his thigh.

Nick hissed and focused on Lexie's bent head, the shimmering colors in her brown hair. He forced himself to breathe and control the pain.

She hung up the phone, then she looked up at him. "I'm so sorry."

The pain didn't matter anymore. Taking hold of her face with his free hand, he said, "You saved our lives with a stapler. What the hell are you sorry for?" He wasn't sure he could have gotten to his gun fast enough.

"I didn't want you hurt because of me! You knew he meant to shoot me and—" She shuddered.

He ran his hand over her clenched jaw into her hair and pulled her head to rest against his stomach. "I love you, Lexie. No way was I letting that prick shoot you. He's hurt you enough."

She lifted her head to look up at him. "I was terrified when he shot you and then rage took over. I couldn't let him kill you or hurt . . . You love me?" Her voice trailed off.

Nick checked to make sure Livingston was still passed out. He kept his gun ready just in case. He wasn't afraid of love anymore; there was no room for fear with Lexie. She was too alive, too vital, and too goddamned courageous. He had to be as strong and fearless as she was. She made him willing to risk anything, even his heart, to hold her. He leaned down and said, "You love me too, Lexie. You don't ever have to be afraid to love me or be loved by me. You're everything I want in a lover." He brushed his mouth over hers just as they heard the sirens of the police cars roaring into the parking lot.

Four months later

She sat on the cold bench, watching the waterfall in the colored lights. The nights were cool, and she shivered. The little park was empty now. This afternoon it had been filled with people celebrating a family reunion. Lexie had arranged it as the event coordinator. She loved her job. She loved her life. She had a small apartment, she dated Nick, she had friends. Her book was done, and while she was waiting to hear from publishers, she had started another one. She felt whole and happy.

William Harry Livingston had been arrested, and the charges against her were dropped. She'd only gone back to her apartment in Santa Barbara to make arrangements to store her furniture. Not long after that, she had moved to San Diego and taken the job at Sand Castle Resort. Nick and Mac had outfitted her apartment with an excellent security system, but most nights she slept with Nick by her side. No man, no person, had ever made Lexie feel strong and self-confident, and yet safe, like Nick did.

She shivered again in the cool spray from the waterfall. Her parents were still trying to get her to return to Santa Barbara, but they no longer tried guilt. They were horrified to realize she had been in serious danger and they hadn't believed her.

Her mom had finally insisted that Larry and Amber grow up and stop leeching off her. Her dad had admitted to Lexie that he was terrified of losing her mom after the heart attack. He cried, and Lexie began to realize that she hadn't been the best daughter either. She should have realized the trauma her parents were going through.

"Lexie."

Her heart tripped, the same as it always did when he called her name.

Nick walked to stand in front of her.

She smiled. She didn't know why he wanted to meet her here tonight, but he knew how much she loved the little resort park. "Is your class over already?" She'd watched him many times when he worked out, sparred, or taught. She was always stunned at the power and grace in his moves.

"It's over." He reached down and pulled her into his arms. "You're cold."

She pressed her face into his t-shirt. "Not anymore. Hmm, you smell good." He had showered at the studio after his class.

He put his hand on the back of her head. "You love it here by this fountain, don't you?"

She looked up at him. "Yes. It's where I found myself that night, then I found you."

He smiled. "Come here." He dropped his hand, pulling her closer to the fountain.

She laughed, hanging back. "The water is cold!"

Nick turned, looking at her. "That night, when I went after you and saw you standing in the water, I knew then. I was in love with you. And each day, I love you more."

Her heart melted. "I love you, too."

He reached into the pocket of his pants and pulled out a small box.

Her heart stuttered.

Nick opened the box and pulled out a ring. It sparkled in the moonlight and caught all the colors of the footlights. He reached for her left hand. "Marry me, Lexie."

She stared at him sliding the ring on her finger.

"Here, in the place where we found each other. I don't care if you want a big wedding or a small one. Please marry me."

She lifted her gaze to his face. "Oh, Nick. I love you, and I'll marry you. But can it be small? Just us, your mom, sister and her husband, and my family?"

He frowned. "Including your asshole brother?"

"Yes, including him."

He pulled her close into his arms. "Anything for you." He kissed her.

When she pulled away to get her breath, she teased him. "You didn't get down on your knees to ask me." He knew she didn't care. His proposal was perfect, beautiful. Real.

Nick sank his hand into her silky hair. "That's because I'm going to get down on my knees for something else." He pushed her closer to the fountain.

"Nick!" She felt the rush, the same rush of love and lust she always felt. "It's cold and someone might see us!"

He scooped her up into his arms. "Then we'll go to the room I reserved for us. But I'm going to have you."

She smiled up at him. "You already do."

MY KIND OF
TOWN

Shelly Laurenston

One

"There's blood everywhere."

Kyle Treharne leaned into the passenger side of the overturned car, the driver's side so badly damaged no one could get through the crumpled metal to extract themselves. Not even the female whose fear he could smell. Her fear and panic . . . and something else. Something he couldn't quite name.

"Do you see anybody?" his boss asked. Kyle readjusted the earplug to hear the man better. The sheriff's voice was so low, it was often hard to make out exactly what he'd said.

"Nope. I don't see anyone. No bodies, but . . ." He sniffed the air and looked down. "Blood trail."

"Follow it. Let me know what you find. I'll send out the EMS guys."

"You got it." Kyle disconnected and followed the trail of blood heading straight toward the beach. He moved fast, worried the woman might be bleeding to death, but also concerned this human female would see something he'd never be able to explain.

Kyle pushed through the trees until he hit the beach. As he'd hoped, none of the town's people or resort visitors were hanging around, the beach thankfully deserted in the middle of this hot August day. He followed the blood, cutting in a small arc across the sand, the trail leading back into the woods about twenty feet from where he'd entered.

He'd barely gone five feet when a bright flash of light and the missing woman's scent hit him hard, seconds before *she* hit him hard. He should have been faster. Normally, he would be. That scent of hers, though, threw him completely off balance, and he couldn't snap out of it quick enough to avoid the woman slamming right into him.

Her body hit his so hard that if he were completely human, she might have killed him.

But Kyle wasn't human. He'd been born different, like nearly everyone else in his small town. They might not all be the same breed, but they were all the same *kind*.

Still, his less-than-human nature didn't mean he didn't experience pain. At the moment, he felt lots and lots of pain as he landed flat on his back, the woman on top of him.

Yet the pain faded away when the woman moved, her small body brushing against his. She moaned and Kyle reached around to gently grip her shoulders.

"Hey, darlin'. You all right?"

She didn't answer. Instead, she slapped her hand over his face, squashing his nose. Putting all her weight on that hand, she pushed herself up.

Between her fingers, he could see the confusion in her eyes as she looked around. Blood from a deep gash on her forehead matted her dark brown hair and covered part of her face. Bloodshot, slightly almond-shaped brown eyes searched the area. For what, Kyle had no idea. A cut slashed across her top lip, and although it no longer bled, it had started to turn the area around it black and blue.

Damn, little girl is cute.

"Uh . . ." He tapped her arm. "Could you move your hand, sweetheart?" The question came out like he had the worst cold in the universe. "I can't really breathe."

She didn't even look at him, instead staring off into the forest. "Dammit. It's gone." Putting more pressure on his poor nose, the woman levered herself up and off him. "Damn. Damn. Damn." She stumbled toward the forest, and Kyle quickly got to his feet.

"This isn't my fault. It's not," the woman blurted.

Poor thing, completely delirious from all that blood loss and muttering to herself like a mental patient, Kyle thought.

Then she stopped walking. Abruptly. Almost as if she'd walked into a wall. "Damn," she said again.

Knowing he had to get her to the hospital before she died on him, Kyle put his hand on her shoulder, gently turning her so she could see him. "It's all right, darlin'. Let's get you out of here, okay?" He slipped one arm behind her back and the other under her knees, scooping her up in his arms.

Hmm. She feels nice there.

Kyle smiled down at her and, for a moment, she looked at him in complete confusion.

Then the crazy woman started swinging and kicking, trying to get out of his arms. Although she had no skills—she did little more than flail wildly—he couldn't believe her strength with all the blood she'd lost, but he quickly realized someone else had caught on to her scent, too, and was heading right for them.

Kyle gripped the fighting woman around the waist, dragging her back against him with one arm. Ignoring how much her tiny fists and feet were starting to hurt, he turned his body so she faced in the opposite direction and with his free hand, swung up and back, slamming the back of his fist into the muzzle of the black and orange striped Yankee bastard hellbent on getting his tiger paws on the woman in Kyle's arms. Tiger males only had to get a whiff of a female and they were on them like white on rice. The fact that this woman was full human and an outsider didn't seem to matter to some idiots.

A surprised yelp and the Yankee cat flipped back into the woods. Kyle rolled his eyes. He loved his town but, Lord knew, he didn't like the Yankees who often came to call. All of them rude, pretentious, and damn annoying.

Kyle walked off with the woman still trapped in his arm until she started slapping at him.

"Hands off! Hands off! Let me go!" After all that blood loss, she seemed completely lucid but quite insane.

Even worse . . . he'd recognize that accent anywhere. A Yankee. A *damn* Yankee.

Kyle dropped her on her cute butt, and she slammed hard into the sand.

After a moment of stunned silence, she suddenly glared up at him with those big brown eyes . . . and just like that, Kyle Treharne knew he was in the biggest trouble of his life.

No, no. *That* was not a normal-sized human being. Not by a long shot. Her Coven had warned her, "They grow 'em big in the South, sweetie," but she had no idea they grew *this* big.

Nor this gorgeous. She'd never seen hair that black before. Not brown. Black. But when the sunlight hit it in the right way, she could see other colors *under* the black. Light shades of red and yellow and brown. Then there were his eyes. Light, *light* gold eyes flickered over her face, taking in every detail. His nose, blunt at the tip; his lips full and quite lickable.

"You gonna calm down now, darlin'? Or should I drop you on that pretty ass again?"

Emma Lucchesi—worshipper of the Dark Mothers, power elemental of the Coven of the Darkest Night, ninth-level master of the dream realm, and Long Island accountant for the law offices of Bruce, MacArthur, and Markowitz—didn't know what to say to that. What to say to *him*. Mostly because she couldn't stop staring at the man standing over her.

Routine. This should have been routine. A simple search for a power source, necessary so they didn't have to worry about blood sacrifices. Their last two power sources had dried up fast. Faster than usual, so they'd gone searching outside of their hometown. They simply didn't mean to go *this* outside their hometown. And somehow the Coven had opened a doorway they now had to scramble to close. Leaving dimensional doors open for too long led to all sorts of problems.

Using a few location spells and some powerful runes the Coven possessed, Emma had located the spot somewhere on the coast in the Carolinas. Normally, Emma's role simply involved her finding out the where, and someone else in the Coven would solve the problem.

Just as at her day job, Emma handled the minutiae. The details. The little things. Someone else handled the more dramatic or interesting things. And this time would have been no different if it hadn't been for one little problem . . .

"North Carolina? In the South? Oh. Um. Well, you know, I really shouldn't take any more time off work." If she'd said London or Paris or even San Francisco or Chicago, there would have been a full-on screaming match about who should go or not go. Even her high priestess, Jamie Meacham, would have had to at least go toe to toe with her cousin, Mackenzie Mathews.

So, in the end, Emma ended up trapped on this little excursion because no one else wanted to head on down South to take care of such a minor situation.

Of course, Emma still wasn't quite clear how her "minor situation" went into full-blown catastrophe in seconds. One moment she was typically lost, unable to find the town called Smithville anywhere on any of her AAA maps although a giant "welcome" billboard told her that was exactly where she was. Then, like a stray dog, it came out of nowhere, stepping right in front of her beige rental car. She could have stopped in time but, unlike a stray dog, it charged her. Head on. Slamming into the hood of her car and crumpling it around her. Trapping her. And killing her if she hadn't moved quickly. As the metal buckled and screamed around her, she called to her sisters. Called to them and took their power, yanking it clean and surrounding herself with it. Letting the power of the Dark Mothers flow through her.

She woke up outside the crumpled remains of her rental car with no idea how she got there, lying in a pool of her own blood. Yet she could feel her strength returning, feel the protective power of her Coven healing open wounds and reviving dwindling blood.

Her body still needed to heal completely, though, because while the doorway had been closed—sending her careening into this gigantic malcontent—the thing that had tried to kill her still ran loose. She had to get to that thing before it killed someone. She didn't know if her Coven had unleashed it when they opened that doorway, but she sure as hell couldn't leave it to go wandering around some dinky little Southern town like in some horror movie.

Swallowing hard, Emma forced words out of her throat. "I need to go." It was the most she could manage at the moment as her insides repaired themselves.

"Yup. You sure do." He crouched in front of her, and she silently sighed in relief when she finally saw the Smithville County Sheriff's Department logo on his T-shirt. Originally all she saw was a beautiful man in black jeans, black boots, and a perfectly fitted black T-shirt. Black in the middle of August didn't make sense to her, but he did look good.

One of his big hands reached out, and she immediately reared back. He blinked in surprise and said, "Don't worry, darlin'. No one's gonna hurt you. I just need to look at your head. And then we need to get you to the hospital."

"No," she forced out, sounding way tougher than she felt. "No hospital."

He grinned and she felt her skin tingle.

"I love how you think you've got some say here, darlin'."

Big strong hands that could probably wring her chicken neck, gently lifted her hair off her face. She frowned, deeply, not because he touched her, but because he might notice exactly how quickly the cut on her head was healing. Hell of a lot faster than it should.

She slapped at his hand. "Stop touching me!"

When he sighed, she wasn't sure why he sounded so exasperated. Weren't cops trained to deal with difficult victims? Jamie and Mac had been. A cop and a firefighter, respectively, the two of them could handle most situations Emma and the rest of the Coven would run screaming from.

"Are you going to keep being this difficult?"

"Yes," she said simply.

"Fine, then." Without another word, he put his arms around her, lifting her up as he stood.

"Wha . . . what are you doing?"

"Taking you to my truck so I can get you to the hospital. I don't want to wait anymore for EMS. And stop wiggling, woman." She didn't, but he pulled her closer into his body. "What did I just say?"

She glared at him, unable to say another word.

"Oh, good. You can follow orders."

Son of a—

"And don't curse at me in your head." Freakishly light gold eyes stared down into her face. She'd never seen eyes that color before in her life. " 'Cause I know you are."

She rolled her eyes and he raised one coal-black eyebrow. After nearly a minute of mutual silent staring, he nodded and walked on and Emma sulked.

Sulked because she was simply too weak to fight anymore. Between the blood loss and what she'd already done to close the door, she could barely keep her eyes open. In fact, maybe a little nap would—

"Oh, no you don't. I need you awake, darlin'."

Sighing, she forced her eyes open. "Stop calling me darling."

He chuckled and pulled her tighter into his wonderfully warm body. "Fine, then. I'll call you exactly what you are . . ."

Emma waited for it. If she were home, she knew exactly what he'd call her. What she'd been called before when she ignored a strange drunk guy on the street or when she didn't step off the gas fast enough at a changing light. But the next word out of his mouth had her stiffening in his arms.

". . . Yankee."

And what bothered her most was how disgusted he sounded.

Two

"You do know she should be dead, right?"

Kyle nodded. "Yeah. I know."

Dr. Dale Sahara, a Harvard-trained physician whose head Kyle had dunked in a toilet when he found out the big-haired bastard had been messing with his baby sister, removed his latex gloves. "And yet, she seems to be healing quite quickly."

"How quickly?"

The big man shrugged and tossed his gloves into a bright red trash can. "I only had to put two stitches in her forehead, and her lip didn't even need a Band-Aid once I wiped off all the blood."

"How is that possible? There was blood all over her car. All over her. And her car's totaled."

"I understand that. I'm simply telling you what I saw once I cleaned her up."

"What about internal damage?"

A sudden tic started in Sahara's jaw, and Kyle knew he'd asked the pompous bastard one too many questions. Good. He hadn't liked Dale Sahara in high school, and he sure didn't like him now.

"You don't think I checked for that?" Sahara snapped.

Kyle gave a casual shrug. "Just making sure you're paying attention, Doc. You know, doing your job."

The man's hand curled into a fist, but he still seemed to keep control. Although, Kyle had to admit, he did love messing with the man. The lions always made it so easy.

"All I know, Deputy, is that the woman is healing more quickly than seems normal."

"But she's not—"

Sahara didn't even let him finish. "No. She's full human."

"That's what I thought."

"Well, aren't you a smart alley cat."

Kyle's eyes narrowed. "Don't make me shove your head in the toilet again, Doc."

"I'd like to see you try," Sahara snarled, his fangs peeking out from under his lips.

Chucking his half-empty Coke can across the room and into the trash, Kyle walked over to Sahara, but one of the nurses stepped between them.

"Now, y'all cut that out right now. You're acting like a couple of dogs fightin' over some bone." She nodded at Kyle. "You better go check on her, Kyle. Your little human is gettin' awfully squirrelly. Keeps bitchin' her phone doesn't work and she wants to leave."

Kyle nodded. Her phone would never work around here. The town owned satellites to ensure it. "I'll handle it." He walked around the pair, heading back to the woman's room, but as he passed, he slapped the back of Sahara's big lion head with the palm of his hand.

And if the nurse hadn't grabbed the doc, holding on for dear life, that would have been one ugly fight.

Emma didn't get out much, she knew that. Admitted it openly. But when she did venture from her house, she was a watcher. That's what she did. She watched and she studied and she stared. But only when no one was looking.

Yet in all the years she'd stared at others, Emma had never

seen so many good-looking people in one place before. The nurse . . . gorgeous. The doctor . . . gorgeous and so damn sweet. And that deputy guy . . . well, he went beyond gorgeous, but he was anything but sweet.

What disturbed her about him, though, was the fact that he kept staring at her, which really didn't make sense considering how gorgeous the nurses were. Except for the whole covered-in-blood thing, Emma should have been as invisible to these people as she was to everyone else in the world.

Emma, always a realist, wasn't perfect but a mutt—half Italian, half Chinese. Everyone gave her that look when she told them her last name, like they kept expecting it to end with "Ling" or "Chen." But other than that, Emma was nothing more than a nice girl from Long Island. An accountant who never cheated on her taxes although she knew how to work a buck, she held a nice, safe job in a big office building with many lawyers and accountants who didn't know she existed. She made decent money and didn't have any insane debts. She even drove a safe beige Toyota and lived a safe beige life. As one of her bitchy cousins once said, "You could make dull an Olympic sport."

No. Emma needed to get out of this town as soon as she could manage. It was giving her a complex. No one needed to be a Plain Jane in a land of beautiful people. That's why you'd never catch her in South Beach, Florida, or hanging out at some hot New York club. Nothing like having the pretty people ignore her.

Sliding off the bed, Emma grabbed her jeans. Probably once she got out of the hospital, her phone would work, too. She couldn't get a connection, and no one would give her a damn phone. She'd never been told no so many times in her life, and always in the nicest way possible. She'd yet to get one cross word from anybody.

Emma struggled into her jeans, pulling them up under her way-too-big hospital gown. Frowning, she reached for her blood-covered T-shirt. She'd rather not put it on, but she didn't have much choice. So, grabbing the hospital gown at the neck, she began to pull it down. She'd nearly cleared her breasts when the words "What exactly are you doing?" stopped her.

Holding the gown up against her, Emma spun around and found the deputy standing there with his arms crossed over his chest and his body leaning back against the door, legs casually crossed at the ankles. Emma had the disturbing feeling he'd been standing there the entire time she'd been busy putting her jeans on.

"You gonna answer me?" he drawled, his voice low, his freaky light gold eyes sweeping up her body.

"No."

Chuckling, he stood up, arms and legs uncrossing. He kind of unwound from the spot. Then he walked across the room toward her, and Emma couldn't help but take a step back, her eyes searching the room for another way out.

"Now, you're not going to try and get around me, are ya, darlin'?"

If Emma were back in New York and some enormous guy asked her that same question, she'd be screaming "fire"—since screaming "help" or "rape" barely warranted a raised eyebrow where she came from—and trying to dig his eyes out. But something about this guy . . . something she couldn't quite understand had her frozen to the spot. Like the time she got cornered by a pissed-off Rottweiller behind her father's pizzeria. She'd known then if she made one move it would go for her throat.

Frighteningly, this guy gave her the same nervous tic.

That big body stood over her, those light gold eyes staring into her face. "You insist on being difficult, don't you?" He took another step closer, and she could feel his body heat, smell his scent . . . and oh! But wasn't that nice.

Emma swallowed. "Difficult?"

"Yeah. Difficult." He took the T-shirt from her hand and tossed it back in the chair she'd originally left it in. "By trying to leave before the doc says it's okay." Those big fingers took firm hold of her hospital gown, and Emma suddenly stopped breathing as she waited to see what he'd do. Although she kind of knew what she'd like him to do . . . but that seemed wrong. She'd known this guy all of two seconds. She and her last boyfriend didn't start sharing a bed for three months after they started dating. When she mentioned this to her Coven during a casual dinner, they'd all simply stared at her, like she suddenly started speaking to them in Cantonese. So Emma didn't have sudden rushes of sexual passion—until now.

Gently, the deputy pried the gown from her fingers and slowly pulled it back onto her shoulders. His face completely impassive, he turned her, and she felt those fingers tie the gown back. She thought he'd stop there, then she gave a little squeak when she realized he'd crouched down behind her and grabbed hold of her jeans.

"Hold up!" She grabbed his hands through the gown. "What the hell do you think you're doing?"

"Just helping you out."

"I don't need your help," she yelped even as he pulled out of her grip and slipped her unzipped jeans back down, lifting each foot to remove the denim completely.

"There. Isn't that better?"

She turned around and glared at him, her face brutally hot. "No!"

He grinned at her and she almost smiled back. Almost.

"Now," he said while still crouching in front of her, dangerously near her pussy, "I don't want any more talk about you leavin'. You're staying until me and the doc say otherwise."

"What?" Panic. She was experiencing deep, bone-crushing panic. "You can't keep me if I don't want to stay."

"Oh, we sure can, darlin'. Ain't that right, Doc?"

Emma's head snapped up and, sure enough, the very gorgeous Dr. Sahara stood in the doorway, smiling at her. She got the feeling he'd been standing there the whole time the deputy had his way with her jeans. Did these people not make noise? Was this a Southern thing? Like grits and ham hocks?

"Now, Miss Emma," Dr. Sahara sweetly chastised, "we need to make sure you're okay before we let you go."

"You . . . you said I was okay. You said—"

"I said there was nothing obvious. But we'll want to keep you for observation. We wouldn't want something horrible to happen to you after you leave us. Would we, Deputy?"

"No. We want her safe and sound."

Emma looked down and realized that yes, the deputy had said that into her crotch. She'd never had this happen before. Standing so close to two men, rife with testosterone, who treated her like they thought she was hot. No one ever treated her like that, mostly because she blended into the woodwork. No one noticed Emma. They never had. And to be honest, she'd gotten quite used to it and preferred it that way.

She pushed past the man at her feet. "I appreciate your concern, gentlemen. But I really think—"

"This isn't up for debate, darlin'."

Emma stopped and turned to look at the deputy. The man took his time standing. That long body of his was one big piece of rippling muscle, slowly unwinding to his full height. She almost moaned. She'd never seen a man so beautiful before. But there was something else about him. Something she couldn't quite put her finger on.

She did know one thing, though. He'd regret it if he made her get mean.

He'd regret it a lot.

One black eyebrow peaked as he stood in front of her, grinning down into her face. "Stop threatening me in your head. 'Cause we both know you are."

Emma didn't even want to know how the hell the man did that.

Three

The last spoonful of imported Belgian chocolate pudding hovered near her mouth, her eyes were glued to the getting-odder-by-the-minute deputy. "What?"

"I asked how many brothers and sisters you have."

"Why?"

"Why what?"

"Why would you ask that?"

He blinked, staring at her like he didn't quite understand her. "Because that's polite conversation."

Maybe in the South, but where she came from it simply meant you were being nosy—and up to something.

"Are you going to answer me?"

Emma's eyes narrowed. "I have a few."

The deputy blinked again and then he sort of smiled. But it was definitely a "this girl is weirding me out" smile. "You have a few brothers and sisters? Your parents didn't give you a specific number?"

"They did. I'm simply not inclined to give it to you."

"Are you always this difficult to talk to?"

"Yes."

"Fine." He threw his hands up in frustration. "No more personal questions."

"Thank you."

She glanced at the Belgian pudding waiting to be eaten and realized she no longer wanted it. Carefully, Emma placed the spoon back on the tray, and the deputy stared at it.

"You gonna eat that?"

Emma scratched her head, avoiding any bumps or sore spots from the accident. "Uh . . . no."

Kyle grabbed the spoon covered in chocolate pudding, plopped it into his mouth, and, leaning back in his chair, casually sucked it clean. He did it so casually, she felt like they'd known each other for years. This should be where she went running for the hills. This should be where she contacted the state police to come rescue her from Insaneville, North Carolina.

Instead, for the first time in her life, all Emma wanted to do was jump into the man's lap, toss that spoon, and replace it with her tongue. She wanted him. She wanted a man who continually referred to her as "Yankee" or "darlin'."

No. No. It was time to go. Now. Before she made a complete and utter fool of herself in front of a bunch of beautiful people.

"I think in the morning I'll get another rental car and head to the airport in Wilmington. Head on home." That would give her the night to find her little "friend," kill it, and get that off her conscience before bailing this little freak town.

The deputy slowly pulled that spoon from his mouth, gave it a few extra swipes with his rather abnormally long tongue, smacked his lips, and said, "No."

Emma waited for more but it didn't come. "What do you mean . . . what do you mean no?"

He shrugged. Slowly, casually . . . annoyingly. "I mean no. You ain't goin' anywhere."

"You can't keep me here against my will."

"Why not?" He knew it was wrong, but he sure did enjoy watching her get all wound up and cranky when she didn't get what she wanted.

"What do you mean why not? It's against the law."

"I am the law, little gal," Kyle stated calmly, wishing she'd left him a little more of that pudding. For a hospital, they had the best food. But his kind, especially the snobby Prides, expected only the best, including imported chocolate pudding for their rare and usually brief hospital stays. "At least around here I am."

She stared at him for a moment, then she blinked and quickly looked away, doing anything and everything to avoid looking at him directly.

"I'm relatively certain," she ground out, her eyes focused across the room, "that's kidnapping."

"Not really." Kyle couldn't figure her out. She didn't seem scared of him, but she definitely didn't seem comfortable either. "It's for your own good. The doc said he didn't want you going anywhere until he was sure you were okay."

"For how long?"

Until I'm ready to let you go. "A few days."

Her eyes grew huge behind all that hair, and Kyle wanted nothing more than to comb that mess out of her face. By the time they moved her from emergency to her own room, she'd finger-combed all that hair in such a way he could barely see her gorgeous eyes. He hated it.

"A few days? I can't stay here a few days."

"Why? You told the doc you were on vacation. 'Just following where the sun leads' were your words, I believe. So what do you care if you stay here a few days or not?"

That seemed to stump her. "Uh . . ."

"Is that how you ended up in our little town, Emma? Following where the sun leads?"

She pushed her near-empty food tray away. "Yeah. Sure."

"Don't lie to me, Emma."

She glared at him through all that hair. "I'm not."

Kyle sighed. "Fine."

"I need to call my friends," she stated flatly. "I can't get a connection on my cell phone."

Her friends? Why not her family? Now that he thought about it, she hadn't said one word about her family. Most people, human or otherwise, wanted to see their family after an accident. Of course, she hadn't mentioned a boyfriend or husband either, which he found very comforting.

"Sure. I'll let you call your friends. As soon as you tell me why you're here."

"I'm on vacation."

"It's never a good idea to lie to the law, Miss Emma."

"It's never a good idea to hold someone against their will, Deputy. And yet, you don't seem to have a problem with that."

For someone who didn't give him much eye contact, she sure didn't back down easy. Standing, Kyle leaned over the metal rails of her hospital bed. "Let's try this again. Tell me why you're here."

She stared up at him, her eyes locked with his as she slowly crossed her arms under her chest. "I'm. On. Vacation."

Kyle nodded and stepped back. "All right, then. Hope you like this room. You'll be seeing it for quite a while."

"What does that mean?"

"It means until I get a straight answer from you, you're not going anywhere. So get comfortable."

He walked to the door. "I'll get some books and magazines from the shop to keep us entertained."

She didn't answer him, just turned her head and looked out the window.

Emma closed the door of her hospital room bathroom. She groaned when she realized it didn't have a lock and knew she couldn't waste any time.

Flipping open the cell phone she'd snagged off the deputy's jeans when he'd been leaning over her and denying Emma her personal freedom, she quickly dialed a number and waited.

Her high priestess answered. "Meacham."

"Hey, Jamie. It's me."

"Em." The woman let out a deep, relieved breath. "You had me worried, girl."

"I had *you* worried?"

"But you're okay, right?"

"Yeah. I'm fine. In the hospital."

"Oh, sweetie—"

"No. No. Nothing like that. This local deputy found me and insisted on bringing me here. I think they're all a little freaked out I'm healing so fast. You wouldn't know anything about that would you, chief?"

Jamie gave a low chuckle. "Just trying to help."

When Emma had called on them, all she needed was their protection. Her body's sudden ability to quickly heal was merely Jamie showing off. "You helped, all right. Now they're suspicious as hell. And to be quite honest—"

"Yeah."

"These people are freaking me out. They're all so nice. But maybe a little *too* nice. And everyone is *huge*. Like, abnormally huge. And they're not on any maps. I mean, I searched every map, and nothing."

"What are you saying?"

"Two words. Government. Experiment."

"Did you hit your head a little hard on that steering wheel, hon?" Jamie asked. "Maybe crack your skull open?"

"I don't appreciate your sarcasm."

Jamie laughed. "Look, I warned you they were nice down there. And remember my cousins from Alabama? They're huge. They grow 'em big in the South. And most of those small podunk towns aren't on the maps."

"Podunk? What podunk town has Gucci, Versace, and Prada stores on its Main Street?"

"I don't know. Maybe they're like the Hamptons of North Carolina?"

"Then why won't they let me leave?"

"Whoa. Who won't?"

"The deputy and the doctor. They say I can't leave."

"Let me see if I understand. After a major car accident that should have killed you if it weren't for your Coven, but which still left you covered in blood, the doctor and the deputy won't let you leave the hospital? Those *bastards!*"

Emma gritted her teeth. "I'm hearing that sarcasm again."

* * *

Kyle picked up an issue of *Elle* magazine and debated whether Emma read this sort of stuff. She didn't seem real "fashion forward," as his baby sister called it. The jeans and T-shirt she had on when he found her were baggy and pretty boring. At the same time, she didn't seem like a scrub, either.

"Why can't you buy porn like the rest of us?"

Kyle sighed and didn't bother to turn around. "Why are you here?"

Tully Smith, his stepbrother and the mayor of Smithville, walked up to the magazine rack and grabbed a copy of *Architectural Digest*. It had been a dark day in Smithville when Kyle's daddy married Tully's momma. But Kyle and Tully had only been seven at the time and unable to prevent it, although they'd tried. Still, Kyle loved his momma more than he ever thought possible. From the first day, she never allowed the word "step" to be used in their home unless they were climbing some to go to their rooms. They were family, she'd say. No matter the differences. No matter the species.

"It's all over town some human crashed near the beach. And that you beat up one of our visitors."

"I didn't beat him up, I broke his nose. If I beat him up, there would have been lots more blood. Besides, he was charging her. I had to do something."

"I'm not arguing with you. I know how those big, dumb cats can be."

Kyle glared and Tully pretended to look appalled. "Of course I didn't mean you, little brother."

Three months apart, and the man insisted on calling him "little brother."

Grabbing a bunch of random magazines from the rack, Kyle headed toward the cashier. "You still haven't answered my question. Why are you here, canine?"

"I would like to meet our little visitor."

Not in this lifetime. Tully came from a long line of Alpha Males. Sometimes it seemed that's all the Smiths birthed. But in order to become the Alpha Male of any of the Smith Packs littered throughout the States, you had to have something the rest of the dogs didn't. Sure, they were all tough, strong, and pack oriented. But Tully was smart. Street smart. The kind of wolf that during a drought somehow always found water and food while other Packs were fighting over every drop and slowly starving to death. No way would Kyle let the conniving bastard near Emma.

"Forget it. She's recovering from the accident. I don't need you in there bothering her."

Tully followed him over to the counter. "Now, now, little pussy. No need to get all territorial. I'm only doing my job. We both know it's strange she's here. And yet here she is. So the Elders want me to meet with her."

The Elders represented each Pride, Pack, Clan, and anything else lurking in their town. No matter their differences, they always worked together to protect the town.

"Right now my only concern is making sure she doesn't go wandering off. She seems real curious."

"The town's on high alert that a human's come to call. So you shouldn't be too worried. Doubt you'll see Randy Cartwright running down Main Street, giggling like an idiot while trying to bring down a bleeding antelope."

The brothers looked at each other and snorted out in unison, "Hyenas."

"Look, Emma, wait a day or two until they're sure you're okay, then come home."

"I can't. Not yet."

Jamie paused, then asked, "What aren't you telling me?"

Emma winced. "Nothing?"

"Emma . . ."

"Okay. Okay. Something, I think, tried to kill me. Maybe."

"This isn't that government-experiment theory again, is it?"

"No. Although I'm still right about that," she muttered.

"What was it?"

"It looked like a dog. An Old Schuck, maybe?"

"Have those even been seen in the last . . . I don't know . . . six hundred years?"

"I'm just telling you what I thought I saw. It looked like a big, shaggy Old Schuck."

"Are you safe? If someone's conjuring demon dogs from the pits of hell—"

"I'm fine," she answered quickly. "Everything's fine. I'll take care of it."

"I'm sensing you don't want me to come there."

"You're being paranoid." No, Jamie wasn't being paranoid, but no point in getting her all upset. The woman could be dangerous on her best days; no use risking an entire town when Emma could take care of the situation herself.

"I've got it all under control."

"Even though you're being held against your will by evil government forces busy creating giant, friendly Southern guys?"

"I'm hanging up now."

"Okay. Okay." Jamie laughed. "Before you go, the others will want to see you. Tonight."

"Why?"

"To make sure you're okay. And stop sounding so surprised. It's giving me a complex. Your place later. Okay?"

Finally, Emma laughed. "Yeah. My place."

"Good. Talk to you later."

"Okay." Emma grabbed hold of the doorknob, blinking when she noticed it was engraved with the hospital logo. That seemed a pricey expense for a local hospital. "Later, Jamie." She closed the phone and opened the door, coming face-to-face with an abnormally large chest. The phone snatched from her hand, Emma made a weird little squeak before raising her eyes up a delectable body to look into the deputy's handsome face.

"Theft," he said calmly, "is a hangin' offense in Smithville, sweetheart."

And Emma knew he was dead serious.

* * *

"You can't do this to me!"

He didn't even look up from the circle-track-racing magazine he had in his hands. "Yes. I can."

Emma stared down at the handcuff securing her right wrist to the metal frame of the bed. Still not quite believing what was happening, she clanged the metal cuff against the metal frame, which extracted a healthy growl from the deputy.

"Stop doing that. It's annoying me."

Too angry to be wary, Emma slammed the cuff against the metal again.

His head snapped up and those light gold eyes locked onto her.

Eep!

"I said, don't do that."

"And I said, let me go."

With a smirk, the bastard went back to his magazine. So Emma jangled the cuff.

His growl turned into a snarl. "You do know I can make this much worse for you?"

"And you do know I can sue you, this hospital, this weird little town, and anybody else I can think of? Do you know that?" She didn't know where these balls she suddenly had came from, but she had to admit she enjoyed them.

"And I can charge you with theft. Maybe you're hoping to see the inside of our jails."

"You'd put me in jail?" She couldn't keep the shock out of her voice. She was Emma Lucchesi. Boring Emma Lucchesi. Except for her tendency to speed on the Long Island Expressway, Emma never had any legal problems. She sure as hell never went to jail!

"It's crossed my mind." He leaned back in his chair. "Or you can tell me why you're here and we can forget all about your thieving ways."

"First off, I *borrowed* that phone. And second, I'm on vacation. Besides, I wouldn't have stopped in this town if I hadn't gotten lost and crashed my car."

"Which reminds me . . . How did that happen? The crash, I mean."

"Dog."

"Dog?"

"A dog ran out in the middle of the road. I swerved to avoid it."

"You sure it was a dog?"

"Yes. I'm sure it was a dog." From the seventh or eighth level of hell, but a dog.

He didn't argue with her, which made her more nervous than if he had.

His head tilted to the side as he studied her. "Why do you wear your hair in your face like that?"

Shocked again, Emma reared back a bit. "I'm sorry?"

"Why do you wear your hair like that? Can you even see?"

"Of course I can see!"

"Really? 'Cause you remind me of one of those sheepdogs, but I heard they can't see unless someone grooms their hair."

She took a deep breath and said, "Can we stop talking to each other now?"

"Why? I was enjoying our conversation." And she had the feeling he meant that.

"Well, I'm not. In fact, you're starting to annoy me. And I don't usually say that to people, even when they are. But you? You need to hear it."

"Fair enough." He went back to his magazine and didn't say another word.

Emma picked up one of the magazines he'd bought for her. She rolled her eyes at the fashion model on the cover.

"Not your thing?" And she realized even when she thought the man didn't pay any attention to her, he did.

She shook her head, tossing the magazine aside and searching through the rest of the pile. "Nope." She grabbed *U.S. News & World Report* and rested back against the pillows.

"Hmm. A thinker," he muttered and Emma almost laughed. But then she nearly choked when he added, "I like thinkers."

Four

Kyle heard her sigh in her sleep one too many times. He could not stand it. Pushing himself out of the chair, he left Emma's room. If he wanted to get any sleep tonight, he'd have to find another place to snooze, because every time the damn woman sighed, he got harder and harder until he was pretty sure he might explode.

He couldn't go far, not with her being pretty tricky. He still hadn't figured out how she got his phone off his jeans without him knowing. If she got out, he might have a hell of a time tracking her. And then he'd have to fight off every damn predator in town to protect her. One whiff of her delicious scent and they'd be all over her, too. He simply wouldn't tolerate it. Which was one of the reasons he'd handcuffed her to the bed. Well, that and she looked damn tasty wearing his handcuffs.

Stepping outside, Kyle breathed in the fresh air and felt the knots in his shoulders start to unwind a bit. He couldn't help but smile. He sure did love this town. Always had. Tourists came and went. Always in their fancy cars, with their annoying Yankee accents, and they brought in good money. But nothing about their lives outside of Smithville ever interested Kyle. Not when everything he wanted or needed was right here.

Even as he had that thought, a deer came running by, followed closely by the Smith Pack, Tully leading them.

As soon as he caught his brother's scent, Tully stopped, letting the Pack go on without him. He trotted up to Kyle, his one stupid hoop earring hanging from the tip of his dog ear. He was one of the few shifters Kyle knew who insisted on wearing identifying jewelry while animal. Their baby sister called him Pirate Dog.

Tully dropped his front down while his ass swung in the air. Kyle shook his head, but he couldn't fight the smile. "I can't. Forget it."

Charging forward a bit, Tully nipped at his jeans and jumped back.

Well, a man did have to eat.

"All right. Fine." Kyle pulled off his T-shirt. "But we can't go too far from the hospital. I gotta keep my eye on Little Miss Trouble in there."

Kyle shucked his clothes, tossing them in a safe bin beside the front door. The hospital staff used it when they needed to go for a run or get in some hunting. Shifting, the black cat took off after his brother, tackling him and tossing him ten feet before tearing after the hot meal running away from them.

Emma slept. She knew she did because she was awake in her dreamscape. As a controller of her own dreams, she'd built her dreamscape from the bottom up, and she absolutely loved it. A perfect aqua blue ocean, blue sand, a low-hanging and giant light burgundy moon, and palm trees. She didn't come here every night, but when stressed, she headed to the one place where she felt calm.

Of course her Coven sisters weren't letting her rest yet. They wanted to see her, to make sure she was really okay. So they kept calling to her, like someone leaning on her doorbell. Grudgingly, she used her power to yank her Coven from their realm into hers.

"Emma!" Seneca Kuroki threw her arms around Emma and hugged her tight. "Oh, God! I'm so glad you are okay. I was so worried."

Emma gave Sen another two seconds before she gently but firmly pulled the woman's arms off her. "I'm fine, Sen. Really."

"Wow, Em. You really did a lot with this place," Kendall Cohen remarked softly, looking around Emma's dreamscape.

"Thanks."

"I see the Master of Dreams title was fairly earned." Jamie grinned at her. "You look okay."

"I'm fine. That hillbilly Nazi took the phone from me."

"Probably because you stole it."

"I borrowed it. But do you think he listens? No. He just handcuffs me to the bed like a common criminal."

As one, her Coven turned to face her, clearly no longer interested in the surrounding beauty of the place she'd created.

She stared back. "What?"

Jamie tilted her head to the side, and Emma could see her desperately trying not to laugh. "He handcuffed you to the bed?"

"Yeah. So?"

Kenny placed her hands on her hips. "Isn't that a tad kinky, Em? You know . . . for you."

Wearing a T-shirt that read "I *am* Lord of the Rings," Kenny remained the biggest geek Emma knew. At thirty-two, Kenny seemed to be comfortably staying in her tomboy phase, not only with her short, shaggy haircut and geek T-shirt, but also those very worn jeans, bright red high-top Keds she'd drawn dragons all over, and a leather armband Ken once drunkenly admitted made her feel like "a total warrior chick." Kenny even turned her one wasted year at MIT—with that whopping 1.7 GPA—into a gaming career that made her more money than seemed humanly possible. It still boggled Emma that there were game packages in Europe and Asia with Kenny's name on the cover. And Emma would bet cash that

Kenny had fallen asleep on her couch with her four-thousand-dollar computer in her lap. Of the five of them, Kenny was the only one fully dressed rather than in nightclothes.

"If it were you, Kendall, maybe. But this is me we're talking about. Me and kinky . . . not close friends."

They all watched Seneca, the pretty waitress from Manhasset and the necessary balance of good for their dark little Coven, spin around them. Literally. "I feel so free here!" More than thirteen years since Sen led their old high school in a cheer, and still the woman acted like pom-poms were permanently attached to her.

Kenny crossed her eyes and sighed. If they weren't in the same coven, Kenny probably would have beaten Seneca to death a long time ago. Sen's bone-deep perkiness wore on Kenny's nerves something awful. Emma didn't mind Sen, though. She was just so damn cute, it was hard not to like her.

"Come on, Em. Give it up. You and the deputy doing something morally reprehensible with those cuffs?" Mackenzie Mathews, dressed in loose sweatpants and a tank top, stood next to her cousin. Actually, she stood over her. Except for the fact both women were black and related by their mothers, there was very little else in common between them. Mac, a good six-foot-three in her bare feet, always kept her head. She rarely panicked, never became hysterical, and kept her cousin in check. Her straight black hair barely reached her shoulders and the blue tank top she wore showed the very large and powerful muscles she got from her hard work. Jamie, on the other hand, stood a good five inches shorter than her cousin, her long hair curly and usually in a ponytail for work. A lighter brown than Mac and a hell of a lot curvier, Jamie remained their "loose cannon." The woman had immense power and knew how to use it. But it was her Coven that kept her from doing something incredibly stupid. It was her Coven that kept her from becoming evil and trying to take over the world.

"As you see"—Emma wanted her privacy, so time to hurry this along—"I'm fine."

When no one said anything, Emma's eyes narrowed. "What?"

"You really think we did this?" Jamie asked.

"Do I think we opened the doorway? Yeah. Do I think we unleashed that thing . . . That I don't know. But if I were a gambler I'd probably put money on it."

"Jamie thinks someone wanted us down here." Mac adjusted her wide stance and rubbed her left lower back. The wound she had there still hurt even after five months, although they were starting to think it was more in her mind than a true physical pain. Not surprising. After what happened. After the attack.

"Has anyone approached you? Or said anything?" Jamie walked over to her cousin and placed her palm flat against the spot where a blade had been brutally shoved between two ribs. Her hand glowed for a moment, then she said softly, "There. That should help the pain." It wasn't until that horrible night at the hospital, waiting on Mac's doctors to come out of surgery, that the Coven realized how much Mac meant to Jamie. No matter how much Jamie might deny it.

"No." Emma answered Jamie's original question. "I've only dealt with that idiot cop and the hospital staff. But they do seem real curious why I'm here. Like they're not big on strangers."

"Wait," Kenny interrupted. "Are you trying to say they don't 'cotton to outsiders 'round here'?"

Emma laughed. "Yeah. That's about the size of it."

"Well, you're a better woman than I, Em." Kenny watched Seneca spin by her again. "I would be freaking out right about now with my ass trapped in North Carolina." Ken stuck her foot out and Seneca gracefully leaped right over it, turned, and gave Kenny the finger. Then the little brat did the Cabbage Patch at her.

Emma rubbed her eyes. "Why would anyone mess with us?" True, to the rest of the world, Emma was invisible. She didn't exist. She, like her reliable Toyota, was beige. But her Coven . . . well, that was a different story. Most witches stayed out of their way. Good or evil, they all gave the Coven of the Darkest Night a wide berth. In their minds the fact that Emma's coven didn't firmly play for one side or the other bothered most covens. Especially after that one incident that got them banned for life from the Green Man Festival.

But for Emma and her sisters it wasn't a simple case of black or white, good or evil. Because sometimes, when things went bad, you did what you had to do. Emma's Coven wasn't afraid to fight mean. Hell, they were good at it.

So exactly what idiot would be fool enough to lure them to this boring town in the middle of nowhere, North Carolina? And . . . why the hell had she been stupid enough to agree to come?

Kyle slammed his paw against Tully's muzzle, ripping his claws through the fur. Tully flipped back, but came at him again. Kyle didn't wait. He went to the tallest tree and climbed it, dragging his prize with him. Once he found a comfortable limb, he lay down to eat. The wolves circled under the tree, watching him, waiting for him to drop some morsel and planning. As always, the hunt went from simple fun to deadly dangerous once they had their prey in their sights. Out-of-town shifters learned fast that Smithville wasn't a leisurely town when it came to the hunting. It often turned mean and vicious with so many different breeds fighting over the prey. But for Kyle, that's what he loved.

Enjoying his warm meal—especially once it stopped squirming—Kyle chewed and stared, keeping a lookout for any other hungry predators. Once, one of the tourist-tigers had leaped up and snagged Kyle's meal right from him before landing back on the ground like nothing had happened. And more than one lion had climbed up after him. He'd given his prize up since the fuckers were so big, but they could never get down from those trees again, which Kyle found immensely entertaining.

Soon another prey charged by and Tully's Pack went after it, leaving Kyle to his hot meal. He ate until he was full and then he leaped down from the tree, leaving his prize behind. He didn't finish it so, in theory, he could share . . . but he didn't share. Wolves shared. Lions shared when there was enough to go around. He, however, did not share unless he was human— and his momma slapped him in the back of the head telling him to act right.

Kyle sauntered back to the hospital, only a mile or so away, and found another tree right outside the Yankee's room. Taking a limb not too far from the ground, he got comfortable and watched the woman. He could see her lying in her bed, asleep, handcuffed to the railing. The thought had him purring, moments before he dropped off to sleep.

Lying against her blue sand, Emma stared up at the sky she'd created. A little too bright. She took it down a notch until the sky became more a pale navy than a bright cerulean.

Emma had two days. Two days to destroy whatever had tried to kill her and to get home. After that, her Coven would be coming for her, and she'd prefer to avoid that. The five of them together could cause all sorts of problems. From the time they'd all met in ninth-grade Social Studies, they'd been a functioning unit. A business partnership, almost. Each serving a purpose, each fulfilling a specific role. Emma always knew, though, if it weren't for the Coven they probably wouldn't be friends. They were too different and had very little in common except the witchcraft.

Jamie always said they were more family than friends. Friends you chose, while family was forced upon you. Still, Emma liked them all and tolerated them fairly well. And she liked that no matter what, they watched out for each other. They definitely treated Emma better than her own siblings did.

It didn't even occur to Emma to call her own blood relatives after the accident. They always thought her weird and said it often, especially when the wine began to flow at family dinners. Her parents tried to make it easier on her, but they all knew she didn't belong. Kind of like the runt of the litter.

Emma shook her head, not wanting to think about it anymore. She came to her dreamscape to relax and just be, and that's what she planned to do.

A rabbit darted past her and Emma watched it with a smile. She did love rabbits. They were the only pets she ever had. Dogs were way too messy and cats simply freaked her out. They always stared at her like they knew she'd been up to something. Considering she was usually up to very little, that reaction seemed strange. Rabbits, however, were cute and fluffy and didn't have claws. You just had to watch out for their sharp teeth, and their feet could kick you pretty good. It was their only defense, though, against animals higher on the food chain.

Like the giant black cat racing past her.

Emma blinked and sat up straight. Why in hell was there a panther in her dreamscape? She never had cats in her dreamscape. Not that she could stop them if they wanted in. Animals could come and go as they pleased through anyone's dreams, but she'd never had some big jungle cat come charging into her sacred space.

Even more disturbing, the cat caught the rabbit, shook it, tossed it in the air, caught it, and started shaking it again. Emma squealed, horrified, and the cat spun around, the poor rabbit still in its mouth. It stared at Emma and she stared back. From muzzle to ass it had to be well over six feet and easily weighed two hundred plus pounds. Its tail alone looked to be about four to five feet. Still, like most things in the universe, it didn't even notice her until she made that stupid noise.

She wasn't going to run. This was her dreamscape, goddammit! She created it. She controlled it.

The panther spat out the rabbit, and the bunny took off.

Then the big cat walked toward her, its big paws slapping against the sand as it moved closer and closer. Emma still held her ground, refusing to run. But every chant she tried simply didn't work. She used all her tricks to push the fucking thing out of her dreamscape and out of her head, but nothing worked.

Finally, it stood in front of her. Cold light gold eyes stared at her, watching her with an intense curiosity that was making her extremely uncomfortable.

Emma glared at it. "Go away," she ordered it. "You're not welcome here."

It made a rather rude snorting noise like it didn't believe that for one second. Then it stepped closer to her, its smooth black fur brushing against her skin as it rubbed up against her, its large head pushing into her as it moved around her body. It purred and nuzzled the back of her neck, its breath warm and sweet against her flesh.

Emma felt naked. Since it was her dreamscape, she'd changed into a dark red bikini after her Coven left. A bikini she'd never have the guts to wear in the real world. Now she tried to conjure a parka and full body armor, anything to protect her soft, exposed flesh from those *really* giant claws. But she couldn't focus. Not when she couldn't look away from the beast moving toward her.

The cat brushed against her leg and then side, moving around her and rubbing itself up against her body. She swallowed back a lump of panic as its tail dragged along her thighs and up across her chest, settling around her neck. The tip brushed the flesh right below her ear. And, surprisingly, that felt kind of nice.

Settling down behind her, its body snuggled up against hers, the cat rested its head comfortably on her thigh. Then he purred.

Oh! And wasn't *that* an interesting feeling.

Trying to control her breathing, Emma glanced down at the big cat. "Comfortable?"

In answer, the cat rubbed its head against her thigh, and then licked the back of the opposite knee.

"Okay, feel free to stop doing that."

In response, it slid its head up her thigh, and Emma put her hand on his snout to halt its progress. "Don't even think about putting your nose there. A girl's gotta have some dignity."

A grumble came up from the cat's chest, and she wondered if that was its laugh.

The fact it didn't try to take her arm off had her smiling a bit, so Emma gently ran her fingers across its head. When it merely snuggled in closer, she dug deep into its coat. Its muscles rippled under her fingers and the purring became decidedly louder. She tickled the backs of its ears and massaged its big neck.

"You are the cutest thing, aren't you?"

All seemed to be going well . . . until it started moving up her body. Emma's hand froze as the big cat dragged its head across her stomach and chest while the rest of it unwound from behind her and slowly moved over her.

Emma slapped her hands against its shoulders, trying to push it off. Unfortunately, the big bastard wouldn't budge, and panic had settled in quite nicely.

She really had no idea how to handle this. Except for what she'd learned from occasionally being too lazy to change the channel when a documentary on jungle animals came on TV, Emma knew next to nothing about the animal kingdom and what to do when a big cat decided to use your body as a scratching post.

The cat loomed over her now, staring down at her. Nope. She didn't like the look in those eyes one damn bit.

Clearly it was time for one of her full-blown panic attacks. She hadn't had one of those since Jamie "accidentally" took the Coven to hell in the eleventh grade—something they still hadn't completely forgiven their high priestess for.

Before she could lose all rational thought and start screaming, those scary cat muscles under her fingers rippled and the fur . . . retreated, sliding back inside the cat's body. Then the cat face hovering over her began to shift and change, as did the cat body sliding between her legs.

Then he was there. The good-old-boy deputy now stared down at her, his naked body fitting comfortably between her legs. The only thing that didn't change . . . those eyes.

He gave her that slow, easy grin of his and said, "Hello, darlin'."

"Uh . . . Deputy."

"If I'm gonna dream about you, the least you can do is call me Kyle."

"Kyle." How pathetic. Now she was conjuring up strange hillbillies in her dreamscape. Had it really been *that* long since she'd last gotten laid? Was she truly this pathetic?

He glanced down at her body. "I *like* this bikini, Emma." And it sounded like he sort of growled that compliment. "You look really good in it."

She rolled her eyes. Yup, she'd become *that* pathetic.

What else would her dream Kyle say? Maybe he'd tell her she was hot and he wanted to fuck her all night long. Ooh. Or maybe he'd say, "I've been waiting my entire life for you, Emma Lucchesi."

Pathetic. Pathetic. Pathetic.

Putting all his weight on one arm, Kyle brought his other hand up and brushed his big fingers across the exposed skin of her shoulder and down her arm.

"So soft," he murmured.

She snorted a laugh and he looked at her, still smiling. "What's so funny, darlin'?"

"Me. My dreams. I mean, since I'm going hog wild, I should have conjured up Ares or Thor. Or had all three of you!" She nodded her head. "Now that is dreaming, my friend."

"You think you can handle all three of us?" he teased.

"Hey. It's my dreamscape. I'm a frickin' goddess of love here."

"I had no idea Yankees could be so funny. Especially you New York types."

"It's how we survive the rough-and-tumble streets of Long Island."

Okay. She'd admit it. This was strange and fun. She couldn't remember the last time she'd dreamed about another human being. But it *had* been ages since she'd been with a man, and to be quite honest, she was a little horny. Had been since she saw the deputy standing over her at the beach.

Hell, what was she fighting here? It was merely a stupid wet dream. She might as well enjoy it before she woke up in her continually empty bed.

Slipping her arms around his neck, Emma smiled up into his surprised face.

She sighed. "I have to say, you are really hot, Deputy."

"Why thank you, ma'am."

"You're welcome." She cleared her throat and said, "Kiss me, Kyle."

He grinned, slow and lazy, his head dipping down and his lips hovering right over hers. "Where I come from, we always try and do what the lady asks."

Emma's eyes closed as his breath brushed her lips. "Good to know."

He didn't dive right for her lips like she thought he would. Instead, he brushed his forehead against hers, nuzzled her chin with his nose, and rubbed his cheek along her jaw. He moved slow and easy, like he had all the time in the world.

It dawned on Emma she had no control over Dream-Kyle, which seemed strange. She had control over everything else in her dreamscape but the animals. Maybe the fact she'd first envisioned him as a panther caused this, but she couldn't seem to rush him. Couldn't seem to force him to do anything she wanted.

When his lips finally touched hers, it was nothing more than a gentle caress. Their breath barely mingled.

Her body moved under his, trying to get closer, and wetness began to seep from between her legs. Frustrated, she tightened her arms around his neck and tried to pull him closer, but he only smiled.

"Easy, darlin'. There ain't no rush."

"I'm from New York. We move much faster there."

"That's a real shame," he murmured as he lowered their bodies to stretch out on the sand. "Y'all don't know what you've been missing."

Before she could respond, he kissed her. No mere touching of lips, this. No, there was real intent and hunger behind this kiss, and Emma immediately opened her mouth to him. His tongue touched hers and she groaned, desperate for more. Desperate for him. As his tongue explored her mouth, he pried her arms off his neck, gripping both her wrists in one big hand while pinning her arms over her head.

In real life she'd be terrified if some guy she barely knew held her down like this but, as Kenny would say, "Fuck it." It was her dreamscape, and if Dream-Kyle wanted to be all alpha dog on her, who was she to argue?

Besides . . . she liked it.

Kyle's free hand slid down her neck, her shoulder, and settled on her breast. He squeezed and Emma arched into his hand, a soft moan torn from her throat. Strong fingers toyed with her nipple until it stood hard and ripe. That's when Kyle stopped kissing her. Panting, she stared up at him.

Kyle squeezed her nipple again between his thumb and forefinger. Emma gasped, desperately fighting to pull her hands out of his grasp, if for no other reason than to get herself off.

Kyle lowered his head, and she watched his lips wrap around her bikini-covered breast. He sucked hard and Emma felt herself unraveling. She slammed her thighs together, trying to create some friction, trying to throw herself over the edge. But then Kyle's free hand was there, forcing its way between her legs and under her bikini bottom. He slid two big fingers inside her pussy, and his thumb played mercilessly with her clit.

The rush of power slammed through her and Emma turned her head, burying her face in her upper arm. Emma bit hard into her own flesh to stifle her cry as the orgasm roared through her. So intense, she tried to pull away, but Kyle wouldn't release her. His hand tightened on her wrists, his mouth on her breast, and his fingers found a spot inside her that he caressed over and over again.

She didn't know if she came again or if it just kept on rolling. All Emma knew was that she'd never felt anything like it before.

In dreams or out.

Finally, the strength of her orgasm forced her teeth to tear past skin, the pain shoving her right out of her dreams and right back into her hospital room.

Jerking awake, Emma looked into strange hazel eyes.

"Who . . . who the hell are you?" she panted out.

"And a good morning to you, too, sunshine. Hope I didn't scare you." A slow, easy grin spread across a handsome face. "I'm Tully Smith, Kyle's bigger and much better-looking brother."

Five

Kyle snapped awake and, for the first time in his entire life, he lost his grip on the limb his body lay across—and fell out of the tree, hitting the ground hard, panting and goddamn horny. His eyes flickered around as he desperately tried to get his bearings.

He looked up into the faces of two nurses he and Tully once had quite a good time with at one of the town's annual barbecues.

"Hi, Kyle," one said, laughing as they walked around him. "Good thing it's warm out this mornin', huh, darlin'?"

That's when Kyle realized he'd shifted back to human sometime during the night. He'd never done that before. However he went to sleep was how he woke up.

It must have been because of that damn dream that seemed so real he imagined he could still feel the sticky wetness of Emma's pussy on his fingers.

How he'd gone from chasing rabbits to making one hot, adorable Emma Lucchesi come, he had no idea. He didn't appreciate the damn dream ending, either, before he had the chance to bury himself inside the woman.

That bikini. That bikini had been his undoing. Once he saw her in that damn red bikini, he couldn't keep his paws off her. Hell, what red-blooded American male could?

Plus, for once, she didn't look panicked or scared or shy. Instead, she seemed damn relaxed and comfortable. She even hit on him. That's when he knew it was only a dream. But why should he fight a good wet dream?

Lord in Heaven, he thought those sounds she made while sleeping were sexy. Those didn't hold a candle to the sounds she made while coming.

Never before had Kyle regretted a dream ending as much as he did this one. Especially when he felt like he could still taste Emma's skin on his tongue.

Nothing had ever tasted sweeter.

Blinking hard to snap himself out of it, Kyle sat up. He needed to distract himself before he did something stupid. Like storm into Emma's room and take her right there in her hospital bed.

No, no. Bad idea. He'd have a hot breakfast first, like the elk he could smell somewhere nearby, and then he'd be right as rain and would be able to face one Emma Lucchesi—hopefully not wearing that damn bikini.

He'd never survive her in that bikini.

"We're not blood. Me and Kyle. His daddy took it upon himself to defile my momma. To ruin her pure innocence."

Laughing, Emma asked, "Um . . . she already had you. So how innocent could she—"

"She was innocent and I won't hear any different. This is nothing more than an unholy alliance as far as I'm concerned."

For some unfathomable reason, Emma liked Kyle's brother. She definitely liked him way more than she liked Kyle. Tully could talk to anyone, it seemed. Emma always had a hard time holding conversations. Small talk had never been her friend, but Tully Smith made it easy even while she knew his presence here wasn't merely altruistic.

Besides, around Tully she didn't get all . . . squirmy.

"Don't you have a baby sister, though, because of this unholy alliance?"

"The only good thing to come out of it, if you ask me."

"What about your real father?"

"Ah, yes. My real father. Well, Miss Emma, he's what they would have called in ancient times a bastard. And we avoid each other's company as much as possible."

Tully looked at her hospital door. "You gonna stand out there all day, hoss, or are you coming in?"

Emma frowned and glanced at the door. "Who are you talking—"

The door opened and the biggest man Emma had ever seen in her entire existence walked in carrying the duffel bag she'd brought with her from New York.

So tall, the man's head nearly touched the ceiling; so wide she wondered how he got through the damn door. Well into the three-hundred-pound range but without an ounce of fat on him, his body wasn't awkward because of its size. Instead, it was perfectly proportioned.

Like Kyle, this man wore black boots, black jeans, and a black T-shirt with the Smithville County Sheriff's Department logo stitched in white on the front. But he also had on a black baseball cap with the same logo.

Brown hair, brown eyes, and, except for that rather permanent-looking frown on his face, incredibly handsome.

"Miss Emma, this is Sheriff Bear McMahon. And yes, Bear's his real name. Bear, this is Emma Lucchesi our little accidental visitor."

The sheriff touched the rim of his hat. "Ma'am."

Holy shit. Emma had never heard a voice that low before.

Say something, you idiot. Don't just stare at the man. "Nice to meet you, Sheriff."

"I'm glad you're here, Bear." Tully stood up. "I want to take our Miss Emma to breakfast in the cafeteria, but your deputy has made that impossible."

"What?"

Tully took Emma's hand and lifted it so Bear could see the handcuff.

"And," she added, a bit desperately, "to be quite honest, I really have to go."

Dropping her duffel bag on an empty chair, Bear sighed and walked over to Emma.

"Some days I wonder 'bout that boy."

"I know," Tully agreed with a small smile that didn't seem at all brotherly. "I don't know how you trust him with human lives."

As Bear leaned over to let her loose, Tully gave her a slow wink and she nearly shivered. Dangerous. This man was very nice and very dangerous.

"There." Bear removed the cuffs and slipped them into the back pocket of his jeans.

Emma scooted off the bed and grabbed her duffel bag. "Thanks."

"We'll wait outside until you're done," Bear offered.

Tully snorted. "We will?"

With a low grunt, Bear grabbed Tully by the back of the neck and shoved him out the door.

Emma nearly sprinted to the bathroom and gratefully used the toilet, trying hard to keep her relieved sighs to herself. Once done, she dropped the bag on top of the closed toilet and reached back to untie the gown. That's when she felt it. A deep, painful sting. Panic swept through her, and she practically tore the gown from her body. She stood in front of the mirror over the sink and raised her left arm.

Then she stared.

She stared at the clear bite mark on the inside of her upper arm. Right where she'd put it when Dream-Kyle made her come. Of course, with her arm handcuffed to the bed, that was physically impossible to do in her sleep unless . . .

Well, this just got horribly weird.

Kyle walked into Emma's hospital room freshly showered, dressed, and fed, only to find the woman and his favorite pair of handcuffs gone.

Finding her gone only irritated him a little. The lingering

scent of his mongrel brother and that flea-bitten bear, though, had him spitting mad.

"Bastards."

Focusing on Emma's scent rather than Tully's or Bear's, Kyle found them easily enough. They sat at a long table in the cafeteria eating a typically large Smithville breakfast.

Kyle hung back by the entryway and watched Emma, all that hair still partially covering her face. Like a sucker punch to his gut, all those intense feelings from the dream came rushing back to him, holding his body and his mind hostage.

Damn the woman. Damn her to hell and back.

Without a word, Kyle stormed over to the table and sat in the chair opposite from Tully and catty-corner from Emma. Bear, by his very nature and size, always needed more space, so he sat three chairs over.

"I turn my back for ten seconds," Kyle stated while grabbing a link sausage off Emma's plate, "and you disappear on me."

Emma picked up a slice of toast and bit into it, all while staring at him, but she didn't say a word.

"Lord, little brother, you sure are cranky this lovely summer morning."

Without taking his eyes off Emma, Kyle said, "Shut up, Tully."

"I wonder what has you so tense. Could it be the daily stresses of your job? Are your Wranglers too tight? Has that stick up your ass gotten bigger?"

Emma laughed, and Kyle turned on Tully like a rattler on a mongoose.

"Go chase your tail, mongrel."

"Go climb a tree."

"Go chew a toy."

"Go play with yarn."

They were ten seconds away from going after each other with fangs and claws whether completely human-Emma was there or not, but the growled "Y'all" immediately calmed them down. Only Bear had that ability. The man could make "y'all" sound like the scariest thing ever.

Kyle glanced at his boss. "Hey, Bear."

"Kyle."

And that's all Bear said. A man of few words, Sheriff McMahon kept the town safe and everyone in line simply by being what he was . . . a big bear. They were the perfect breed for sheriff. No affiliations except with their own kin. No Packs, Prides, or Clans to speak of. They didn't like anyone, really, even each other, so favoritism was never a big problem. And whether human or bear, they were enormous, so even tigers at sometimes seven hundred pounds when shifted had to think twice before challenging them. Bear's ability to defuse brawls between lions and hyenas had become legendary.

As long as you stayed out of their way and didn't make too much noise when they were around, brown and black bears made great law enforcers.

Bear took his position from Momma McMahon, and one day Bear's fifteen-year-old son, Luke, would probably do the same. If for no other reason, the McMahons really didn't feel like going anywhere else and starting over. Bears liked their lives simple and quiet. And Kyle's boss was no different.

Sopping gravy with his biscuit, Bear asked, "Can you explain to me, Deputy, why Miss Emma was wearing your handcuffs this morning?"

"She stole my phone."

"Borrowed," she squeaked in. "I *borrowed* your phone."

Bear silently chewed his biscuit for several long seconds, then said to Emma, "You do know stealing is a hanging offense around here, don't ya?"

Emma threw up her hands. "It is not! And stop saying that. You're freaking me out."

Going back to his biscuits and gravy, Bear grumbled, "I'm just sayin' . . . it could have been worse for ya."

Even though she rolled her eyes in exasperation, Emma still smiled. A smile that had Kyle staring at her like a lovesick cub. He didn't even realize it until Tully kicked him under the table to snap him out of it.

Completely oblivious, Emma sipped her orange juice and said to Tully, "Finish your story."

"Oh, yeah. Anyway, I was a tender fifteen. She a saucy eighteen-year-old—"

"Not that," Emma laughed. "I meant about your family."

"Oh. Well. You've got your Carolina Smiths. North and South. Your Alabama Smiths. Your Tennessee Smiths. Your Kentucky Smiths. And your Texas Smiths, but they ain't real friendly. As well as Florida, Detroit, and, of course, the West Virginia Smiths."

Kyle glanced at Emma and shrugged. "Of course."

Emma giggled as Tully continued.

"But it all started right here when the first Smith arrived on these shores about four hundred years ago."

"You can trace your family back that far?"

"Most of us around here can."

Emma shrugged. "I know I have a great-aunt on my dad's side who lives in Sicily and a cousin on my mom's side in Jiaoling Prison for gunrunning."

Kyle sighed. "Well, isn't that a lovely tale to tell your grandchildren one day."

Emma held her arm up so Kyle could see her wrist. "Did you notice this? I'm bruised from your stupid handcuffs."

"Then you shouldn't steal," he said while stealing another sausage link off her plate. "So . . . did you sleep well, Emma?"

Emma choked on her juice, waving Kyle away when he went to pound on her back.

She'd been trying all morning to forget about that dream and praying he didn't remember. The more she thought about it, the more she realized she must have pulled the poor sap right into her dreamscape. Based on the way he was looking at her, though, he hadn't forgotten a damn thing.

Wiping her mouth with a linen napkin embroidered with the hospital's logo, Emma muttered, "I slept well. The beds here are very soft and comfortable. For a hospital and all."

"We do like our creature comforts," Tully offered after sipping his coffee. "When you check out of the hospital, you can stay at the Smithville Arms and—" Tully abruptly stopped speaking, those dangerous hazel eyes locking on Kyle. "Do that again and you'll lose a leg, son."

That's when Emma knew Kyle had kicked his brother under the table.

"Mind your own business or I'll rip out your throat."

Emma had seen a lot of fights between men. Before college, she worked in her father's Manhasset pizza parlor every summer. After eight o'clock on a Saturday night, after a few pitchers of beer, there was always a fight between two or more guys. Lots of bullshit threats thrown around. Occasionally the cops called. But something about these two squaring off felt different.

It felt . . . deadly.

"Y'all," Bear sighed again, either not feeling the tension or not caring. And like that, the deadly moment ended as quickly as it had come.

Bear finished off his juice and stood up, pulling his baseball cap out of his back pocket. "I'm done eating. I'm going back to the office. Nice to meet you, Miss Emma. See ya at the office, Kyle. You coming, Tully?"

"Nope. I think I'm going to spend a little more time with our Miss Emma."

Our?

Kyle hadn't felt this pissed since a bunch of hyenas surrounded him and took off with his deer. He'd hunted it, run it down, torn it open, and then these scavengers came out of nowhere and his one to their twenty didn't stand a chance. He had to let his prize go.

He'd be damned if he did the same thing with Emma. He especially wouldn't give her up to Tully. The woman deserved better than a dog.

Emma leaned forward, dropping her head in her hands, her fingers rubbing her eyes in obvious exasperation. "Look, Deputy, I'm really fine and I think—"

"Why do you always have your hair in your face like that?"

Her hands froze and, after several seconds, brown eyes stared at him through her fingers and all that hair. "What is your obsession with my hair?"

He ignored her question to ask his own. "You do know you're pretty, don't you? You're not insecure about that, are you?"

Emma glared at him. "I don't think you said that loud enough. Utah missed out."

"If you don't believe me, ask Tully. He'll be honest."

A look of horror spread across her face and a strangled sound came out of her throat. "No!"

Tully grinned. "Ask me."

Kyle turned to his brother. "Do you think Emma's—" He stopped speaking. He had to. The large piece of ham that hit him in the head completely distracted him.

Tully snorted out a laugh and looked away.

Kyle squinted at Emma. "Did you just hit me with pork?"

"I had to."

"You *had* to?"

"Yes. You wouldn't shut up," she squeaked.

Tully laughed harder and Kyle joined him. It had been a long time since they found something to laugh at together. Most of the time it was more about keeping territory, fighting over prey, or getting the bigger piece of their momma's pecan pie at Thanksgiving dinner.

"It's not funny," she yelped.

"Actually . . ." The brothers looked at each other and said in unison, "Yes, it is!"

Growling, Emma poked at what was left of her food. "Let's just leave Tully out of this."

"Why? What are you afraid he's going to say?"

"It's not what he'll say. It's what he won't say. It's The Pause."

Kyle and Tully glanced at each other. "The Pause?" Kyle asked, finding himself damn entertained by this woman.

"Yeah. The Pause."

"And what is that exactly?"

Emma tucked her legs up under her and sat back on her heels. "It's when someone asks you a question that you start to answer honestly and realize you can't, you stand there staring blindly for two seconds too long and your true answer becomes clear."

When neither brother said anything, she elaborated. "For instance, 'Honey? Do I look fat in this?' And your only response is to stare for more than fifteen seconds because you're scrambling for an answer. Like this . . ." Her face went perfectly blank under all that hair. Then she shrugged. "That's The Pause."

It was the most the woman had said at one time, and he found it . . . wonderful. She wore her nuttiness well.

"So, you were afraid Tully would give you The Pause if I asked him if you were cute?"

"It's possible. And I'm already too traumatized to have to stress over that as well."

"Sweetheart," Tully drawled, "you're not cute. You're hot. There's a difference. And I prefer hot any day."

Emma snorted. "Yeah. I'm sure that line gets you a lot of booty, Tully, but it won't work on me."

Tully leaned back in his chair and laughed. "Lord, woman. You are adorable." He looked at Kyle. "Let's keep her."

Kyle shrugged. "Okay."

"Wait. Wait. Wait." Emma shook her head. "I thought we discussed this. You can't just keep me."

"Why not?" Kyle and Tully asked together.

" 'Cause I'm not a stray cat or something you found by the side of the road."

Tully grinned. "You mean like Kyle?" Tully leaned over and said, "His daddy don't like to talk about it, but he picked Kyle up over on Jessup Road hidin' under a car."

Kyle wanted to be mad, but he couldn't. Not with Emma around. "Yeah. And your momma told me she got you from the pound. Had you fixed there, too."

Emma scratched her forehead while pushing her food tray away. "You two slam each other with the weirdest insults."

Six

Emma, her hand on her hospital door, stopped and turned around to look at Tully. "I'm sorry. What?"

"I said I have to get back to my office."

"Before that."

"That being mayor is a lot of work."

She frowned. "Mayor of what?"

Kyle laughed so hard, she knew someone must have asked the question before.

With a small snarl, Tully answered, "Of Smithville."

"Oh, I see."

"Come on." Kyle shoved Tully hard, but the big man barely noticed. Boy, these Southerners were a tough bunch. "I need to talk to you outside for a sec, Mr. *Mayor*." As the pair headed down the hallway, Kyle threw over his shoulder, "And don't try sneaking off, darlin'. Unless you're just in the mood for me to hunt you down."

Emma didn't answer Kyle, too busy staring at his ass as he walked away. Jeez, the guy could really work a pair of jeans.

"Get control of yourself, you idiot." It was one thing to fool around with a guy in her dreamscape. A whole other thing to try it on this plane of existence. The risk of rejection was too great; she immediately dismissed the idea. Emma didn't do embarrassment well. Actually, she didn't do it at all.

Sighing in resignation, she opened her hospital-room door and stopped.

"Uh . . ." She looked up at the number on the door to see if she had the wrong room. Nope. Right room.

The two very old women stared at her and she stared back.

"You must be Emma," one of them said.

"Yes. I am."

"I'm Sophie Winchell and this is my sister Adelaide." The second sister merely nodded in Emma's direction but apparently didn't feel the need to speak.

"Can I help you?"

"Oh, we're just here to visit. We heard you had a very bad accident."

"Around here that's big news." The other sister finally spoke, and Emma wished she hadn't. It sounded like someone shredded her vocal chords with a cheese grater.

"That's very nice of you."

"Not really," Adelaide admitted. "We just wanted to get a look atcha."

And that's when Emma knew. "Well, thanks for the welcome, sisters."

Sophie smiled but her sister sneered. "We ain't your sisters."

Emma sighed. "I see." All that light and love among certain covens, and still sometimes they could be the biggest bigots when it came to those who worshipped the Dark Mothers. "So then why am I here?"

The two sisters looked at each other and then Adelaide helped her sister out of the chair. Sophie used a cane, while her sister appeared to be as strong as an ox despite her obvious age. "You're here, dear, because we need you. Because we need your Coven."

The two women neared the door and Emma moved aside to let them pass. "They're not coming."

Sophie stopped and her sister began to say something, but Sophie cut her off with a raised hand. Adelaide might be the enforcer of their coven, but Sophie was definitely their high priestess.

"You should come stay at our hotel, the Smithville Arms, when you get out of here, dear. I think you'll like it. I think you'll definitely like this town. It's a good, safe place for our people."

Sophie raised her hand to pat Emma's cheek, but Emma stepped back and away.

The old woman smiled. "We'll talk when you feel better, dear." Without another word, the two women left.

"Looks like the big pussy's got a crush."

Kyle bared his fangs. "Stay away from her, Tully."

Tully gave a rough laugh. "I ain't a hyena, friend. I don't take what ain't mine."

"Who said she's mine?"

"You do. You're acting like you did last night when you dragged that gazelle up the tree so my Pack couldn't get to it. Besides"—Tully lifted his nose in the air and cast around—"something's not right in this town, little brother. You and I both know it. Soon everyone will know it. We can smell it on the wind. Feel it tremble beneath our feet in the dirt. There's something the Elders aren't telling us." Cold wolf eyes looked at Kyle, and he realized there was little connection between some fun-loving dog and the wolves that roamed Smithville. Although he did love watching Tully go all cranky when Kyle called him Fido.

Ambling off down the road, Tully said, "And what do you wanna bet, little brother, your Miss Emma is at the heart of it all?"

Emma stared out the window of her hospital room at the rapidly darkening sky. Seemed like it would be a stormy night.

The sky turned black quickly, nearly making Emma forget

it wasn't even late afternoon yet. Trees swayed as the wind picked up, and she studied the forest behind the hospital.

Placing her hands against the glass, she leaned in closer and narrowed her eyes a bit, trying to see well into the trees. That's when she saw it. Two burning, bright red spots of light. Her nose touched the glass as she leaned in more. The light disappeared and quickly reappeared. *Blinking?*

Holy shit.

Emma stared hard into the growing darkness, her focus on those red spots and a powerful spell on her lips. But before she could unleash it—and possibly destroy the entire forest in the process—a strong arm reached around her, the fingers touching the glass.

"I guess you're going to see one of our storms, darlin'."

Her entire body tensed and she barely stopped herself from spinning around and screaming.

Kyle's hand fell to her shoulder. "Are you all right?"

She looked back at the spot where she saw those red eyes and, not surprisingly, they were no longer there. *Damn.*

"Yeah. I'm fine."

He turned her to face him, his gaze searching her face. "Are you sure? You went tense on me awful fast."

Emma took a deep breath to calm her nerves and immediately realized *that* had been a big mistake. Having Kyle this close to her, smelling so very nice, did nothing for her composure.

Maybe she simply needed to admit she wanted the man. A lot. And if she were like the women in her coven, she would have had him by now. She wasn't them, though. She was Emma. Boring, plain, safe Emma. Christ knew that wouldn't change anytime soon, since it hadn't changed for thirty-one years.

"I'm fine, Deputy. Thanks," she tacked on for no particular reason. Emma moved to step around Kyle, but he stepped in front of her and blocked her path.

Confused, she stared up at him. "What?"

"Tell me, Emma. Did you dream last night?"

She blinked and lied. "Not that I remember."

"Did I mention, Emma, I can tell when you're lying?"

Unable to help herself, she raised an eyebrow in disbelief. "Is that right?"

"Yup. I sure can."

"I'm not lying," she calmly lied.

He stepped toward her and Emma immediately stepped back.

"I think you are."

Emma shrugged, even as she kept backing up and he kept moving forward. "You believe what you want to believe."

"I do."

Her back slamming into the wall behind her, Emma could only stare up at Kyle as he stood in front of her, blocking her way out with his big gorgeous body.

"Are you trying to intimidate me or something?" 'Cause it was kind of working.

Kyle shook his head. "No."

"So what are you doing?"

"I don't rightly know." He slipped his hand behind the back of her neck, his fingers massaging the tense muscles while holding her in place. "But I do know what I want to do."

Then he leaned forward, his eyes locked on her lips. Emma knew she should do something, but her brain took that moment to completely shut down on her. She ended up watching Kyle lean down until his lips were barely a breath away from hers.

"You gonna stop me, Emma?" he whispered softly, his lips barely touching hers.

Emma was confused. Hot, horny, and confused. She didn't know what he was talking about because she kept waiting for him to goddamn kiss her. "Stop what?" she finally asked.

Kyle grinned. "Good girl."

He kissed her and Emma realized she might be in the biggest trouble of her life.

She tasted the same now as she did in the dream—amazing. He coaxed her lips open with gentle swipes of his tongue, and she responded with a heartfelt groan. Her hands reached up, and one dug in his hair while the other gripped his shoulder. He used his free arm to pull her small body tight into his.

Her tongue shyly touched his and his knees almost buckled, because she went from shy and delicate to hot and demanding in seconds.

Kyle had finally begun to realize something about his little Emma Lucchesi. Although definitely shy and cautious, once you got past those walls she'd built up . . . Lord, you were in heaven.

Her fingers dug into his shoulder and hair while her tongue boldly stroked his. She wanted him. And Kyle was more than happy to accommodate her. If he could only maneuver her over to the bed. A bit small, but it would do to get this first time out of the way . . .

"And how's our Miss Emma today?" Dale Sahara asked, pushing through the door of Emma's hospital room.

Kyle pulled away from Emma, his fangs bursting from his gums as he snarled his displeasure at Dale. "*Get. Out.*"

"All righty then," Sahara said, turning right around and walking back out.

Realizing his fangs were out, Kyle hugged Emma to his body, his chin resting against the top of her head. It took much to get the cat in him leashed.

He didn't know what this woman had done to him, but he knew he had to get himself under control. She was human. A human who wasn't staying. Flash his fangs or his claws, and he'd have a very big problem on his hands.

"I'm sorry, Emma," he whispered into her hair, barely forcing his fangs back.

Those hands that had gripped him like her life depended on it moments before now landed on his shoulders to push him away.

"Don't apologize," she said. But she wouldn't look at him. "It's not a big deal."

She tried to walk around him, but he grabbed her arm and turned her to face him.

"What's going on?"

Still without looking at him, using her hair to hide her face, she said, "Nothing."

"Don't play this game with me, Emma." He tipped her chin up with his knuckle. "Tell me what's going on."

She blinked once, and then she lied. "I gotta pee. Is that okay with you, Deputy?"

He couldn't exactly argue with her on that one, so he released her. She didn't run like he thought she might. Instead she walked away from him, throwing over her shoulder, casual as you please, "When I come out, you won't be here anymore."

The quiet closing of that bathroom door sure did sound mighty final.

Seven

"I have no idea what I did, but I screwed it up somehow."

"Maybe you should have kept those lips to yourself, big brother," Katie Treharne-MacClancy teasingly chastised. "You know those weak, full-human women can't handle the mighty men of Smithville."

"You come up with the biggest load of—"

"Besides," she cut in, "maybe you took her by surprise. You should try again."

"Nah. She made it clear she doesn't want me trying anything again."

"I'm sorry, Kyle." And she meant it. That's why he loved his baby sister. She got the best of both cat and dog emotionally and was a gorgeous woman. Unfortunately, her shifted self had not been so lucky. Funny looking didn't quite describe the awkward mix of cat and canine his parents had forced upon his poor baby sister. Especially her snagglefang. The snagglefang broke his heart and made him laugh at the same time.

As a deputy, however, no one dared push his Kit-Kat past her tolerance point. Unlike her brothers, she put up with a lot more, and the town loved her for it. Unlike her brothers, however, when Katie snapped . . . well, it was never pretty, although he and Tully often found it damn entertaining.

"Don't be sorry, Kit-Kat. It isn't your fault. It's *his* fault."

"Who?"

"His. That big, shaggy-haired, interrupting bastard."

Katie laughed. "Do you mean Dale?"

"If it hadn't been for that lazy, twenty-hour-sleeping son of a bitch, I wouldn't have to spend the night in this goddamn SUV." He moved around again, trying to get comfortable in the front seat.

"That seems a little unfair, big brother."

Kyle had to spend the night in his SUV, staring at a dark hospital and hoping Emma would walk by her room window every once in a while. As far as he was concerned, *that* was the only unfair thing here.

"The man's an asshole."

"Kyle Treharne! You stop that." But he could hear his sister trying desperately not to laugh. "Now, if I were you, I'd go back in there and show that Yankee what a nice Southern boy can do for a gal."

"I better not, Kit-Kat. Getting involved with a full-human who doesn't plan on staying? A very bad idea."

"How do you know she won't stay? Maybe she'll stay for you."

"I've barely known the woman five minutes."

"And?"

"What do you mean, and?"

"I mean, maybe she's the one for you, if you'd stop being a gawd-darn cat for two seconds."

His sister always wanted to believe in love at first sight. Shame Kyle and Tully knew better.

"Oh, yeah. I'm sure when she finds me eating a whole deer on my dining room table, she'll say, 'Well hey, pretty kitty. Make sure to save me some.'"

Katie sighed, long and loud. "Kyle—"

"Forget it, Kit-Kat. I'll just keep my dumb hick ass out here. And leave her adorable Yankee ass in there. Then tomorrow, I'll send her on her way."

"As always, you're as hardheaded as Daddy. But, and I'll leave you with this, Kyle, 'cause I gotta go kick a little hyena ass downtown, there are more than one or two humans who live in this town, and they seem quite happy with their mates. Definitely happier than your miserable cat ass. But don't worry, darlin', I say that with love."

Laughing, Kyle hung up the phone.

True enough, there were full-humans mated to shifters, but that was rare and most of those full-humans were more animal than human in their soul. Whether it was in the way they moved or lived, they were comfortable with both sides of their mates.

Emma didn't seem comfortable with much of anything, so Kyle didn't really expect her to understand or accept what he was and always would be. No, he was better off waiting for the right leopard to come walking through his door. He needed a predator in his bed. A female who could handle a Pride of lions running by her front door in the morning and not start screaming when Tully showed up covered in blood, his Pack in tow, looking for cold beer and some of their momma's key lime pie.

Knowing he'd made the best decision, Kyle settled back in his SUV, very glad he'd run home and put on his sweats so he could be comfortable. Because it would definitely be a long, lonely night.

He didn't come back. Not that she wanted him to, but . . . he didn't come back.

You threw him out, you idiot.

What was she supposed to do?

Toss his fine ass on the bed and fuck him within an inch of his gorgeous life?

Oh, yeah. Sure. Rolling her eyes in annoyance, Emma tossed the magazine against the opposite wall as lightning outside her window lit up the entire room.

She jumped from the explosion and sighed when the hospital's electricity went out. *How could they not have a generator?* Or maybe they did and it wasn't working. But why wouldn't it?

Taking a deep breath to calm the warning bells screaming through her system, Emma used the lightning outside her room to illuminate her way to the window. More lightning flashed by, and even in her current state Emma had to admit how beautiful the natural power of the goddesses could be. This was where they ruled, and this was where some of the energy and power that her coven tapped into came from.

Emma placed her hand against the glass, fingers spread out, palm flat. She focused her thoughts, her energy, and called down the lightning. Multiple strikes slammed into the ground outside her window, moving closer and closer to her as her spell gained momentum. Then, when it got close enough, Emma called a strike right to her. It hit the glass, sending electricity through it and into her. Emma gritted her teeth and reveled in the feel of the Dark Mothers moving through her. She lifted her hand and watched white sparks flicker between her fingers.

With another deep breath, she centered herself. Focusing all her energy and strength, streaming it, making it even more powerful. Then Emma spun around, unleashing that lightning on the thing that had just launched itself at her back.

The thing that had already tried to kill her once.

Its black, filth-encrusted fur sizzled as its body flipped back and slammed into the opposite wall. It moved and, in a panic, Emma hit it again with the remaining energy in her body.

It twitched and Emma jumped. Good gods, the thing wasn't dead. After all that, it wasn't dead.

It blocked the door to the hall, so she ran for the bathroom, slamming the door as the beast crashed into it. Anything natural or from this plane of existence would have disintegrated instantly from all the lightning she'd poured into it. Instead, this thing still fought even while its unholy body dissolved around it.

Unholy. Unnatural. Goddess, did they actually do this? Did her Coven conjure this thing?

She couldn't worry about that now. Not when it kept throwing itself against the door, trying to get in. She knew that it would try to kill her until it took its last breath.

Emma only had one way out and she took it, scrambling up onto the toilet and pushing the lone window open. Shoving herself through, she slipped on the toilet lid, and suddenly Emma had the ground rushing up to meet her as she tumbled out—head first.

He'd been seconds away from contacting the Water & Power guys to tell them the generator at the hospital had failed again when he saw the vicious lightning strike slam right outside Emma's window and then ricochet up, slamming through the glass and into the hand Emma had pressed against it.

Kyle was already moving when he saw Emma turn, faster than he'd ever seen her move. In fact, he didn't know humans could move like that.

That's when he saw it. Some kind of big black dog stood behind her. Kyle had never seen it before. It wasn't local. To be quite honest, he didn't know what the hell that thing was. He only knew it moved on Emma with unholy speed. But she used the lightning she'd pulled into her body and slammed the thing back away from her—twice. Then Emma ran. Not out the door, but into the bathroom.

Kyle changed direction and went around the hospital. He found Emma tumbling out the window, head first, as the thing inside her room raged and slammed into the bathroom door, nearly taking it off its hinges.

Sliding under the window, Kyle caught Emma in his arms before she hit hard, pain-inducing earth.

She screamed, fighting him.

"Emma! It's me!"

Those brown eyes of hers looked up in shock. Then her small hands grabbed his shoulders.

"We've gotta—"

"I know, darlin'." He placed her on her feet. "Move."

He didn't have to tell her twice. She took off running, heading around the hospital building.

"Get in!" he yelled over the storm that seemed to have worsened in the last three minutes. Emma pulled the passenger side door open and scrambled into the front seat. Kyle got in and slammed his door, turning the key he'd left in the ignition. The SUV rumbled to life and Kyle pulled out onto the road. Emma looked through her window, then she kneeled on the seat, her knees pushing into the leather.

"It's behind us."

"It won't be for long. Buckle up, darlin'."

She did as he ordered and once she was securely in, he made a wild turn into the woods. One small hand gripped the armrest between the seats while the other gripped the handle over the door that Tully always called the "oh shit!" bar.

Emma didn't say anything, which Kyle appreciated.

He made a few more wild turns, knowing he couldn't stop until he heard it. Knowing he wasn't safe until he heard it.

As soon as he'd stepped out of his truck to get Emma, he'd sensed them heading toward the hospital. They'd known an outsider had come to their town. Not sweet little Emma but something else. Something they'd have to kill.

Now that he had Emma, Kyle knew some of them would split off to protect his back while others would continue on to track and kill that thing. So when he heard it over the driving rain, he breathed a sigh of relief.

Tully's howl. Calming him as it never had before.

A roar answered Tully's howl. A loud lion roar. Followed by another roar. The roar of bears.

Kyle slowed down his truck and passed through two boulders leading to his house. On top of it stood Tully, his small hoop earring glinting as lightning flashed nearby.

He nodded at Kyle, his wolf head dipping just a bit to let Kyle know they were watching out for him and that Emma would be safe.

Because at the moment, that's all Kyle really cared about.

Eight

Emma didn't look at Kyle when he pulled the passenger side door open. She couldn't. Instead she sat in his SUV, her entire body shaking. Not from fear, although she was woman enough to admit she was scared shitless, but from shame. What if her Coven *had* done this? What if, in their quest for power, they'd unleashed this thing on Smithville? They'd put all these people in danger. Bear. Tully. Dr. Sahara.

Kyle.

"Come on, Emma."

Strong arms slipped under her knees and her back, easily lifting her out. A few steps took them to the porch of a small house while he tried his best to protect her from the rain with his body.

He carried her up the stairs and pushed the door open. Without a key.

She nearly moaned in despair. Kyle, who didn't exactly seem to be much of a trusting fellow, felt comfortable enough in his town to leave his door unlocked for hours at a time.

Kyle stepped into his house, reaching over to flip a switch. No lights came on, and he sighed. "Electricity's out here, too."

He released Emma's legs and slowly lowered her to the ground. "Wait here." Gentle fingers brushed against her cheek, and he disappeared into the darkness.

She shouldn't stay. She should leave. She was putting Kyle in danger, and she'd never forgive herself if something happened. "Kyle, maybe I should—"

"Don't even think about leaving," his deep voice replied from the darkness as he easily moved around the house with absolutely no light to see by.

She really hated when he got that tone. "Look, I'm just trying to protect your egotistical ass. It's not safe for me to be here."

"I don't need your protection. And you couldn't be safer."

Emma looked at the open door and wondered about making a run for it. Then she heard the howling.

"Wh . . . what was that?" Was it that thing coming for her?

"Wolves. Nothing to worry about."

"Are you sure?"

"Very."

"Aren't they dangerous? I thought they were . . . uh . . . predators or something."

"They like to think so, but I consider them more scavengers myself."

After several moments, a match flared and met paper. The fireplace burned to life, and Emma looked at the room she stood in for the first time.

"Wow," she muttered as she examined what she could see. "This is really cute."

Kyle stood and walked over to her. "Cute? I wasn't going for cute, darlin'. I was going for rugged and manly."

This didn't surprise Emma. All made from highly polished and gorgeously put-together wood, the floors, ceiling, and furniture looked as if they could handle any abuse. One big picture window looked out over the forest surrounding Kyle's property, with smaller windows dotting the rest of the house. Not a big place at all, with the living room flowing into the dining room, which flowed right into the kitchen, a hallway led off, and she assumed that it led to Kyle's bedroom. The enormous couches and chairs were plush and begged her to stretch out and take a quick nap.

Yeah, this place wasn't big or fancy, but it was beautiful.

"Well . . ." she teased, trying to lighten a mood that could definitely turn sour, "you definitely managed cute."

Grinning, he stepped around her and closed the door. "You must be freezing."

"No. Just a little chilled." She stepped over to the fireplace and looked at the pictures that were on the mantel. The first one that grabbed her eye was the picture of Kyle with his arm around a young woman. Since it still was kind of dark, Emma leaned in closer, trying to get a good look without setting herself on fire by falling into the fireplace. Who the hell was this woman? And why the hell did Emma care?

"That's my baby sister," Kyle's voice announced in her ear.

Emma barely stopped herself from jumping out of her skin. The man moved without making a sound. She found it unsettling.

"Um . . . yeah. I can tell," she lied. "You two look alike."

"Actually, she looks more like Tully. She's our half sister. Born after my parents got married."

"She's really cute."

"Yup."

Clearing her throat, Emma looked at the other pictures. "Wow," she exclaimed again. "Did you get this at a wildlife reserve or something?"

She took the picture off the mantel and crouched in front of the fireplace for a better look. She'd never seen anything like it. Two wolves. Two black panthers. And one . . . Her eyes squinted. *Jesus, what is that thing?* It kind of looked like a big cat, but its ears were weird and it had a bit of a snaggletooth problem. Whatever it was, they were all together. Practically snuggling. She'd never seen panthers and wolves "snuggle."

Kyle crouched next to her and smiled at the picture. "Reserve? Yeah, something like that."

"It's just . . . I've never seen these kinds of animals together in one picture. And this wolf looks like he's . . . posing?" She could almost hear it growling, "Cheese!"

Her eyes narrowed. "What's on that wolf's ear? Is that an earring?"

With an awkward laugh, Kyle took hold of the frame. "Yeah. Sure. Like a pirate dog." He stood and carefully placed the picture back on his mantel.

"So," he said, staring down at her, "you're a witch."

That wasn't really a question, now was it?

"Whatever gave you that idea?" She tried to make that sound light and airy, like Seneca would have. Of course, that girl could talk herself out of any situation. That's how they got out of hell. From what they knew, Satan still spoke of Sen kindly.

"What gave me that idea? I saw you manipulate lightning."

"Oh." She waved that away. "That's like juggling."

"Juggling? You expect me to believe that?"

With a deep sigh, Emma walked over to one of Kyle's couches and dropped onto it. "No. I don't expect you to believe it."

He crouched in front of her, his big fingers touching her cheek gently. "Then tell me what's going on, Emma."

Nine

Kyle reared back. "What do you mean no?"

"I mean no. I'm not telling you anything."

"Why the hell not?"

Emma stood and walked around him. "Because it's none of your business."

"It is now."

Rubbing her hands over her face, she said, "Kyle . . . don't make this difficult."

She hadn't called him by his first name since that hot dream. He liked when she said his name. Even when she snarled it.

"Emma, I wish you would trust me."

"You don't trust me."

He cringed inside and worried about where this might be going. "What do you mean?"

"Oh, come on." She turned around and faced him. "Do I look stupid to you?"

"No, but—"

"I know what's going on."

"You do?"

"Yeah." She raised herself on her toes so she could look him squarely in the neck. "Government. Experiment."

It took him a second, but when he laughed in her face . . . no, she didn't take that well at all.

"I'm leaving."

"And going where?" he demanded as she snatched open the front door. And just as quickly she closed it again.

"There's a wolf in front of your porch."

Kyle cleared his throat. "Yeah?"

Her eyes narrowed and she growled between clenched teeth, "Government. Experiment."

"This is not a government experiment. It's the South. There's a lot of nature and . . . stuff around."

"Nature and stuff?" Nope. She didn't sound like she believed him at all. "Do I look like an idiot to you?"

"Of course not."

Kyle's phone went off, and he snatched it off his jeans.

Emma held her hand out. "That's for me."

Now Kyle narrowed his eyes and answered. "Hello?"

"Hello. Can I speak to Emma, please?" said a female voice.

He handed the phone over and Emma took it from his hand and walked out of the room. The bathroom door slammed shut, and he was about to go over there and shove it open, since he had no locks on his doors anyway, when his landline rang.

"Yeah?"

"Hey, big brother."

Kyle smiled. "Kit-Kat. What's up, darlin'?"

"Bear wanted me to let you know everything's okay. That thing . . . at the hospital. She fried it."

"But it was still fighting. It came after us."

"It did," his sister agreed. "Until I took a shovel to its head. Again and again and again. Then it stopped fighting completely. Miss Sophie and Miss Addie are heading over here now to deal with the remains, which I have to say . . . smell damn funky."

Kyle's smile turned into a grin. He absolutely loved his baby sister.

"Aren't you just the handy girl."

"I am. Now the question is, are you all right? Heard you were the white knight and rescued our little Miss Emma."

"Something like that."

"Well, you can tell her the coast is clear."

Kyle frowned. He knew if he told Emma that she'd leave. And he didn't want her to. "Maybe. Sure. But she isn't feeling real friendly at the moment."

Katie took a deep breath. "Kyle, I've heard rumors."

"What rumors?"

"Well, I'm sure you've figured out she's a witch."

"Duh."

"The Coven and the Elders are fighting it out. The Coven wants your little helpless victim and her coven to take over for them."

"She's hardly helpless. And what do the Elders have to do with who takes over and who doesn't?"

"That's what I was thinking. But it turns out that this new coven don't worship that wood nymph goddess. Artie something?"

Kyle rolled his eyes. "Artemis?"

"Yeah. Her."

"You never did pay attention in mythology class."

"Boring. Anyway, they apparently worship the darker goddesses. Which I find damn fascinating."

Of course she did. Katie loved trouble.

"The Elders aren't happy, but the Coven is standing firm."

"All right. Thanks for letting me know what's going on."

"You going to tell her the truth?"

"What truth?"

"About why this town needs a coven."

"No. That's not my responsibility."

"Kyle—"

"No. 'Cause to be honest, baby sister, I don't think she has any intention of staying. And it'll be a cold day in hell when I tell a Yankee anything that could put my town at risk."

"Suit yourself. But Tully says you like her."

"You and Tully mind your own damn business."

"Fine. Be that way." His sister hung up the phone, and Kyle sighed.

Damn family.

"Why did I suddenly roll out of bed?"

Emma closed the bathroom door. "Bad dreams?"

"Emma."

"Okay. Okay. That thing that tried to kill me. It tried again. I think I got it, but I had to pull some mighty power to make it happen."

"What did you use?"

"Lightning."

"Ooh. Using nature. Good move." Jamie could be entertained by the strangest things.

"I don't know if I killed it, though. And I don't know if we conjured that thing."

"How bad is this?"

Emma took a breath. "I'd say not that bad 'cause I know we could handle it, except for one thing."

"Which is?"

"Another coven. An older one. Living here. Came to the hospital to check me out. And I don't know why."

"Maybe they wanted to make sure you wouldn't be any trouble. You know, protecting their town."

"Maybe. Only it didn't feel that way. I'd swear they were expecting me."

"Really?" She could hear the interest in Jamie's voice. "I'm not liking the sound of that, sweetie."

Cringing, Emma said, "You're coming down here, aren't you?"

"What do you think?"

Emma thought about it a moment, then nodded. "It's probably for the best. Even if I killed this thing, Jamie, we need to make sure there's no more."

"You're worried about that little town."

"It's a nice place. Weird. But nice. If we unleashed something here . . . we have to clean it up. We have to fix it."

"We will. I promise. Look for us tomorrow. We'll be there."

"I know you will."

"Are you okay?"

Emma closed her eyes. "I feel raw. Angry."

"It's all that power you used, combined with the fear. What you're feeling is normal. It'll dissipate."

"When? 'Cause I don't like it."

"Hard to tell. Jogging helps, though. Or sometimes I do yoga."

"Yoga? Did you just recommend yoga to me?" Even as she said the words, Emma could hear herself getting louder and could feel more anger than she normally ever had to deal with bubbling up inside her.

"Uh . . . Em?"

"Is there anything about me that says I like to twist myself into a pretzel? Seriously. Because I'd like to know."

"Well, sweetie, it was just a suggestion."

"A *stupid* suggestion."

"Okay. On that note, I'm going to let you go get some rest or something before we get into a really ugly fight and hex each other over the phone."

"Fine. Whatever." Emma slapped the phone closed and tried to get control of her running emotions. Tomorrow she'd have to apologize to Jamie, but at the moment, if the woman happened to be standing right in front of her, Emma felt pretty confident she'd punch her lights out.

Liking the idea way more than she should, Emma snatched the bathroom door open to find Kyle standing there.

And that's when she absolutely lost it.

Emma pushed past Kyle and stormed back into the living room. "Were you listening to my phone conversation?"

"No," he answered honestly. "I wanted to see if you were hungry. Or if you needed some dry clothes."

She spun on him and threw his phone right at his chest. "Don't lie to me!"

Kyle took a deep breath. "Emma, I know you've had a long night."

"Yeah. And?"

"So maybe you should calm down."

Emma marched up to him, her small but surprisingly strong forefinger slamming into his chest, punctuating each word she spoke. "Don't. Tell. Me. To. Calm. *Down!*"

"Don't yell at me, and stop poking me with that damn tiny finger."

Emma's eye twitched, and Kyle watched as she took her forefinger and slowly moved it toward his chest.

What the hell is she doing?

After what seemed like hours, Emma's small finger poked his chest. Hard.

Kyle lightly slapped her hand away, getting good and pissed off himself. "Stop it, Emma."

She poked him again.

"I said stop it."

And again. "If it's annoying you so much"—and again—"then stop me your damn self."

And again.

Like that, Kyle's control snapped like dry wood during a summer heat wave.

Without thought, only animal instinct, he grabbed hold of Emma's hand and yanked her close. She gave a startled gasp but said nothing else. He needed her to say "Stop." He needed her to say it before it didn't matter what the hell she said.

Instead, she looked up at him, her lips slightly parted.

"Emma." He growled her name. Snarled it. She didn't run. Didn't try and pull away. No. Instead, the crazy little Yankee raised herself the smallest bit on her toes, her eyes staring straight at his mouth.

"Damn it!" was the last thing he said before he claimed her mouth with his. Like everything else about their relationship, even their kiss was a fight. Their tongues sparred for dominance while Emma pushed that soft little body against his and wrapped her arms around his neck.

The last thing his rational mind thought or, in this case, prayed, "Please, Lord. Don't let her change her mind."

Asshole, asshole, asshole. Kyle Treharne was such an asshole.

Didn't stop her from wanting him, though. She wanted the man more than she'd ever wanted anything before in her life.

She especially wanted him like this. Kind of wild and out of control. Emma had never had a guy treat her like he couldn't wait to fuck her. She'd always had polite, kind sex with polite, kind guys who acted like they couldn't wait for her to meet their mother. Taking her to bed seemed perfunctory, not something they had to do before they lost their minds.

Kyle pulled out of their kiss with an angry snarl that should have had her running back out into the storm. Instead, she worried he might be trying to bail on her. He pushed her back several feet until the back of her legs hit the couch. With one shove, she landed on the big sectional. Before she had a chance to get back up, he was on top of her, his mouth devouring hers, his hands damn near everywhere on her body. She felt completely naked but she still wore her wet oversized sweats.

Big hands slipped under her sweatshirt, pushing the thick cotton up until her breasts were exposed. Never really needing a bra before anyway, she'd decided to forgo one during her hospital stay. Kind of Emma's way of running wild. So worth it, if Kyle's groan of appreciation told her anything.

His mouth skimmed across her upper chest, his rough tongue leaving a wet trail along her heated flesh. The tip of Kyle's nose tickled her already-hard nipples and she couldn't help but giggle. Then he sucked one into his so-warm mouth and Emma gasped, her back arching, pushing her closer to him. Her hands, originally gripping the arm of the couch, now gripped the back of Kyle's head, forcing him closer to her, demanding what he seemed more than ready to give.

A rumbling purr resonated from him and right into her, setting her entire body on fire. She wrapped her legs around Kyle's waist and her hips pushed against his like he was already fucking her. Like he was already inside of her, buried deep.

Releasing one breast, he leaned up and kissed her again, stopping only to pull her sweatshirt completely off. Then he went to her other breast, and Emma wondered exactly how much more she could take. Her need to come was nearly wiping out her sanity, and yet he kept playing with her.

He slid his fingers down her stomach, under the sweatpants, and under her panties. Two fingers pushed inside her, and Emma cried out, clinging to him tighter, one hand still digging into his scalp, the other leaving nail marks in his shoulder.

His fingers fucked her hard, not remotely gentle. And she didn't want him to be. She wanted him to fuck her so hard she would scream his name and promise to buy him a Florida condo. She wanted the son of a bitch to fuck her raw. She knew he would, too.

"God, Kyle!"

Her plea ripped another growl from him, and he released her long enough to sit back on his haunches so he could pull down her sweatpants. He got them down as far as he needed them to be, then he reached for her.

She grabbed his hands and he snarled at her. "*What?*" His voice might sound like he was pissed off, but his light eyes were begging her not to stop him. Pleading.

"Con . . . condoms," she stammered out.

He blinked, like he'd suddenly come back into the room. Then he scrambled off her and disappeared into the blackness. She'd never seen a man move so fast—and, even more importantly, he was moving that fast for *her*.

Before she could even think about what she might be doing and if she should stop, Kyle was back. The box of condoms hit the floor right by the couch and then he landed on top of her again. He kissed and licked her neck, then he bit it.

Emma whimpered and clung to Kyle. A few more seconds

and she'd start begging. A few more seconds and she'd promise the man absolutely *anything*.

Kyle could smell her lust for him, and it pushed him past the point of being human. His cat side took over his human body with every intention of having the hot little thing desperately pushing his sweatpants down.

Naked and warm and so wet Kyle thought both his heads might explode, this little gal had brought out a side of him he'd always had under serious control.

With only a touch and a kiss, this woman had ripped away all of that, leaving the raw animal behind.

His sweats pushed down *enough*, Kyle slammed that stupid condom on and shoved her back down to the couch, moving over her. The last remnants of his human self yelled at him to slow down, to take it easy, but he couldn't. Especially when she reached for his cock with both hands while spreading her legs wide. Her pussy glistened at him in the firelight, and he snarled.

Before her hands could get a firm grip, he grabbed her wrists and pushed them above her head, pinning her to the spot and reminding him of that wonderful dream. He placed the tip of his cock against her wet slit, and while they both watched, he shoved into her hard.

"Damn!" he groaned.

"God!" she screamed.

He stopped. Lord, he didn't want to hurt her. But she looked at him with such horror, he did all he could to rein himself in. Until she said, "*What . . . what are you doing?*" She fought the hands holding her down.

Kyle looked down into her face, where the beginning of tears filled her eyes. He knew then he had to let her go. He wouldn't hurt Emma. Not for anything.

Then she said, "Please, Kyle. *Please.*" He stared at her, and suddenly he realized what he was seeing. Not pain or fear . . . but hunger. Hunger for him. The same hunger he had for her. They wanted the same thing, the same way.

That was all he needed to know.

Releasing her arms, Kyle ordered, "Grab your knees, darlin', and lift 'em."

After one startled look, she did what he ordered and wrapped her hands around her knees, lifting them up so her thighs cradled his hips. He placed his hands on either side of her chest.

Staring down at her, he prayed his fangs wouldn't come out. "Hold on."

With that, he drove into her as hard as he wanted to. Emma screamed, her back arching, her fingers gripping her knees tighter. He slammed into her again and again. By the fourth stroke she was coming, and he wasn't nearly done.

Emma couldn't have stopped that orgasm if she tried. Never in her life had she been fucked so hard, and wow . . . did it rock, or what? She pulled her knees higher, allowing him deeper inside her body, and her orgasm simply kept rolling along.

"Look at me, Emma."

She didn't realize she'd closed her eyes and had turned her head away until he said that. Emma looked into Kyle's face, and another wave slammed into her.

No one had ever looked at her like that. No one.

"That's right, darlin'," he groaned. "That's right."

His hips pistoned against hers, pushing his hard and oh-so-large cock inside her again and again. She felt ripped from the inside out, and goddamn, but nothing had ever felt so fucking good before.

"Again," he ordered. "Come for me again."

Oh, he must be joking. She shook her head no, unable to speak the word.

"Again, Emma. Now."

It was like the bastard owned her body. And maybe, at the moment anyway, he did. That was the only way she could explain how he managed to pump another blinding climax out of her. This one stronger and more powerful than the last.

"Oh, yeah, darlin'. Yeah." Then his back arched and he came, his body shaking as he exploded inside her. He pumped his hips two more times before crash-landing right on top of her.

And Emma only had one question on her mind as her body worked to recover . . .

Did he just hiss at me?

Ten

He had to get off her. He really did. But still . . . she was so warm and soft. And he was so damn comfortable.

"Can't breathe."

Damn.

By sheer force of will, Kyle pushed himself up and off Emma, throwing himself back so he rested against the opposite end of the couch.

Breathing hard, their sweatpants down around their ankles, the two stared at each other for what felt like hours as opposed to the few seconds it actually turned out to be.

Then Kyle watched, fascinated, as Emma grabbed hold of the sofa pillow and covered her pretty, sweat-drenched face with it. There she was . . . Painfully Shy Emma. He had to admit, she was just as dang cute as Demanding, Bitchy Emma.

"I can't believe I did that," she groaned. "I want us to be clear"—she peeked over the pillow—"I do not do this often or anything."

Kyle nodded. "I could tell."

Emma slammed the pillow down onto her lap, covering up that pretty little pussy. "What the hell does that mean?"

Okay, exactly when did this conversation go wrong? How did he manage to do that so easily with her?

She struggled to sit up, but her body was not exactly cooperating. "Well?"

Shrugging, he told her, "Darlin', you were a little too tight to be well used."

Clearly confused, she stared at him. "Huh?"

Unable to feel stressed about anything, Kyle sighed out, "Your pussy, sweetheart." He stretched against the couch like the big satisfied cat he was at the moment and smiled. "Tight and perfect."

A small grin turned up the corners of her mouth. "Oh. Well, thanks . . . I guess."

They stared at each other for a moment and then, with a tiny squeak, she covered up her face again with the pillow and turned her entire body away like she was trying to curl into herself.

Lord, if it wasn't her hair hiding that face, it was a damn pillow.

"What now?"

"Nothing," she mumbled into the pillow.

Still too mellow to worry about much of anything, he removed the condom and wiped himself off with a tissue before dumping it all in the trash can right next to the couch. With another too-relaxed sigh, Kyle leaned his head back against the armrest and stared up at the ceiling. He and his brother had built this house together, with his sister occasionally stepping in to cause additional problems. They did a nice job and only got into five or ten actual fistfights over the two years it took.

Emma moved and he knew—*knew*—she was going to run out on him. Even if she had to brave that nightmare storm to do it.

He slammed his foot down onto the lowered sweatpants she'd been desperately trying to pull back up and locked his sights on her face.

"Eep!" At least that's what it sounded like she said.

"What are you doing?"

"Um . . . I . . . uh . . ."

"You weren't thinking about leaving, were you?"

"Well . . . ya know . . ."

"Cause you're not going anywhere."

"Well, I don't want to put you out or anything. I can stay at a hotel or—"

"We ain't done, Emma."

Her entire body tensed at his words, and her small hands grabbed tight hold of that damn pillow again. "No?"

"No." Not remotely done.

"Oh. Okay."

She looked away, unable to meet his eyes. No. This wouldn't do. He didn't want to deal with Painfully Shy Emma when it came to sex. He wanted the ballbuster. He wanted the woman who wouldn't let him get away with a goddamn thing.

"Come here," he ordered.

"Uh . . ."

"Now, Emma."

"Stop ordering me around. It's annoying the hell outta me." Ahhh. There she was—his little ballbuster.

"Come here, Emma," he coaxed, "and I'll make it worth your while."

Her lip caught between her teeth.

"Don't make me wait, darlin'. I hate that."

Using her hands, she pushed herself up until she rested on her knees. She moved forward and he shook his head. "Leave the pillow."

Emma actually looked down at it like he'd asked her to leave her oxygen tank behind while going underwater. Eventually, though, she dropped it and moved forward again.

"Wait."

She sighed in frustration. "What?"

"Take the sweatpants off. I want you naked."

"Oh." With less hesitation, she shimmied out of her sweatpants. Watching made his cock hard again, and her eyes widened when she noticed.

"Now, come here."

She shuffled over to him on her knees while he pulled his

sweatshirt off and tossed it across the room. By the time she reached him, he'd kicked the pants off and slipped another condom on.

"Can you handle another ride?"

With a chuckle, she looked away from his direct gaze. "The way you talk is . . . uh . . . interesting. Most of the guys from my neighborhood just say, 'You wanna fuck again or what?'"

"Don't compare me to Yankees, and you didn't answer my question."

Emma's nipples stiffened and she gave a small nod, her eyes focused intently on his cock.

"A hard one?" he pushed, enjoying the blush creeping over her entire body.

"Yeah. Sure." She swallowed and licked her lips, her big brown eyes still locked on his cock like she couldn't wait to get to it. "Why not?" she asked *it* as opposed to asking him.

"Then bring that pretty little ass over here."

Emma crawled into his lap and he held his cock, wordlessly telling her to impale herself on it. She did, slowly, and they both groaned at the contact.

Once he had her right where he wanted her, Kyle reached up and did what he'd been aching to do since he met her—he pushed her hair off her face. She pulled back a bit, but he wouldn't let her go. Instead, he pulled her down for a kiss while keeping her hair off her face. First, he'd fuck her again. Then he'd fuck her in the shower. Both would involve getting her hair wet—sweat from the workout and water from the shower—so he could easily comb it out of his way to get a good long look at that pretty face.

"It's gonna be slower this time, Emma," he said between kisses.

"Okay."

"Harder, too."

Fresh, hot wetness coated his latex-covered cock, and she panted. Her hands reached up and gripped his biceps, her fingers digging into the skin.

"You up for that, Little Emma?"

She groaned and said, "Are you going to keep asking me questions, or are you going to get to it?"

"Anything you want, darlin'. Absolutely anything." And then he gave her exactly what she wanted for the rest of the night.

Eleven

All night. They'd gone at it all night.

She'd heard about having sex all night but all her—few—past boyfriends usually passed out by one or two in the morning. Not Kyle. He kept going until about seven when, while showering together—which involved him licking her clean from head to toe—she finally begged him to let her sleep.

Five hours later and she had the overwhelming desire to make a run for it. Especially since she had no idea where Kyle was at the moment. She didn't want any uncomfortable morning-after conversations. She really didn't want any "pauses."

Without bothering to think about it too much, she slipped out of bed intent on finding her clothes, but she froze when she saw the big window above Kyle's bed. With the sun shining bright she could see a sparse forest with lots of tall trees taking up most of the view, but off to her right she could see the beach. The man had an ocean view. She used to dream about having a house with an ocean view, but on Long Island she'd need a few million to make that happen.

Shaking her head at the distraction, Emma remembered her clothes were still on the living-room floor.

"Shit, shit, shit," she muttered to herself while quietly stepping out into the hallway. She looked around and didn't see

Kyle. So, moving quickly and silently, she tiptoed down the hall and through the living room. Her clothes littered the floor and she grabbed at them, piling them in her arms.

She tiptoed over to the front door and pulled it open. Bright sunlight nearly blinded her, and the sound of the close-by ocean filled the house. *I love it,* she thought, a split second of regret cutting through her.

She shook her head. *No feeling sorry for yourself.* She'd get dressed, head back to the hospital and get her stuff, then get a hotel room at that Smithville Arms place. By tomorrow morning, she'd be on a plane back home with her Coven and that would be that.

Nodding her head, she took a step out the door.

"Now, did I tell you to get dressed, darlin'?"

Emma turned and slammed right into Kyle's chest. She never heard him come up behind her. She didn't even realize he'd been in the house, much less in the room. Wearing a pair of black sweatpants that rode low on his hips and nothing else, Kyle stared down at her.

And that's when Emma realized she was in deeper than she should be. Way deeper than she should be. Because nothing, absolutely *nothing*, had ever looked so damn beautiful as this man in sweatpants.

Before she could do something stupid—like throw herself at him and promise never-ending love and fidelity—Emma burst out in one quick rush, "I was thinking I should go back to the hospital or get a hotel room or something." *So that I can avoid this particular morning-after conversation as if my life depended on it.*

Kyle's light gold eyes watched her, like someone might size up a lobster in a tank for dinner.

"So you're just going to leave, Emma?" he finally said while gently pulling her back into the house. "Walk out on me?"

"I wouldn't put it that way."

Reaching around her, he slammed the door shut.

"Then what way would you put it?" he asked, his fingers sliding across her jaw and down her throat. Emma's toes curled against the hardwood floor. "You had your fun and now you're going to go sneaking out on me?"

Was he kidding? "It's not like that."

Slowly, Kyle moved in on her, and Emma moved back and around as he maneuvered her away from the door. "My momma warned me about city women like you."

Emma clutched her clothes to her chest as she stumbled away from him. "Actually . . . Long Island is more of a suburb."

"She said y'all come down here for some good-ol'-boy lovin' and then you leave us. Alone . . . and broken."

A rather unladylike snort burst out of her, and Kyle sighed. "Now you're laughing at me?"

"I'm not laughing at you. I just . . ." She watched as Kyle took hold of her sweatshirt with two fingers and tossed it over his shoulder. "Look, Kyle—" And there went her sweatpants.

Emma's ass slammed into something hard, and she turned to find the dining-room table behind her. *Uh-oh.*

"I won't be tossed aside, Emma. Used for my body."

She turned and slapped her hands against his chest. "Stop it. Right now," she demanded, even while she laughed. Even while she squirmed.

"We're not done, Emma."

"We have to be."

Kyle shook his head, his disheveled black hair falling in front of his eyes. "Nope. Sorry. Can't do it."

"What do you mean you can't—hey!" How she ended up flat on her back on that dining-room table, she had no idea.

Kyle threw her legs over his shoulders and licked the inside of her thigh. "Come on, darlin'," he teased. "Give it up to ol' Kyle."

"You start referring to yourself in third person and we are so going to have a problem."

"Okay. I'll stop. But only if you promise to spend the day

with me." He grinned at her. "Ya know, so I don't feel so used."

"Okay. If you're—oh!"

Before she could finish her sentence, Kyle pushed her legs against her chest and leaned down. He brushed his mouth against her pussy, and she whimpered.

"You're already so wet, Emma." He looked up at her, and she didn't quite know what to do with the heat she saw in that handsome face. And all of it for her, apparently. "Have you been thinking about me this morning?"

Had she been thinking of anything else?

She nodded, not sure she should risk speaking.

"Did you touch yourself while you were? Did you make yourself come?"

"I haven't done that with my hands since I gave myself carpal tunnel a couple of years ago."

He stood there for a second, his mouth so close to her clit she thought she might burst out of her skin if he didn't touch it, or stroke it, or *something*. But then he started laughing. So hard, he finally laid his head on her stomach, his arms resting on the table.

Confused, she stared at him. Then her eyes widened and she said, "No, no! I got carpal tunnel from typing too much at my job!"

Kyle laughed harder. He hadn't laughed this much in a long time. And never with a female he'd been sleeping with. Getting off and getting out being the way of most residents of Smithville, both male and female.

Emma, though . . . Emma was different. Being with her felt so good. He could relax, and not once did she try and go for his throat or try and take his deer. But in no way was she boring in bed. A little shy at times, but once he got her hot enough—which didn't take much—her shyness went right out the window.

"Come on, darlin'." He wiped tears from his eyes, then

slipped his hands under her body and lifted her into his arms. "Let's take this to the bedroom."

She buried her face in his neck. "Good. I need a pillow."

Kyle coughed to stop the laugh about to come out. "Don't be embarrassed, Emma." He wrapped her legs around his waist and headed to his bedroom. "You can say whatever you want to me. Don't forget that."

"And you won't laugh?"

"No. I'll probably laugh, but it'll be with love."

"Gee, thanks, Kyle."

He laid her gently on the bed and stretched out with her. "Now, darlin', don't be mad." His cell phone rang and he snarled. "I'm not answering that."

Kyle leaned in to kiss her and Emma put her hand over his face. "Aren't you supposed to be protecting and serving?"

"Emma—"

"You have to answer the phone, Kyle. What if there's a big bank heist or something?"

He laughed again, hard, but she only stared at him and he realized she probably wouldn't get the joke.

With a sigh he said, "Fine. I'll answer the damn phone."

Reaching over, he grabbed his cell from the nightstand. "Yeah?"

"It's Bear. There's an Elder meeting in an hour."

"So?" Bear had to go to those on occasion, as did Tully, but even though Kyle's daddy was a member, they'd never asked Kyle to attend before.

"They want you there."

"Bear—"

"Did I make it sound like this was open for discussion? In an hour, cat."

Kyle snapped his phone closed and looked at the woman lying next to him. The *naked* woman lying next to him.

"You've gotta go?" She sounded half disappointed and half relieved.

"I have a meeting in an hour."

She started to sit up. "Then I better—"

He tossed the phone to the floor and laid his hand against the soft skin above her breasts. "What exactly led you to the conclusion you were to get up?"

"Christ, you are so damn bossy!"

"Yep."

"And it's really annoying."

"So I've heard." He leaned over and licked each nipple. She groaned and he smiled. "An hour, Emma. We've got an hour to play." He gave her a light push back to the mattress. "So keep that adorable ass right where it is till I'm done with it."

Twelve

Emma stepped out of Kyle's SUV and closed the door, but she leaned back through the open window.

"I'll be fine. I don't need you baby-sitting me."

Kyle frowned, looking around at the nearly deserted streets. "Are you sure you wouldn't rather wait at the house?"

"Yeah. I'm sure. I'm just going to get some breakfast, or it might be more of a brunch."

"All right." That frown on his face seemed to be getting worse and worse, but she had no idea why. "But don't go wandering around without me."

"Why?"

He stared at her. "Why what?"

"Why don't you want me wandering around without you?"

"You ask a lot of damn questions."

"Yeah, and you never answer them."

Quiet for a long moment, staring off down the street, Kyle seemed to finally come to some conclusion. "Tonight."

"Tonight what?"

"Tonight I'll answer your questions. Tonight I'll tell you anything you want to know."

"O . . . kay."

"Don't panic on me yet."

"Government experiment," she whispered.

Kyle's frown deepened even more. "Again with that?"

She shook her head. "Forget it."

"Good. Now come here and kiss me."

Chuckling, Emma lifted herself up so she hung half in and half out of his SUV window. Kyle leaned across the seats and kissed her, his mouth warm and delicious. She loved how he kissed her. Like he actually enjoyed it. Like he could do it for hours if she let him. Which was why it took her a good twenty seconds to realize he was slowly pulling her back into the SUV.

"Oh, no." She pulled away laughing. "I'm hungry . . ." His eyebrow peaked. "For food!"

"Fine. Be that way."

"I will." She again stood safely on the outside of the SUV. "Go to your meeting, you're already late."

"All right. You got my cell phone?" She held the small black device up. He'd handed it to her and told her to use Tully's number to contact him. "Call me if you need me. Okay?"

She knew he meant it, and that felt really nice. She nodded. "I will."

Before Kyle walked into the Smithville Junior High classroom where the Elders held their monthly meetings, he felt damn good. Emma, with her quirky sense of humor and slightly obsessive nature, turned out to be quite the match for his cranky-cat personality. She constantly made him smile, and when she irritated him, she still made him smile.

In short, the woman rubbed up against him in the nicest way possible.

Of course, if she hadn't gotten him all sappy with images of all the things he planned to do to her tonight, he might have seen all this coming. But he walked into that room completely unprepared.

"Well, boy?" his father demanded.

Kyle stopped in the doorway and stared. "Well, what?"

"Did you do it?"

Concerned what his father might actually be asking him, Kyle looked to Tully and Bear, both standing off in a corner. The look his brother gave him had the hairs on his neck standing up, and he started to feel angry before he even knew why.

"Did I do what, Daddy?"

"Did you send that little witch packing?"

Emma kept her head down, read her magazine, and ate her breakfast. She knew they were all watching her, she simply didn't know why. Had they never seen a half-Chinese woman before? Or maybe it was because she was the smallest adult woman in town. Whatever the reason, she didn't like it.

The fist slamming down on her table had Emma almost flying out of her chair. She looked up into a slightly familiar face. Maybe one of the nurses at the hospital? Then Emma realized the woman wore the black baseball cap, T-shirt, and jeans that seemed to be the uniform for the town's sheriff's department, although the baseball cap was a tad too big for that head.

"Don't y'all have something else to do?"

It took Emma a moment to realize the woman wasn't speaking to her, but behind her. Emma looked over her shoulder and stared at the three . . . uh . . . men? Yeah. Very femme men.

"We were only trying to be neighborly," one said, and the other two gave high-pitched giggles that Emma found extremely disturbing.

"Go away, Mary Lou Reynolds, or I'll make you cry again."

Holy shit! This is a woman?

Emma tried not to look surprised and then she tried not to rear back as the woman leaned over her chair slightly and gave a seriously unholy grin. It seemed wider than normal.

"So, tell us, darlin'. Is it true what they say about Kyle Treharne? Is he the wild ride we've always heard? Or were you a little too tame for him?"

Nope. She didn't know what to say to that. Emma didn't have confrontations. Hell, people barely noticed she breathed, much less got in her face. She could toss a spell, but the satisfaction would be fleeting. Especially if they decided to burn her at the stake or something.

So Emma merely stared and wished her Coven were around. They did all the ass-kicking when necessary, and Emma lied to the police. A very symbiotic relationship.

But as she watched a pepper shaker fly past her and slam right in the middle of the woman's forehead, she realized that sometimes help came from the strangest places.

Mary Lou screeched and grabbed her forehead while the other two women—or whatever—giggled hysterically.

"Now, listen up," the female deputy barked. "First off, never mess with the tourists. And second, don't ever talk about my brother again. Either one. Don't even breathe around them. Or they'll be finding parts of you around town for decades."

Interesting. Based on what Emma knew of the law, threatening bodily harm in front of witnesses . . . not really a good thing. *Of course, 'round here, phone stealin' is a hangin' offense.*

"Now get out of my sight."

The three women, after a little more glaring, skulked off. And it was definitely "skulky."

The deputy pulled out the chair and dropped into it. Literally. Kind of like a load of bricks, she sort of landed in the seat. "Sorry about that, darlin'. Some people just don't know any better."

"It's okay," Emma finally managed.

"My name is Katie Treharne-MacClancy. I'm Kyle and Tully's baby sister. You look cute in my way-too-big-for-you clothes, by the way."

Emma glanced down at the oversized white T-shirt and

enormous blue boxer shorts she had on. Kyle had given her these when her sweat clothes suddenly went missing from his living-room floor. "Thanks." She motioned to the now-empty chairs behind her. "And thanks for that."

"No problem. It's part of my job. Besides, I hate those bitches. Just downright mean. But all their kind is."

Emma blinked. Their kind? Funny, they all looked white to her.

"Lord, you sure are a little thing. I can see why Kyle's keeping you close."

Once again, not sure what to say, Emma gave a small shrug.

"Kind of shy, too, huh? I used to be shy. Sort of. Okay, not really." Katie grinned, and Emma saw Tully's grin with Kyle's eyes. A very nice mix on a woman.

"So," and Katie took a sausage off Emma's plate, the way Kyle had, "you in love with my big brother or what?"

Emma stared at the pretty woman. And she kept staring.

"Lord, girl. You look like a deer caught in headlights."

Emma cleared her throat. "Kyle and I barely know each other."

" 'Round here that don't count for much. You'll find the people of Smithville make up their minds right quick. We see something and we just go for it. Like a cheetah after a zebra."

An interesting analogy that had the table of men next to them laughing.

Katie winked at the men and smiled at Emma. "Come on, darlin'. I'll show you around our fair town. You might find it very interesting."

Her appetite gone, Emma pushed her plate away. "I think I already do."

"You said they were evil."

Miss Sophie sighed. "You never listen, do you, Jack Treharne? I said, they worshipped the Dark Mothers. I did not say they were evil."

"There's a difference?"

"Trust me when I say there's a very big difference." Miss Sophie glanced at her sister. "All of you need to face it. Our Coven is gone. And every day, Addie and I get weaker."

"There are other Covens," Bear's momma, Gwen, cut in. "From good Southern families."

"Who?" Tully asked. "The hippies? You can stand that smell? 'Cause I can't."

"We could ask them to bathe," Miss Gwen offered hopefully, "and ask 'em not to wear that pawhatsit oil."

"Patchouli, Momma," Bear laughed. "It's called patchouli oil."

"Well," Kyle's daddy groused, "they gotta be better than these devil worshippers."

Finally Miss Adelaide slammed her hand down. "None of you are listening. This isn't up for debate. This isn't something we can go off and think about for ten years while you all fight for territory and a hunk of zebra carcass. Times have changed, and this town must change with it if it hopes to stay the same. There's evil at our borders, and it will get in. This Coven, they could be our only hope."

Kyle sighed. "I've seen Emma . . . protect herself. She's powerful, but I don't think she's as powerful as you seem to think she is, Miss Addie."

"On their own, they're powerful, Kyle." Miss Sophie rubbed her forehead, clearly tired. Twenty years ago she'd been spry and strong, but her age had caught up with her. "But it's the coven working as one that makes them the allies we need. Together they can protect this town from those covens you don't want anywhere near this place. Covens who make them seem downright cuddly."

"Why would some Yankees wanna stay here?" Jack pushed, clearly not willing to give up the fight on this. "Especially a bunch of New Yorkers."

Miss Addie snorted. "How could they resist all this Southern charm?"

* * *

"And the first Smithville settlers landed right here in 1610."

Emma frowned up at Katie. She had to frown up because the woman was huge. "In 1610? I thought the first U.S. settlers didn't land on Plymouth Rock until 1620 or so."

Katie shrugged. "We don't make a big deal of it, but we were here first."

With a nod, Katie started trudging back over the sand. "Come on. I'll take you over to the Smithville museum." She turned and faced Emma while walking backward. "I think there are some old photos there you'll find very interesting. Then we can go shopping. Tiffany's having a sale."

"Smithville has a Tiffany's?"

"Sure. Don't you have one in New York?"

She fought the urge to say, "Yeah, but it's New York," because she knew how snobby that would sound. Instead she said, "Oh. Yeah."

Emma really didn't know what the hell was going on, but she couldn't shake Katie or the feeling Katie wanted to show her something. Needed her to understand something. Emma tried to hint at her government experiment theory, but Katie only stared at her.

Trying her best to keep up with the much taller woman's long strides, Emma studied her. Although beautiful, the woman still looked like she could lift a Hummer over her head for laughs. Emma had always thought Mac had a strong body, but Mac and Katie had one big difference.

Mac didn't make Emma nervous.

Not that she thought Katie would do anything, but the potential to do something lay right under the woman's skin. It didn't escape Emma, either, that she'd felt the same way when she met Kyle and Tully. Something raw and predatory she couldn't quite put her finger on. And the more she thought about it, the more she realized everyone in town had the same vibe flowing through them.

A quick jaunt back onto Main Street in Katie's truck, and they soon pulled up in front of the Smithville County Museum.

Like all the county buildings in Smithville, Emma now realized, the museum reeked of old money and powerful influence. Lots of marble and Italian tile. When Emma noticed they had a whole wing dedicated to Pollock, Monet, and Van Gogh—originals, no less—she knew she was way out of her league financially in this town. Although she did have a framed Monet poster on her hallway wall.

"Now, you could spend a couple of days really exploring this museum, but I thought I'd show you this wing. It's my favorite. It's all about the history and whatnot of my town."

Politely, even though convinced she'd be bored out of her mind, Emma walked down the hall, glancing at the extremely old pictures. Some clearly dating back to the late 1800s. As her eyes passed each photo, she suddenly stopped and took a step back, staring intently at the shot of six women dressed in ceremonial robes. She recognized the emblem on their clothes from one of her history of witchcraft books. An old, powerful coven, they worshipped Artemis mostly, disappearing around 1892 or so. Except the photo was dated 1905.

Yet even that wasn't what caught Emma's interest. It was the big lion pride asleep in the background. Emma leaned in closer to see if they had superimposed the images or something. Then she realized one of the male lions had his tail wrapped around one of the witch's ankles . . . and the witch didn't seem to mind.

Emma, heart slamming against her rib cage, took several steps over to another photo, dated 1958. She recognized Miss Sophie and Miss Adelaide immediately. Extremely young and not too bad looking, they sat on the beach with their coven as well as two male lions, a cheetah, a leopard, and a hyena. Not surprisingly, the hyena had his head in Miss Adelaide's lap, while one of the lions rested his majestic head on Miss Sophie's shoulder.

Then it hit her, like a shovel to the back of the head. Pirate dog.

That wolf in Kyle's picture had been posing. He'd probably been saying "cheese" too.

"Witches aren't the only ones who must be silent, Emma." Katie stood next to Emma now, speaking quietly. "Secrets are what keep this town safe."

"Then why are you telling me?"

"You know why, Emma."

Without another word, Emma turned and headed for the exit.

"Emma, wait."

She barely heard Katie's voice through the screaming in her head. Suddenly everything made sense. Every growl, purr, snarl . . . and hiss.

It also explained why Kyle could traipse in and out of her dreams so damn easily.

Emma stormed out of the museum and headed blindly down the street. She would have kept going too, straight back to Long Island, if that hand hadn't grabbed hold of her arm and swung her around.

"Hello, pretty little Emma." The creepy heifer from the diner. "Don't run off. We only want to talk."

With a roll of her eyes, Emma snatched her arm back and marched off. But fingers grabbed at her again.

Emma didn't even think about it, she spun around and let a spell fly, realizing too late that the one grabbing her arm had been Katie. In horror, she watched Katie fly back and slam into the store front windows of a Gucci store.

Glass exploded out and sprayed across the sidewalk. Some of the people on the street ducked to avoid the spray, but none of them ran. None of them screamed. They only waited until the glass settled, and then they all turned and stared at Emma.

It was the snarling, though . . . the snarling and the growling and the palpitating anger swirling around her that convinced Emma she'd just made a very bad mistake.

* * *

"I'll tell her the truth tonight. I was planning to anyway. And then she and her Coven can decide."

His father threw his hands up in exasperation. "Tell them who we are before we find out if they're staying? Have you lost your mind?"

"She won't say anything."

"How do you know? You barely know this woman."

"I know her enough."

"Have you marked her, Kyle?" Miss Gwen asked softly.

"No. I won't do that until she knows the truth. Until I know it's what she wants."

"You're a fool, boy," his father snapped. "Risking this town and your kin on this one woman."

"Just like you did when you were chasing after my momma," Tully murmured.

"That's not the same."

"It's not? Some Smith Packs were ready to kill her for getting involved with you. A cat. Lord knows, I wasn't happy. My momma risked her life to be with you, old man. And don't you ever forget it."

Kyle's father finally calmed down, looking sufficiently chastised by Tully. A few factions of the Smith Packs were notoriously unstable. So although Tully's momma wasn't a Smith by blood, she still had one of Buck Smith's sons. A meaner Alpha bastard few of them knew. He'd threatened more than once to take Tully from her when he found out Jack and Millie were mated and, even more appalling, married. But the town had protected them. No matter the infighting, the town always protected its own.

"Why don't you go get her, Kyle," Miss Gwen said softly. "Get her and when you're ready, tell her the truth. We'll decide what to do from there."

Kyle nodded. "Yes'm."

Walking toward the door, Tully behind him, Kyle heard Miss Gwen snap, "And, Jack Treharne, why don't you take your ornery ass home. Maybe that female of yours can calm you down!"

Kyle and Tully had enough respect for their father not to start laughing until they walked outside.

Emma backed up as they moved toward her. They'd . . . changed, going from human to predator in about sixty seconds or so, shaking off designer clothes while jewelry snapped off wrists and necks and littered the ground.

No, these weren't some cursed "were-animals" or a crazy government experiment. These were a perfectly blended hybrid of human and animal created by nature.

Created by the gods. And protected by them.

I am so screwed.

Looking for any way out of this that didn't involve her killing anyone or getting herself killed, Emma threw up a mystical wall between herself and the animals. They briefly stopped. Not because they walked into it, but because they could sense it. A male lion with a huge mane raised his paw and tapped at the wall. But when his paw slid right through, he followed.

Again the animals moved on her, and again Emma stumbled back, now getting desperate, especially when that lion roared, the sound echoing for miles. But before he could take the next few feet to reach her, three hyenas tried to go around him and get to her first.

The lion snarled and swatted at two of them, knocking them back. Another male lion threw its big body against the third, sending it rolling into the middle of the street. But the hyenas righted themselves quickly and tried for her again. The lions slammed them back, unwilling, it seemed to give up their prize. Several female lions joined the fray, as did a few tigers.

It turned ugly fast, and Emma stared in shock as the animals tore into each other, the lions standing in front of her. She knew they weren't protecting *her* as much as they were protecting their dinner.

Before she could think about running or doing anything, for that matter, a hand slapped over her mouth and dragged her back around a corner.

"I swear, Lucchesi. I leave you alone for two seconds and you get into all sorts of shit."

Emma almost dropped from relief at hearing that familiar voice whispering in her ear. She turned and threw her arms around strong shoulders.

"I've never been so glad to see you."

Mackenzie Marshall looked down into Emma's face and shook her head. "First you started that pit fight in hell, and now this."

"I think they're arguing over which bits of me they get."

"They're gettin' nothing. Let's go." Mac took her hand and proceeded to pull her toward the waiting SUV the Coven had rented, but the locals realized she'd left and came after her, moving around that corner like a combat unit.

At that moment, Jamie stepped out of the SUV, the expression on her pretty face making it crystal clear she'd tear the town apart to protect her Coven. Emma had to move fast. She stepped in front of Jamie and took her hand, ripping the power from her high priestess. The essence of it tore through Emma's body, shocking her with the richness of it. No wonder Jamie never seemed to have a moment of doubt about the path she'd chosen. When you wielded that much power, you didn't question a damn thing.

Jamie's knees buckled, and Mac caught hold of her. "Emma!"

"Trust me," Emma begged as she raised her free hand, fingertips up and palm flat. She aimed at the street in front of them, imagining herself grabbing hold of the Main Street asphalt the way she might grab a sheet on a bed and yanking it up and off.

The hard concrete heaved and, like an ocean wave, raised up nearly twenty feet high . . . and froze. It even arced over like a wave.

"Holy shit," Mac muttered as she handed Jamie off to Kendall, who shoved her into the front passenger seat of the vehicle.

Emma started to follow Kenny into the backseat but stopped when she saw a tiger leap up onto the concrete . . . and over, heading straight for Mackenzie.

"Mac!"

Mac turned, her fist already swinging wide and slamming into the tiger's jaw. The added fire spell really kicked it up a notch, though, knocking the animal back across the street.

"Time to run away," Mac yelped, jumping into the driver's seat while Emma slammed her door shut. "Hold on." Putting the vehicle in reverse, Mac looked over her shoulder and hit the gas.

"Here, hon. Drink this." Seneca put a cold bottle of apple juice in Emma's hand, knowing what she'd done had drained her. Emma gave her a grateful smile.

"You okay?" Kendall gruffly asked.

"Um—" She didn't have a chance to answer as Mac suddenly spun the car around, causing all of them to scream and grab hold of armrests or seat belts. Then Mac took off down the highway.

Mac glanced at her cousin, reached over, and slapped her face. Hard. "Wake up, cuz."

Jamie opened one eye and glared at Mac. "Don't. Hit. Me." She reached up and rubbed her temples, then took the bottle of juice Sen offered her before glaring at Emma. "And what the fuck were you thinking?"

"I had to do something. You had that look in your eye. That 'I'm going to destroy this entire town for my own amusement' look. But they were only reacting to something I did." Something she knew Kyle would never forgive her for.

Jamie didn't argue, which meant Emma had been right. "Whatever. Are you okay?"

Emma sipped her juice and shrugged. "I've been better. How did you guys find me, anyway?"

"We didn't," Mac answered. "It was more like we stumbled upon you. We had just turned onto that street when we saw you tossing the residents around."

Emma closed her eyes in horror. "Don't remind me."

"Don't sweat it, sweetie," Jamie said softly. Emma gave her high priestess two more minutes before she passed out cold from exhaustion. "We'll figure it out. Then we can decide if we want to wipe this town and all these freak people from the face of the earth."

"That's lovely, Jamie," Kenny sighed. "Reminds me of 'We Are the World.' "

"I'm sure she didn't mean it," Seneca chimed in.

"Giggles doesn't think you mean it."

Sen slapped Kenny's arm. "Stop calling me Giggles."

Grateful to have her bickering Coven with her, Emma finished her juice and stared out the window as the town of Smithville whizzed by and out of her life forever.

Thirteen

Everyone thought Jamie had fallen asleep again until she suddenly grabbed hold of the emergency brake and yanked it up. The SUV spun in a tight circle, coming to an abrupt halt right beside a tree. A few more feet and they would have been wrapped around that tree.

Mac gripped the steering wheel and her emotions . . . barely. "Have you lost your mind?"

"Don't you hear it?"

Mac glared at her cousin. "Hear what?"

"Them. They're calling for us."

And before any of them could ask who "them" might be, Jamie had already pushed open the passenger door, and stumbled out of the vehicle.

"Where the hell is she going?"

They all unbuckled their seat belts and followed, watching as Jamie tripped and stumbled through the woods, heading to who knew where but moving incredibly fast for someone who should be weak if not completely passed out.

"Jamie, wait!" But it was as if she couldn't hear them, moving through the trees until she went over a ridge and they lost sight of her.

"God," Mac muttered, running up the ridge after her

cousin but stopping suddenly at the top, Seneca and Kenny nearly colliding with her.

Emma made it up the ridge last, standing in mute shock for several long seconds before following her Coven down to where Jamie stood.

A graveyard. Their high priestess stood in the middle of a graveyard, powerful magick emanating from the land and out. Into the trees, the grass, the flowers. It hung off limbs like icicles and dusted the ground like snow. Emma had never seen so much concentrated energy in one place before. It almost blinded her.

Even the few seconds Jamie let the power wrap around her had rebuilt the energy she'd lost when Emma snatched it from her, explaining the sudden burst of strength and speed.

"This . . . this is amazing." Emma couldn't stop staring. A nonwitch wouldn't see anything except a well-tended but very old graveyard. The Coven, however, saw so much more. Especially Jamie.

"It comes from their bones," Jamie, now back at full strength, offered as explanation. "They die, are buried, and the magick that is inside them naturally, returns to the land."

Mac glanced at Emma and back at her cousin. "How the hell do you know that?"

"They told me."

Emma saw them. The ones who had come before them. The witches who'd protected the land and the people over the last four hundred years. And to be quite honest, they didn't look real happy to see Emma's Coven.

"Should we run away?" Emma asked carefully.

"Why?"

Only Jamie would ask that. Only Jamie wouldn't be freaked out by a crapload of dead witches standing around staring at them.

"We won't hurt you," one of them said. "We've come to help you understand."

Jamie sort of wandered away, touching leaves and tree

limbs, playing with the magick in front of her. So Mac asked the questions. "Understand what?"

"Why you've been brought here."

"We didn't open that doorway, did we? We didn't conjure the thing that tried to kill Emma."

The apparition, a plain, dark-haired woman, smiled, but it wasn't remotely friendly. "Oh, but you did open that door-way. As usual, you ladies play where you have no place. But the doorway you opened allowed darker forces—darker than you, that is—to bring forth that unholy thing to terrorize our town. He had to stop Emma so she couldn't close the door. Others like that one were headed this way."

"Okay," Mac said calmly, "we screwed up. It's happened before, it'll happen again. What do you want from us?"

It moved around Mac, the other visions standing back and watching. Preventing the Coven from leaving. "It's not want, my dears. It's need. We need you to stay. We need you to pro-tect our town."

Kenny scratched her head. "You're dead. What do you care?"

And the subtle award goes to . . .

"When we all came here, we had nothing. Nothing real. Our families had shunned us, our neighbors had tried to kill many of us. When we got here . . . everything changed."

Another apparition with long blond curls, who looked very much like Sophie and Adelaide, stepped forward. "We have families here now. Children, grandchildren, great grandchil-dren. We need them protected from those who would choose to take their power and use it. Who would expose them for their own selfish needs."

"Did you have no daughters, no sons who could take your place?"

Sophie and Addie's sister grinned. "The power of the ani-mal always rules. Every child we bred went on to be a shifter; the only magick they wield is the ability to change from human to animal."

Jamie turned, her eyes nailing them all with one look, and Emma watched a few of the other witches move away from them. "So what's your offer? What do you want from us?"

"Simple. You give up everything to get everything. All this power can be yours, if you're not afraid to take a chance."

A cold smile on her face, Jamie said, "But we have to stay. We have to make this our home."

The dark-haired one nodded. "That's the price you pay. It's a choice you'll have to make. One we all had to make."

"Any regrets?"

"For some. Not for all. But that's for each witch to decide."

"But you don't want us here."

"No. You're not our first choice . . . but you're our only choice. Our only choice if we want to protect this town."

"We're not warriors," Emma admitted.

"We don't need warriors. The town is filled with them. We need witches not afraid to call on the darker powers. Who aren't afraid to kill if it becomes necessary."

Jamie blinked and glanced around. "Why is everyone looking at me?"

"You've been to hell, sisters," the blonde reminded them. "And they've spit you out again. That says much to us."

"It wasn't like that," Sen stated suddenly. And when everyone looked at her, she shrugged. "Well, it wasn't. They were real nice about it. They just asked us not to come back."

"Ever," Mac added. "They specified ever."

The apparition spoke again. "They'll come to you tonight. With an offer. You'll have to decide what you want and what you're willing to lose."

"And if we choose no?" Emma asked, always needing to know the options and the potential outcome.

"Then you go back to your lives."

"But if we stay?" Jamie tilted her head to the side, staring at the apparitions before her with absolutely no fear. "Then what?"

"Only you can decide that, sister."

Another apparition stepped forward, her eyes watching the forest. "They're coming for you. Not to hurt you, but to take you back into town. So they can give you the offer."

"Choose wisely, sisters. There will be no going back."

Jamie gave a small smile. "There never is."

Like mist, they dissipated, and moments later a lioness stepped from the trees, her Pride with her. On the opposite side, wolves. Some hyenas. Some tigers. Even a couple of bears. They moved forward as one, surrounding the five of them and making it perfectly clear . . .

The Coven of the Darkest Night wouldn't be leaving Smithville anytime soon.

Kyle stared up at the immobile blacktop. When younger, he and Tully had surfed waves shaped like this during the summer.

"Well, Miss Addie and Miss Sophie were right." Tully stood next to him, also staring up. It had to be twenty feet high. Apparently it had taken no time for Emma and her Coven to completely destroy Main Street.

I knew I shouldn't have left her on her own.

Tully reached out to touch it, and Bear slapped his hand. "Don't touch it, you idiot."

Rolling his eyes, Tully stepped closer and touched the asphalt. "It's real, all right." And as he said the words, the ground beneath their feet began to shake and rumble. Quickly, they all stepped back onto the sidewalk and watched as the giant black wave shifted and relaxed and slid right back into place.

"Good Lord," Tully muttered.

Bear scratched the back of his neck. "I wouldn't quite say that."

Katie pushed up against Kyle's side. She'd stopped bleeding, and the cuts from the glass were already healing. She flatly refused to go to the hospital, so they'd drop her off at their momma's house and let her take care of Katie's wounds.

"I'm so sorry, Kyle." Katie's head rested on his shoulder. "I shouldn't have said anything, but I didn't understand why we wouldn't tell her the truth."

Tully growled. "It doesn't matter. She shouldn't have hurt you."

"It wasn't her fault. Really," Katie admitted. "She thought I was Mary Lou, which I do find a little insulting, but still . . . no fault of hers."

Mary Lou Reynolds. Hyena bitch.

Kyle put his arm around Katie's shoulders. "It's all right, Kit-Kat. We'll fix this." He looked at Bear. "Where are they?" He wanted to see Emma. If she never wanted to see him again, he needed to hear her say it.

"Probably already back on the main highway, heading toward the airport."

Tully shook his head. "I bet ya fifty bucks they're still here."

"What makes you say that?"

In answer, Tully walked out onto the street. It had already hardened back into place, like it had never moved. "Because, Yogi, the female who controls this much power ain't walkin' away from this town anytime soon."

"Don't call me that," Bear snarled.

"Go home, Kyle," Tully suddenly said. He walked back over to them. "Drop off Katie and then go home."

"No way. I wanna see her."

Tully put his hand on Kyle's shoulder. Probably the only man, besides his father, who Kyle would let that near important arteries. "You'll see her before the night's out. But you've gotta trust me, little brother."

"But—"

"You go over there now, and that Coven of hers will think they need to protect her from you. As much as I don't like your feline ass, I'd still hate to see my momma cry at your funeral. So let me handle this."

Kyle took his baseball cap off and ran his hand through his

hair. As much as he hated to admit it, Tully was right. If he pushed now, he'd lose her forever. Humans didn't handle the pushing very well. Emma especially hated it.

"Fine. But call me later and let me know what's going on."

"I got ya covered." Tully winked in that really annoying way he had. "Just leave this to the big dog."

Bear walked by them, muttering, "You are the biggest idiot."

The Smithville Arms turned out to be nothing like they expected. It was in no way, shape, or form a "quaint" hotel owned by two little old ladies. It was a resort. An enormous resort with enormous rooms and suites in the main building and family-sized cabins scattered around the property near the beach. As usual, the Coven sent Seneca in to arrange their rooms, knowing she'd get them a good deal, and she did. Because who could do better than free?

A surprising turn of events, especially when they saw their free rooms for the night: a "cabin" that was twice the size of the two-story house Emma grew up in with her parents, four sisters, and two brothers. It boasted a professional-grade kitchen with a fully stocked refrigerator and freezer, living room with leather couches and chairs, giant-screen TV with full cable, high-speed Internet access, a sitting room, a gaming room, and a bedroom with personal bath for each of them.

When Emma saw it, she immediately noted it was a very good thing they were getting the joint for free, because the only one among them who could afford it was Kendall.

Of course, they still had a price to pay because the Coven couldn't exactly leave, either. Since they'd walked into the place, they'd had furry bodyguards surrounding the cabin. Eventually, as their dead sisters promised, a town representative showed up to make them an offer.

Tully.

He and Jamie, after sizing each other up like two gators at a water hole, took their discussion to the front porch, while the rest of them remained inside and indulged in the enormous spread of food Mac made and the Merlot Kenny discovered in the cabin's wine cellar. Yeah. The cabin had a wine cellar.

Bottle two, and Emma wasn't feeling much pain at this point. Just a vague sense of annoyance.

"You made too much food, Mac." They had enough left over to feed them for days.

"I couldn't resist. That kitchen makes me wet. I haven't been able to cook like that since I went on leave."

"What do you think they're talking about out there?" Kendall asked, her head resting against the back of the exquisitely made dining-table chairs.

"Talking? The way my cousin was checking him out, she's probably on her knees giving him a hummer."

"The bond you two have warms my heart," Kenny muttered.

Eventually Jamie came back inside alone, carrying an enormous leather-bound briefcase with her, and dumped it at Emma's feet. "Some light reading for you."

"Huh?"

"They're books. Financial records for this place." Jamie threw herself in a seat beside Emma. "That's the offer. The same offer they've given every coven for the last four hundred years."

"Which is?" Mac pushed.

"This place."

Kenny sneered. "The cabin?"

Jamie shook her head and couldn't keep the smile off her face. "The resort."

They all froze, staring at each other over the piles of half-eaten food.

"You can't be serious?" Kendall argued. "This place must earn a fortune."

"Emma will tell us after she looks at their books. Apparently they pass it down from coven to coven. The money we make will be ours. The only restriction is that we can't sell it to anyone from outside the town."

"And we'll need to stay?"

"And we'll need to stay. We use our powers to protect their borders, to keep whatever is trying to get in out, and basically handle all the mystical stuff."

"And what do we get from them?"

"Besides this place? The sacred space of our choosing, the freedom to worship as we wish, and their physical protection. Which, I'm guessing, is quite mighty."

Kenny sat up straight. "You can't seriously be considering this."

"Oh, yeah. I'm seriously considering it. But we go into this together or we don't go in at all."

Kenny's gray eyes looked away. "We all know you've got enough power to do this on your own. What do you need us for?"

"Without you guys I'm just a crazy witch on a power trip." Jamie shrugged. "You guys protect me from myself. You'll protect them. I can't do this without you. And believe it or not, I don't want to. We may not be best friends or anything, but . . . you're my Coven. My sisters. We either take this journey together or we don't take it at all."

Jamie grabbed the half-empty bottle of Merlot off the table and took a sip. "But we'll worry about that later. Tully and the rest of the jungle menagerie left for the night, so let's decide what we want to do tomorrow."

Reaching over, Jamie topped off Emma's glass. "Here, Em. Drink up."

Emma shook her head, feeling groggy and a little disoriented. "Nah. I think I had too much already."

"Go on," Jamie urged. "Live a little. What's one more glass?"

"What are you doing?" Mac questioned softly.

"Shut up," Jamie said lightly to her cousin before turning

back to Emma. "I mean, if I were you, I'd need a drink. After what that deputy guy did."

Emma frowned. "What he did?"

"He used you, hon. He lied to you."

"Jamie," Mac warned, although Emma wasn't sure why, since nothing Jamie said wasn't true. Although at the moment, Emma wasn't sure why about a lot of things. She especially didn't know why Jamie hit her cousin in the head with a dinner roll.

"He did lie to me, didn't he?"

"He sure did." Jamie filled Emma's glass again. "And if I were you, I'd go over there and I'd tell him exactly what I'm thinking."

"You would?" Something didn't sound right, but as she downed that next glass of wine, Emma didn't care anymore.

"Oh, I totally would. And if you want, I'll drive you over there myself."

Mac shook her head. "How the hell do you know—?"

"Dog guy told me," Jamie snapped while grabbing up a set of keys. "Come on, Em. Let's go over there so you can give this guy a piece of your mind."

"Damn right," Emma snarled, pushing herself up and letting Jamie catch hold of her arm before she hit the floor. "I have a lot I wanna say to that guy Karl."

"Kyle."

"Whatever."

Kyle snarled around the slice of key lime pie he was trying to eat when the knock came again. He didn't want to see anyone tonight. Then he remembered—his family never knocked.

With a forkful of key lime still in his hand, he walked to the door and opened it. Emma stared up at him, her face angry and her eyes glazed. Behind her stood a black woman Kyle had never seen before. Pretty. Tall. And with the eyes of a predator. She sized Kyle up closely and, after several silent moments, grinned. "Emma's here to give you a piece of her mind." She pushed Emma toward him. "Good luck."

Then she walked off, got in the blue SUV she'd left running in front of his house, and drove off.

"Hey!" Emma reached up and shoved his shoulder. "I wanna talk to you, bub!" She stormed into the house and Kyle watched her. Her friends must have brought her extra clothes. She wore the cutest little shorts and a smallish T-shirt that hugged her breasts perfectly. Other than that, no shoes and no bag.

Kyle closed the door and turned to find Emma standing right in front of him.

She punched his chest with her small fist. "You lied to me, Karl Treharne!"

"It's Kyle."

"Did I say I was done talking? Huh?" While standing still, she somehow managed to stumble, bracing herself against his body.

Good Lord in heaven, the woman is drunk off her ass.

"Jamie said I should come over here and tell you exactly how I feel about things. So here I am."

What should Kyle think about a woman who would dump her drunken friend off on his doorstep in the middle of the night? Other than he would make sure she had whatever she needed for the rest of her life, because she brought him his Emma.

"And you're going to listen to what I have to say?"

"Yup."

"Good."

He held up his fork. "Wanna try?"

She dutifully opened her mouth and he worked hard not to moan out loud while he fed her the bite of his mother's key lime pie. She shrugged. "That's good." Then her expression darkened again. "Don't try and distract me!"

"Sorry. Go on."

She stormed into the middle of his living room. And stood there. For a while.

Kyle placed the fork on the side table. "Emma?"

"What?"

He scratched his head, desperately trying not to laugh. She had to be the most adorable drunk he'd ever seen.

"You have something to say?"

"Don't rush me, bub. I'll say it when I'm damn good and ready."

"Okay. You thirsty? Want something to drink?"

"No. I think those two . . . or three bottles of wine I drank is enough."

"That seems like a lot, Emma."

"Well, Jamie kept pouring." She took a step to steady herself. "Okay. So what I want to say is . . . *Where are you?*"

Where he'd been for the last five minutes. "Behind you."

Emma spun around and he barely caught her in time. "Stop moving around like that. Must be some damn animal thing." She pulled away from him. "Anyway, you're a liar, Kyle Treharne. Sure, I didn't tell you anything about my Coven, but that's my prerogative. You, however, should have told me about the freakness that is you. And about this town, which I knew was funky from the get-go. Nobody's that nice!"

"I know, Emma. I'm sorry."

"Don't you dare argue with me on this."

Kyle cleared his throat. "Of course not."

Taking Emma's hand, Kyle started walking.

"Where are we going?"

"We're going to put you to bed, darlin'. Before you hit the floor and break that pretty nose."

"I'm not drunk," she stated right as she walked into the living room wall. "Ow! Dammit! Stop moving the walls around."

Kyle lifted Emma into his arms. "Sorry about that. Totally my fault."

"Damn right it is."

She wrapped her arms around his neck and buried her face into his throat. "You smell good, Deputy."

He practically ran to his bedroom. He needed to get her to sleep soon. Especially with her licking his neck like a kitten. "You taste good, too."

Kyle practically threw her on the bed.

"What?" she demanded, looking so cute and sexy he didn't think he'd be able to keep his hands off her if she kept talking . . . or breathing.

"Nothing. Except you need to go to sleep now, darlin'. For the sake of my sanity."

"Okay." Fully dressed, she slipped under the covers and snuggled against the pillow. "I am a little tired."

Thank God. He knew he couldn't take much more.

"Stay with me, Kyle."

"Emma—"

"Please?" She wiggled a bit. "You can spoon me. Preferably naked, please."

"Okay. But maybe I should keep my clothes—"

"Naked!" she ordered.

With a sigh, Kyle stripped off his sweatpants and got into bed with her.

"Gimme arm," she slurred. He held his arm out and she wrapped it around her stomach. "Closer. Cock against butt, please."

"You're gonna kill me, Emma."

"In the morning that's a definite possibility. Right now I don't think I'm up to it."

Grinning, Kyle snuggled up close behind her, holding her tight.

"Is that you purring?" she asked.

"Actually, no. That's you, darlin'."

"Oh. I didn't know I could make sounds like that. Hey. Wait a minute. This thing isn't transm . . . transmit . . . trans-something, is it?"

"Transmittable? No. It's not. You have to be born this way."

"Are you born furry?"

Kyle kissed her ear to keep himself from laughing at her or being insulted. "Go to sleep, Emma. We'll talk in the morning."

"O—" She never finished the "kay" part since she'd already started snoring.

Fourteen

Emma opened her eyes and immediately closed them again. What cruel person would repeatedly stab a knife in her forehead like that? And had the sun moved closer to the Earth? Because that could be the only explanation for the damn thing being so bright.

Soft lips brushed against the back of her neck. A strong hand gently kneaded her breast.

That better be Kyle or I'm going to lose my ever-loving mind.

"Kyle?"

He sort of hummed in answer and she tried opening her eyes again. "Why am I naked?"

Kyle had one arm around her waist, his hand resting against her hip, and he brushed his fingers back and forth over the area, making Emma pretty tingly.

"You woke up in the middle of the night 'cause all that wine caught up with you. Unfortunately you kind of missed the toilet." She cringed. "I cleaned everything up, brushed your teeth, then gave us a nice shower. No point in putting your clothes back on after that."

"Sorry about your bathroom."

"Don't worry about it, darlin'. Tully can't hold his liquor

either, but he insists on drinking tequila every once in a while. I had to clean up after him for years so our parents didn't find out we were out partying."

"I'm so sorry about last night." She blamed Jamie for all of it. The woman kept filling up her glass with that overpriced wine, and Emma kept guzzling it.

"Don't apologize, darlin'. I'm so glad you came over. Whatever the reason."

Emma pushed Kyle's arms away and turned over to face him. She had to. His seriously hard cock digging into her back kept distracting her from just about everything.

"So you're a . . . a . . . whatever?"

Propping himself up on one elbow, he smiled at her. "Shifter. Yes. I can shift between human and animal. I come from a really long line of whatevers."

"What kind are you? I'm guessing cat since Tully keeps calling you 'pussy.'"

Kyle bit back his snarl. "Black leopard."

Emma cleared her throat, determined to face her fear. "Can I see?"

Watching her closely, Kyle asked, "Are you sure, darlin'?"

"Yeah. I'm sure."

Kyle shrugged and, as he had in her dream, only in reverse . . . he shifted from man to cat.

A big-clawed, big-fanged cat.

Giving off a panicked squeal, Emma didn't even realize she'd covered her face with the sheet. "Go back! Go back!"

After she got herself under control, she peeked over the sheet. Kyle—human Kyle—lay right where he'd been, trying really hard not to laugh at her.

She shuddered a bit. "Well . . . that was interesting."

"It's okay, Emma."

"No. It's not. I'm not usually this big a pus . . . uh . . . wimp."

"You'll get used to it."

She would? She'd be there long enough to get used to it?

Apparently Kyle thought so, and, to her surprise, she wasn't inclined to argue with him about it.

"Do you like being this way?" she asked, trying not to obsess while in bed, naked, with a gorgeous male who wanted her.

"I can't imagine any other way to be. What about you? Do you like what you do?"

"Well, that's just a religious choice. It's not like I'm not human or anything."

"Really?" He raised an eyebrow. "Emma, I saw what y'all did to the street."

"That was more Jamie. I simply ripped her power from her to make it happen."

Kyle laughed and lay back against the bed. "Oh, is that *all* you did?"

"Don't make fun of me."

"I'm not. I'm just always fascinated by how you never see yourself the way the rest of us do."

Plucking at the sheet covering them both, she asked softly, "What do you see?"

"Me?" He reached over and grabbed her around the waist, pulling her onto his lap so she draped over him. "I see a hot little minx with no idea of the power she holds. A woman who can control lightning and turn it into a lethal weapon. A witch whose Coven scares my own father, who ain't ever been scared of a damn thing in his life." He pushed her hair off her face. "I see you, Emma. And I like what I see. A lot."

She blushed. No one had ever said anything like that to her before. Everyone else only saw the dependable, reliable, boring Emma. The Volvo. It seemed like Kyle saw the sporty, bright red, two-door convertible Audi she had buried underneath.

Kyle kissed her forehead. Trailed his lips over each eye and down her nose. His mouth neared her lips and she blurted out, "I have a headache."

Blinking, Kyle pulled back and looked at her. "Oh. Okay. I'm sorry."

She frowned at him in confusion, then she realized how he must have interpreted her statement. "No. No. I mean . . . I have a headache." Emma swallowed back her insecurity. "When I have headaches I sometimes find that . . . uh . . . certain activities make them go away."

"Certain activities?"

"Yes. Activities normally done alone, but a partner could actually be a big help and a lot more fun."

After a brief moment, Kyle grinned. "You mean the activity of giving yourself carpal tunnel?"

"I told you I got that from typing."

"Sure you did, darlin'."

Kyle eased her onto her back, his body held tight against hers. "Now let's see if old Kyle can help you out with that little headache of yours."

She giggled. "You are such a good old boy."

"That I am, darlin'. That I am." He kissed his way down her body, paying special attention to all her favorite little hot spots. Licking and nipping here and there. Eventually his head disappeared under the white sheet, and she bit her lip. She had never seen anything sexier than that man slipping beneath the covers to go down on her.

Kyle's hot tongue swiped long and slow up her pussy, the tip teasing her clit. Oh, and she'd never felt anything better, either. Christ, the man had a way with his tongue. *Must be a cat thing.*

Emma reached back and gripped the headboard as Kyle took another long, luxurious swipe.

He said something against her skin and she panted out, "What?"

Tossing the sheet aside, Kyle looked up at her from her lap and answered, "You taste amazing."

She blushed again. "Thanks."

Big hands slipped under her ass and lifted her up a bit so his tongue had easier access. "Didn't you know that?" he asked between licks.

"Uh, not really."

"We'll have to fix that," he muttered while tossing her legs over his shoulders.

Emma's grip tightened on the headboard, her body rocking into his tongue, pushing against his face as he licked her pussy clean. Or at least tried. The more the man licked, the wetter she became.

She groaned loudly as Kyle pushed a finger inside her. His tongue concentrated on her clit, and another finger joined the first. They pushed in and out of her, then they pushed in hard, stroked inside her, while Kyle sucked her clit.

Emma screamed out her orgasm, her hands releasing the headboard and grabbing onto the fitted sheet under her. Kyle didn't stop, either. He kept nursing at her, stretching her orgasm out until she thought she might literally die from the pleasure of it.

Then suddenly Kyle was over her, his mouth clamping down on hers. She tasted herself and Kyle, his tongue desperately sweeping inside her mouth. Her legs were still on his shoulders, bent back against her. He reached into the night table drawer for a condom. He had it on and was inside her in less than six seconds. Or at least, that's how it felt.

His pace was hard and rough, just the way she liked it. As if he couldn't wait to fuck her. As if she, Emma Elizabeth Lan Lucchesi, made him so crazy he lost control. The thought had her coming again, gasping into his mouth and wrapping her arms around his neck.

Without stopping his hard thrusts, he sat up and grabbed hold of her legs, stretching them out like a V. He fucked her hard, staring down at her the entire time, his fingers tight around her ankles, most likely leaving bruises.

She didn't care. She loved all of it. Emma gave herself up to the sensations, loving the feel of Kyle's cock powering into her again and again.

Not knowing what else to do, Emma again grabbed the headboard and, unconsciously, licked her lips.

Something inside Kyle must have clicked with that one little move, and she saw his eyes change from human to cat in a split second. She also saw fangs when his lips pulled back over his teeth. And she could feel the tips of claws against her ankles where his fingers kept their tight grip.

Emma didn't care. Not at all. So she smiled and then she came. Hard. Kyle right behind her. The two of them cried out as the sensations pounded through them, passing from one to the other.

Kyle arched over her, his satisfied groans almost making her come again. Knowing she had the power to give him that kind of satisfaction the greatest aphrodisiac she'd ever known.

This time, instead of dropping on top of her, he dropped off to the side. Immediately his arm went around Emma and pulled her close.

It took them a while to get their breath back, but once they did Kyle asked, "How's your headache now, darlin'?"

Emma smiled, her lips dragging across his chest where he'd placed her head so she could rest. "Gone."

"Well, you just let me know anytime you need help with a headache. I'll be more than happy to help you out."

"Your selflessness knows no bounds, Deputy."

"This is very true. I'm all about the giving."

She snorted into his neck and ignored his mock gasp of indignation, deciding instead to go back to sleep.

Fifteen

"Guys?"

"Back here."

Emma walked through the living room and dining room of the cabin, into the kitchen, and right out the back door to the porch. Her Coven stood at the railing, staring out at the ocean and the waning moon above it.

Jamie glanced at her briefly before turning back. "Beautiful, huh?"

"Gorgeous."

"So?" Jamie smirked. "Have a good night?"

"Yup."

"Where is the fine deputy, anyway?"

"Out front. Talking to Tully. I guess Tully's here for our answer?"

"Probably."

Seneca grinned. "Did you guys spend all day together?"

"Yup."

"You guys have to see this man," Jamie informed them. "He's gorgeous."

Emma stood next to her high priestess. "Do you really think so?"

"Oh, yeah. I mean . . . *gorgeous.*"

"I'm so glad you think he's gorgeous, Jamie. That means so much to me."

Jamie frowned. "Are you being sarcastic?"

"Very." Emma grabbed Jamie's upper arm, yanked her down, and proceeded to slap the back of her head.

"Hey! Hey!" Jamie pulled away and when Emma advanced on her, she grabbed hold of Seneca and held the much smaller woman up in front of her. "You wouldn't hit me while I'm holding Sen, would you?"

"Wait a second! How did I get in the middle of this?"

"Mac's way too big to grab."

"How could you leave me like that?" Emma demanded. "You got me drunk and you left me with a complete stranger."

"What are you talking about?" Jamie peeked around a struggling Sen. "You're crazy about the guy."

"I know that. But *you* don't know him. You're not supposed to get your friends drunk and leave them to the mercy of guys you don't know. Didn't you learn anything in college?"

"Look, I was just trying to help a sista out. If we left it up to you, you would have run back to Long Island. Besides, I gave him the Meacham once-over," she laughed.

Emma stalked toward her, but Jamie kept a tight grip on poor Seneca. As it was, Emma was only sort of angry to begin with, but when Jamie started imitating Sen's voice and begged, "Please, don't hurt Jamie. She's weak and fragile," all Emma could do was laugh with the rest of her Coven.

"You're an idiot."

"I thought we established this long ago?" Jamie placed Sen on her feet.

"Never do that to me again," Emma warned as she leaned against the rail.

Mac turned to her cousin. "So what's the plan, cuz? Are we staying or going?"

"I don't want to live in the South," Kenny argued.

Jamie patted her shoulder. "I'm sure you'll get used to

phrases like 'Down the road a piece' and 'What are y'all up to?'"

Kenny's head fell forward in defeat.

Putting her arm around her shoulders, Mac gave the woman a brief hug. "Come on, sweetie. It won't be that bad."

"All I'm saying is—Jews in the South. Bad idea, in my opinion."

Mac chuckled. "And when was the last time you were in a synagogue?"

"The day the rabbi told me to get out because I was pure evil. I swear, you ask one little question. But that's not the point. I don't think we belong here."

Jamie gave a harsh laugh. "Sweetie, I don't think we belong anywhere else. There's nowhere else in the world where we fit. And for once, we're not the biggest freaks, which is a nice change of pace."

Mac nodded. "Now there's a goal."

Kenny gave one last-ditch effort. "But our lives are in New York."

"This is true," Jamie agreed. "And what lives we have, huh? I could go back and be shot at some more, 'cause that's always fun. Mac can go back to risking her life dancing with flame, because I hope to bury my cousin before I'm forty. And, of course, we both get paid so well as civil servants. Sen can go back to her fun-filled waitress job and get her ass pinched by strange old men with Mafia connections. Emma could give up the prime bit of meat I dropped her off with last night to return to her exciting life as an accountant for divorce lawyers in Merrick. And, of course, there's you, who never leaves your house anyway."

"But I don't leave my house *in* New York."

Mac rubbed her eyes with the palms of her hands. "In or out, Ken? In or out? Make up your mind."

Kenny started to say something when she caught sight of Seneca grinning up at her. Her eyes narrowed.

"And," Jamie quickly added, "don't *not* do it to get even."

Ken gritted her teeth. "Fine. I'm in." Seneca squealed and threw her arms around Kenny's shoulders. "Hugging! I thought we discussed the hugging?"

Emma gently pulled Sen off Kendall and allowed her to put her arm around her shoulders instead.

Jamie nodded. "Then it's decided. We're in."

They fell silent and stared out at the beach, each lost in her own thought or worry or daydream. They remained silent and unmoving for so long, a small family of deer wandered by.

Mac sighed in wonder. "My God, guys. Look at the beauty of this place."

"The beauty of nature, ladies," Jamie added. "Enjoy the wonder that is the power of the gods."

They did. Until the deer suddenly scampered off and a zebra came charging out of the woods, three female lions hot on its hooves. Unfortunately for the zebra, it didn't realize they'd herded it right toward three other female lions. These were bigger and appeared more powerful. They came tearing out of trees on the opposite end of the beach and closed in on the defenseless animal. The Coven watched as the zebra made a wild turn, trying to outrun the lions, but it didn't stand a chance. One of the bigger ones slammed her paws into its rear flank, sending it tumbling forward. Another large one tackled the zebra, rolling with the white and black striped animal until she could get her maw around its throat. She turned over again and held the zebra in her jaws while hooves kicked out and the poor thing made pained whimpering sounds. Eventually its movements slowed down. It wasn't quite dead, though, when the lions took hold and started tearing it open so they could get to the good stuff inside.

The Coven watched in horror while the lions ate and fought over the carcass right in front of their porch. They watched until the big cats suddenly became aware of them, stopping their feeding frenzy to look up at the women, their gold fur–covered faces soaked in blood. The two groups stared at each other for nearly a minute.

Then one of the lions roared.

As one, Emma and her sisters screamed and charged back into the cabin, Mac and Jamie slamming the door behind them.

Panting and trying not to run back to New York in her bare feet, Emma glanced up and found Kyle and Tully leaning against the counter. The men had discovered the leftovers from Mac's meal the night before and had plates piled high with food they were busily devouring.

With those eyes only the residents of Smithville seemed to have, they stared at Emma's Coven, and the Coven stared back.

"I tell ya, little brother," Tully finally said as he headed off to the dining room with his food, "I'm feelin' safer already."

Emma only had a second to catch Kyle's wink before she had to slap her hand over Jamie's mouth to prevent the woman from finishing the spell that would turn Tully Smith into a poodle.

Epilogue

Five months later . . .

Shaking her head, Emma walked out of the inn and onto the porch. She couldn't take it anymore. The incessant fighting. The constant complaining. It was making her nuts.

"Couldn't take it anymore, huh?"

Emma glanced over at her Coven. They sat on the porch of the main building, Jamie and Kendall in chairs, Mac on the porch rail. Only Seneca remained inside, busy checking in a couple of good old boys who had Jamie practically squirming. Emma had to admit, she'd never—ever—seen so many hot guys in one place. Shifters were literally and figuratively a breed unto themselves.

Still, she knew she had the best of the bunch . . . even when he was being irritating.

Emma rolled her eyes as the snarling in the house became louder.

"You sure they aren't related?" Kendall asked. She motioned to Jamie and Mac. "They fight like these two."

"Some days I wonder." Bodies hit the screen door and Emma stepped aside seconds before a giant ball of snarling, snapping fur bounced out onto the porch and rolled down the steps.

Impassively, they all watched as Kyle and Tully tore into each other. Emma didn't even wince anymore. Their constant arguing, which led to bloodletting, had become as common to her as having a warm body next to her every night. Of course, she enjoyed one way more than the other.

When the pair disappeared into the woods, Emma let out a sigh. "I'm going home."

"Any plans for the night?" Jamie asked.

"Long hot shower and television. Kyle's huntin' tonight."

"Bet you never thought you'd hear yourself say that about a boyfriend, huh?"

Emma laughed. "I never thought I'd say anything about a boyfriend, period. Oh, by the way, there's a barbecue this weekend at Kyle's mother's house if you guys want to—"

As usual, they couldn't say no fast enough. They were never mean about it—even Kenny—they simply hadn't found their place in Smithville yet. Emma, knowing exactly how it felt not to belong, didn't push. She knew in their own time, these women would find their place. Besides, Seneca made up for the rest of them. Especially with the Smithville males. They absolutely *adored* her. In fact, Sen knew about the weekend barbecue before Kyle did.

Emma turned to go, but Sen's startled squeal from inside the inn had the women quickly moving toward the front door. Sen stumbled out, pushing the Coven back. A moment later, two enormous tigers—at least five hundred pounds each—came tearing out of the inn, down the porch stairs, and into the woods.

Emma put her arm around Sen's shoulder. "Are you okay?"

"I just have to get used to them . . . changing in the middle of the inn like that."

"They call it shifting," Jamie said with a smile, straddling the porch rail with her long legs.

"Well, whatever." Sen gave a brave smile. "I'll be fine. I just find all this so exciting!"

Kenny, her feet up on the porch rail as she relaxed back

against the lounger, waited until Sen was stepping back into the inn. Then, an evil grin on her face, she tossed out, "That shipment of gazelles came in earlier. Lots of little baby ones. Real ripe . . . and juicy."

Sen's hand slapped against the door frame. "I hate you," she hissed before storming back into the front lobby.

Jamie shook her head. "You're going back to hell, Ken. And this time . . . they'll keep you."

Laughing, Emma walked down the steps. "See you guys later."

"Night, Em," they called after her.

Heading toward her new car—a cherry red Jeep Cherokee Kyle fucked her in the night she bought it—Emma passed a male lion ambling out of the woods.

"Hi, Dr. Sahara!" she called out cheerfully.

He roared back in greeting and kept going. She'd stopped screaming and running at the sight of him nearly two months ago, which made her very proud.

Yeah, life in Smithville wasn't exactly normal, but she couldn't say it wasn't fun, either.

After beating Tully into the ground, Kyle made it home in record time. He'd planned to go hunting with Tully and his Pack, but he realized he'd rather go home and see his Emma. But she hadn't gotten back yet from the inn, so he climbed his favorite tree and lay out on one of the lower branches so he could lick the wounds Tully gave him.

That didn't take long and he was just drifting off to sleep when the shades in his bedroom opened up. It was dark now, and he could easily see inside his well-lit house. And he got the feeling Emma knew that.

Especially when she started to take her clothes off . . . slowly.

Lord, he absolutely loved that woman. True, all that witch stuff took some getting used to. Especially when she came home the last full moon bruised like she'd been in a fight. She wouldn't tell him what had happened and then never gave him a chance to force the issue. Instead she practically threw him on the dining-room table and had her dirty, horny way with him. She was always so horny after "spellcasting," as she called it. Hungry and horny.

Whatever. It didn't matter. He loved it. Besides, Emma didn't flaunt that side of her life. It was simply part of her, and he loved it like he loved her. Of course, Kyle was on his own for Sunday church, but his momma had learned to let that go.

Funny thing was, Emma still hadn't "officially" moved in. She'd taken one of the houses on the resort property, yet she hadn't even unpacked the boxes she brought back from New York, where Kyle had met her less-than-friendly family. Instead she spent every night in his house and called it "home."

Must be some human thing. She kept saying they had to get to know each other better before moving in together. But Kyle knew all he needed to know. She smelled good. She tasted even better. And she made him laugh. The cat was content, and that's all the cat needed to know.

What he hadn't mentioned to her was that he'd slowly started moving her stuff into his house. She wanted to read the newspaper, and it took her a second to realize she'd turned on her own lamp on his end table by the couch. The drawers he gave her for clothes kept getting fuller. Same thing with her closet. And if she grabbed another book off the bookshelf and exclaimed, "Hey! I have this book," one more time . . . he was gonna laugh at her. And she really hated when he laughed at her.

Kyle watched as she worked her way down to her white lace bra and matching panties that hugged her ass like a tight pair of boy's shorts. He loved when she wore those. She turned her back to him and unlatched the front clasp, slowly pulling the bra off. *My shy little Emma*, he thought with a laugh that came out as a bark.

Her thumbs hooked into the top of her panties and she bent over to slowly lower them. Kyle groaned, enjoying every second of it. Then, without even glancing out the window, she headed off to the bathroom.

Kyle stood up and made a wild leap from the tree branch. He slammed against the side of his house, his claws digging into the wood. Reaching out, he latched hold of the windowsill, pulling himself over. Pushing his paw through the small opening between the window and the sill, Kyle forced the window open enough so he could wiggle his big body through it. Landing silently on the floor, he walked to the bathroom. He could hear the water running and smell Emma's scent mingling with the steam. Purring low, he nudged the door open with his muzzle and entered. He could see her on the other side of the glass door as she soaped her gorgeous little body, and his mouth watered.

The shower door opened out, and as leopard he had no thumbs, so he stood on his hind legs and slapped his front paws against the glass. She turned and looked at him.

"You want something, pretty kitty?"

He roared impatiently and scratched at the glass, leaving marks.

"Okay. Okay. Calm yourself." She laughed as she opened the door and he leaped inside. She stood directly under the spray while he wound his long body around her legs. He licked the back of her knees, and she giggled. "Stop that!"

With one last nuzzle against her thigh, Kyle shifted from cat to man.

She smiled up at him, and his hard cat heart melted while his hard-on doubled in size.

"I'm glad you're home," she said softly.

He pushed her hair out of her face. "Me, too, darlin'."

With a bar of soap and her soft hands, she started to clean him off. He closed his eyes and let her have her dirty way with him, enjoying it all. Until she took firm hold of his cock, and his knees almost gave out.

"Did that hurt?"

"What?" he gasped out as her hand ran down the length of him.

"Those rips you have on your arm from fighting with Tully."

Kyle glanced down and saw the scratches on his forearm.

He wouldn't exactly call them "rips," but he liked that she worried about him. Especially when stroking his cock while she worried.

"Those ain't nothin', darlin'." He leaned down and kissed her forehead, her cheek, then her neck. "Tully can't hurt me. Ain't no dog alive can hurt me."

He bit her neck and she groaned, her hand tightening on him. "He doesn't like to be called dog, ya know? He nearly ripped Jamie's head off when she called him Marmaduke again the other day."

"She keeps calling him that, and I am loving every minute of it," Kyle laughed.

Emma grinned, her small body leaning into his as he stroked his hands over her wet flesh.

"Look, darlin', I don't want you to worry about me and Tully. We just like to argue over stupid stuff. It's instinctual."

She giggled. "Cats and dogs?"

He unwrapped her hand from his cock and kneeled in front of her, kissing her lower stomach and loving that her breath rushed out in a gasp at his touch. "Yankees and Rebels," he whispered.

Her hands tightened in his hair. "You're never letting me forget that, are you," she moaned.

"Nope." He licked her deep, and her hips moved against his face. "Who'd have thought it, darlin'? Me and a Yankee. Momma and Daddy are still trying to deal with that."

"It could be worse," she sighed out while his hands kneaded her adorable little ass.

"Is that right?"

"Yeah. I could be a dog person."

Before she could say another word, he had her slammed up against the far shower wall, with her legs around his hips, his cock buried deep inside her. He stared down into her beautiful face and growled. "*Never* say that to me again."

Then Kyle proved what a cat lover Emma really was.

Take a look at Sylvia Day's
PASSION FOR THE GAME,
available now from Brava!

"Do not be fooled by her outward appearance. Yes, she is short of stature and tiny, but she is an asp waiting to strike."

Christopher St. John settled more firmly in his seat, disregarding the agent of the Crown who shared the box with him. His eyes were riveted to the crimson-clad woman who sat across the theater expanse. Having spent his entire life living amongst the dregs of society, he knew affinity when he saw it.

Wearing a dress that gave the impression of warmth and bearing the coloring of hot-blooded Spanish sirens, Lady Winter was nevertheless as icy as her title. And his *assignment* was to warm her up, ingratiate himself into her life, and then learn enough about her to see her hanged in his place.

A distasteful business, that. But a fair trade in his estimation. He was a pirate and thief by trade, she a bloodthirsty and greedy vixen.

"She has at least a dozen men working for her," Viscount Sedgewick said. "Some watch the wharves, others roam the countryside. Her interest in the agency is obvious and deadly. With your reputation for mayhem, you two are very much alike. We cannot see how she could resist any offer of assistance on your part."

Christopher sighed; the prospect of sharing his bed with the beautiful Wintry Widow was vastly unappealing. He knew her kind, too concerned over their appearance to enjoy an abandoned tumble. Her livelihood was contingent upon her ability to attract wealthy suitors. She would not wish to become sweaty or tax herself overmuch. It could ruin her hair.

Yawning, he asked, "May I depart now, my lord?"

Sedgewick shook his head. "You must begin immediately, or you will forfeit this opportunity."

It took great effort on Christopher's part to bite back his retort. The agency would learn soon enough that he danced to no one's tune but his own. "Leave the details to me. You wish me to pursue both personal and professional relations with Lady Winter, and I shall."

Christopher stood and casually adjusted his coat. "However, she is a woman who seeks the secure financial prospects of marriage, which makes it impossible for a bachelor such as myself to woo her first and then progress from the bed outward. We will instead have to start with business and seal our association with sex. It is how these things are done."

"You are a frightening individual," Sedgewick said dryly.

Christopher glanced over his shoulder as he pushed the black curtain aside. "It would be wise of you to remember that."

The sensation of being studied with predatory intent caused the hair at Maria's nape to rise. Turning her head, she studied every box across from her but saw nothing untoward. Still, her instincts were what kept her alive, and she trusted them implicitly.

Someone's interest was more than mere curiosity.

The low tone of men's voices in the gallery behind her drew her attention away from the fruitless visual search. Most would hear nothing over the rabble in the pit below and the carrying notes of the singer, but she was a hunter, her senses fine-tuned.

"The Wintry Widow's box."

"Ah . . ." a man murmured knowingly. "Worth the risk for a few hours in that fancy piece. She is incomparable, a goddess amongst women."

Maria snorted. A curse, that.

Suddenly eager to be productive in some manner, Maria rose to her feet. She pushed the curtain aside and stepped out to the gallery. The two footmen who stood on either side to keep the ambitiously amorous away snapped to attention. "My carriage," she said to one. He hurried away.

Then she was bumped none too gently from behind, and as she stumbled, was caught close to a hard body.

"I beg your pardon," murmured a deliciously raspy voice so close to her ear she felt the vibration of it.

The sound stilled her, caught her breath and held it. She stood unmoving, her senses flaring to awareness far more acute than usual. One after another, impressions bombarded her—a hard chest at her back, a firm arm wrapped beneath her breasts, a hand at her waist, and the rich scent of bergamot mixed with virile male. He did not release her; instead his grip upon her person tightened.

"Unhand me," she said, her voice low and filled with command.

"When I am ready to, I will."

His ungloved hand lifted to cup her throat, his touch heating the rubies that circled her neck until they burned. Calloused fingertips touched her pulse, stroking it, making it race. He moved with utter confidence, no hesitation, as if he possessed the right to fondle her whenever and wherever he chose, even in this public venue. Yet he was undeniably gentle. Despite the possession of his hold, she could writhe free if she chose, but a sudden weakness in her limbs prevented her from moving.

Her gaze moved to her remaining footman, ordering him silently to do something to assist her. The servant's wide eyes were trained above her head, his throat working convulsively as he swallowed hard. Then he looked away.

She sighed. Apparently, she would have to save herself. Again.

Her next action was goaded as much by instinct as by fore-thought. She moved her hand, setting it over his wrist, allow-ing him to feel the sharp point of the blade she hid in a custom-made ring. The man froze. And then laughed. "I do so love a good surprise."

"I cannot say the same."

"Frightened?" he queried.

"Of blood on my gown? Yes," she retorted dryly. "It is one of my favorites."

"Ah, but then it would more aptly match the blood on your hands"—he paused, his tongue tracing the shell of her ear, making her shiver even as her skin flushed—"and mine."

"Who are you?"

"I am what you need."

Maria inhaled deeply, pressing her corset-flattened bosom against an unyielding forearm. Questions sifted through her mind faster than she could collect them. "I have everything I require."

As he released her, her captor allowed his fingers to drift across the bare flesh above her bodice. Her skin tingled, goose-flesh spreading in his wake. "If you find you are mistaken," he rasped, "come find me."

Take a peek at Amy Garvey's
ROOM SERVICE
available now from Brava!

No one appreciated tradition, she thought with a spark of mutiny as she stepped backward toward the curb. Her gaze was trained on the hotel, counting floors and picking out the windows of the suite where she had grown up. Everyone wanted everything to change, all the time. Newer, improved, bigger, better. It was absurd. Some things deserved to stay just the way they were. And Callender House was one of them. Her father had entrusted her with it, and she wasn't going to let him down.

It was a little disconcerting that she couldn't pick out the old suite's windows automatically, however. Once upon a time, she'd been able to do it in her sleep—she'd spent the first eighteen years of her life there, after all. She took another step backward, craning her neck as she counted up each floor, then over five windows—or was it six? The perspective was a little different now that she was taller.

She stepped backward again, squinting now, trying to remember—until a pair of very strong hands thrust her forward and a cab blared its horn.

She was still stumbling for balance when she heard something else hit the pavement with a wet splat, and then an irritable, "Oh, bloody hell."

Uh-oh.

She grabbed a parking meter to right herself, and turned around to find a cabbie giving her a one-fingered salute as he drove off—and a rock star covered with what looked like a mocha latte, an exploded suitcase, and a dropped backpack at his feet. The sidewalk was littered with jeans and T-shirts.

He looked like a rock star, at least. First there were the faded jeans and what appeared to Olivia like motorcycle boots, black leather that had seen better days and plenty of wear. Then the layered shirts, a long-sleeved gray one under a short-sleeved dark blue one with Mick Jagger's luscious pout on the front. Finally there was his hair, dark and shaggy around his face—and splattered with creamy white foam, just like his visage. And the white snakes of his iPod, which he pulled from his ears and shook over the sidewalk, spraying foam and coffee.

She swallowed hard. "I'm so sorry. *So* sorry. You don't even know . . ."

"I can imagine well enough," he said with a dry smile, shaking latte out of his hair like a wet dog. His eyes were gray, she noticed. Deep, stormy gray, and fixed on her face. "You and that cab would have ended in blood and tears, now wouldn't you?"

"Um . . ." She knew, vaguely, that her mouth was hanging open, but she couldn't seem to close it, much less find an intelligent response. She hadn't expected the British accent. Something inside her melted into a warm puddle.

She'd dreamed about men like him. Well, "fantasized" was probably more accurate. In her sleeping dreams, men tended to be a strange combination of Cary Grant and that guy from the Verizon commercials.

But men like this one, those were the kind in her daydreams. Except this one possibly was better.

And she'd . . . splattered him.

"You're all right, yeah?" he asked, wiping his face. "I didn't mean to shove you quite so hard."

"You . . . Well, you saved me from being hit by a cab." She shrugged as a heated blush spread over her cheeks. "I'm fine. You're . . ."

"A bit of a wreck at the moment, I know." He grinned at her then, a sudden flash of mischief and sunshine. Licking his upper lip, he added with a wink, "Brilliant latte."

Completely cool. Completely confident.

Completely unlike any man she had ever met.

In her head, there was no problem, She would say something witty, or smart, or maybe even flirty. He would lean in and flirt back, invite her to dinner. She would give him a mysterious little wave when she left, maybe flip her hair a bit. In her imagination, hair-flipping got them every time.

But this wasn't her imagination. This was real, right here, right now. This was overwhelming.

Especially when he pulled up the hems of his T-shirts and wiped off his face, revealing a lean, muscled abdomen.

So much for offering him a towel from the hotel. So much for any hope of getting her racing pulse under control.

And he wasn't even going to give her a chance to try. "Bit of a trick, walking backward, yeah?" he said, letting his shirts fall and wiping his hands on the back of his jeans.

"Oh. Right." Her cheeks were on fire. She wouldn't have been surprised to see an actual flame lick the tip of her nose. "That was . . . dumb."

"Not in an empty meadow, maybe." His grin was as lop-sided as the hotel's nameplate and a lot more appealing. "On a Manhattan street now . . ."

"I know. I am sorry." She gestured helplessly at his ruined shirts, at the empty cup on the pavement.

"No worries, love. Pleasure to meet you . . ."

"Olivia." She put her hand in his when he offered it, and an actual thrill of excitement raced through her. Which was silly, because he was simply being nice. It was probably a British thing. Nothing to do with her at all.

"Rhys," he said, and she realized he was still holding her

hand. His was nice, firm and warm and stronger than she would have imagined for a man with such long, lean fingers.

But she couldn't stand here all day holding hands, pining after him like some teenager, even if she wanted to. It was time to step away. Get back to work. Take her tattered dignity back to her office and mend it with a big fat muffin.

Right. She was stepping away now. Yes, *now.*

Except for the fact that it wouldn't be polite to leave him to the scattered contents of his suitcase all by himself, would it?

She untangled her fingers from his and knelt down to pick up a pair of jeans—and found a jumbled pile of boxer briefs beneath them. She dropped the jeans with a little gasp of embarrassment, and looked up to see Rhys grinning at her.

"I'll take the unmentionables, love."

And now, Kathy Love's newest,
MY SISTER IS A WEREWOLF,
coming next month from Brava!

Reaching for her beer, Elizabeth took a sip, and for the first time that night felt a little normal. The atmosphere of the bar seemed to envelope her, like she was meant to be there. A much needed sense of contentment filled her. The talking, the laughter, the smell of drinks and salty roasted peanuts. It made her feel oddly better. This was a good idea—a good distraction. Tomorrow she'd return to her research in a more relaxed and focused state.

Elizabeth smiled as Jill Lewis finally took the stage. The reluctant woman shook her head, glaring good-naturedly at her friends.

"All right!" Jolee cheered from over her microphone, and much of the bar exploded into applause. Elizabeth clapped along with them.

Jolee started the music and the woman's voice filled the room almost from the first note, asking the listeners to go on and leave her breathless. Elizabeth recognized the tune as a song from the radio with a happy, contagious beat. And the woman sang it well—better than well. It was little wonder that her pals had been urging her to get up there. She was great.

Elizabeth looked back to the woman's table of friends to

see their reaction to the woman's fantastic singing. Two of them, a man and a woman, beamed and clapped. While the other at the table, a male, just watched, somehow distant from the other two. The clapping male leaned over to say something to him; and the one who only watched turned toward his friend, giving Elizabeth her first full view of his face.

Elizabeth's smile disappeared. Desire, so strong that it almost made her cry out, ripped through her, shredding any impression of calm she'd found. Every muscle in her body tensed, every sense sharpening until her whole being was centered on the man before her.

Without saying a word to Christian, she rose. Carefully, purposefully, she zigzagged through the tables, her eyes never leaving the man. Just tables away, she stopped herself, fragments of her reasonable mind taking control. She glanced back at the bar. Christian watched her, but when he saw her looking, he busied himself by taking an order from one of the patrons.

Her brother could sense her desire now. Of course he could. Vampires could sense emotions—and she knew hers ran very strong. Shame filled her, but still her gaze returned to the male at the table.

The man was beautiful: dark hair, sculpted features, perfectly shaped lips that any woman would have killed for—yet on him they were sinfully masculine. He was beyond handsome.

But while Elizabeth had seen many handsome men in her life, never had her body reacted like this.

She swallowed. *Control yourself! What was she doing?*

But instead of walking back to her barstool as her brain ordered her to, she took another step toward the table of friends. Then another. She sauntered slowly past the man's chair, not getting too close, not drawing attention to herself—not just yet. She had to assess, she had to watch. Stalk her prey.

She lifted her head to breathe in his scent. The hint of woodsy cologne, the freshness of soap and shampoo, the minty traces of toothpaste. And a warm, rich aroma—a scent that made her want to tip back her head and howl.

She continued around the table until he was directly in her line of sight, and she sat down at an empty table. Eyes trained on him, she studied. Oh yeah, she wanted him.

For just a moment, she closed her eyes as her rational mind took tenuous control. Why was this happening? It was as if the wolf was in control. But that didn't happen. She didn't stay in human form and think like the wolf. She didn't allow that. Some werewolves did. Brody did. He was more wolf than man at all times. She didn't allow that. She didn't.

Her eyes snapped open. The man was looking at her. She'd felt his gaze before she'd actually seen it. Their gazes met; but even in the dim light, she could see his eyes were a mixture of brown and green.

Again her body told her this was what she needed. This was what she'd been wanting. *He* was what she wanted. She continued to stare, meeting his gaze, until he looked away. Still she watched him. Unable to do otherwise. The need was in control now.

She was acting like a bitch in heat. And she didn't care.